# Shiloh
# and Other
# Stories

# Shiloh
# and Other
# Stories

## Bobbie Ann Mason

1817

**HARPER & ROW, PUBLISHERS,** New York

Cambridge, Philadelphia, San Francisco, London

Mexico City, São Paulo, Sydney

Copyright acknowledgments appear on page 248.

*Designer: C. Linda Dingler*

Library of Congress Cataloging in Publication Data

Mason, Bobbie Ann.
    Shiloh and other stories.

    I. Title.
PS3527.A15S5 1982      813'.54      82-47541
ISBN 0-06-015062-9                  AACR2

    83 84 85 86 10 9 8 7 6 5 4

*For Roger*

# Contents

# Shiloh

Leroy Moffitt's wife, Norma Jean, is working on her pectorals. She lifts three-pound dumbbells to warm up, then progresses to a twenty-pound barbell. Standing with her legs apart, she reminds Leroy of Wonder Woman.

"I'd give anything if I could just get these muscles to where they're real hard," says Norma Jean. "Feel this arm. It's not as hard as the other one."

"That's 'cause you're right-handed," says Leroy, dodging as she swings the barbell in an arc.

"Do you think so?"

"Sure."

Leroy is a truckdriver. He injured his leg in a highway accident four months ago, and his physical therapy, which involves weights and a pulley, prompted Norma Jean to try building herself up. Now she is attending a body-building class. Leroy has been collecting temporary disability since his tractor-trailer jackknifed in Missouri, badly twisting his left leg in its socket. He has a steel pin in his hip. He will probably not be able to drive his rig again. It sits in the backyard, like a gigantic bird that has flown home to roost. Leroy has been home in Kentucky for three months, and his leg is almost healed, but the accident frightened him and he does not want to drive any more long hauls. He is not sure what to do next. In the meantime, he makes things from craft kits. He started by building a miniature log cabin from notched Popsicle sticks. He varnished it and placed it on the TV set, where it remains. It reminds him of a rustic Nativity scene. Then he tried string art (sailing ships on black velvet), a macramé owl kit, a snap-together B-17 Flying Fortress, and a lamp made out of a model truck, with a light fixture screwed in the top of the cab. At first the kits were diversions, something to kill time, but now he is thinking about building a full-scale log house from a kit. It would be considerably cheaper than building a regular house, and besides, Leroy has grown to appreciate how things are put together. He has begun to realize that in all the years he was on the road he never took time to examine anything. He was always flying past scenery.

"They won't let you build a log cabin in any of the new subdivisions," Norma Jean tells him.

"They will if I tell them it's for you," he says, teasing her. Ever since they were married, he has promised Norma Jean he would build her a new home one day. They have always rented, and the house they live in is small and nondescript. It does not even feel like a home, Leroy realizes now.

Norma Jean works at the Rexall drugstore, and she has acquired an amazing amount of information about cosmetics. When she explains to Leroy the three stages of complexion care, involving creams, toners, and moisturizers, he thinks happily of other petroleum products—axle grease, diesel fuel. This is a connection between him and Norma Jean. Since he has been home, he has felt unusually tender about his wife and guilty over his long absences. But he can't tell what she feels about him. Norma Jean has never complained about his traveling; she has never made hurt remarks, like calling his truck a "widow-maker." He is reasonably certain she has been faithful to him, but he wishes she would celebrate his permanent homecoming more happily. Norma Jean is often startled to find Leroy at home, and he thinks she seems a little disappointed about it. Perhaps he reminds her too much of the early days of their marriage, before he went on the road. They had a child who died as an infant, years ago. They never speak about their memories of Randy, which have almost faded, but now that Leroy is home all the time, they sometimes feel awkward around each other, and Leroy wonders if one of them should mention the child. He has the feeling that they are waking up out of a dream together—that they must create a new marriage, start afresh. They are lucky they are still married. Leroy has read that for most people losing a child destroys the marriage—or else he heard this on *Donahue*. He can't always remember where he learns things anymore.

At Christmas, Leroy bought an electric organ for Norma Jean. She used to play the piano when she was in high school. "It don't leave you," she told him once. "It's like riding a bicycle."

The new instrument had so many keys and buttons that she was bewildered by it at first. She touched the keys tentatively, pushed some buttons, then pecked out "Chopsticks." It came out in an amplified fox-trot rhythm, with marimba sounds.

"It's an orchestra!" she cried.

The organ had a pecan-look finish and eighteen preset chords, with optional flute, violin, trumpet, clarinet, and banjo accompaniments. Norma Jean mastered the organ almost immediately. At first she played Christmas songs. Then she bought *The Sixties Songbook* and learned every tune in it, adding variations to each with the rows of brightly colored buttons.

"I didn't like these old songs back then," she said. "But I have this crazy feeling I missed something."

"You didn't miss a thing," said Leroy.

Leroy likes to lie on the couch and smoke a joint and listen to Norma Jean play "Can't Take My Eyes Off You" and "I'll Be Back." He is back again. After fifteen years on the road, he is finally settling down with the woman he loves. She is still pretty. Her skin is flawless. Her frosted curls resemble pencil trimmings.

Now that Leroy has come home to stay, he notices how much the town has changed. Subdivisions are spreading across western Kentucky like an oil slick. The sign at the edge of town says "Pop: 11,500"—only seven hundred more than it said twenty years before. Leroy can't figure out who is living

in all the new houses. The farmers who used to gather around
the courthouse square on Saturday afternoons to play checkers
and spit tobacco juice have gone. It has been years since Leroy
has thought about the farmers, and they have disappeared without his noticing.

Leroy meets a kid named Stevie Hamilton in the parking
lot at the new shopping center. While they pretend to be
strangers meeting over a stalled car, Stevie tosses an ounce
of marijuana under the front seat of Leroy's car. Stevie is wearing orange jogging shoes and a T-shirt that says CHATTAHOO-
CHEE SUPER-RAT. His father is a prominent doctor who lives
in one of the expensive subdivisions in a new white-columned
brick house that looks like a funeral parlor. In the phone book
under his name there is a separate number, with the listing
"Teenagers."

"Where do you get this stuff?" asks Leroy. "From your
pappy?"

"That's for me to know and you to find out," Stevie says.
He is slit-eyed and skinny.

"What else you got?"

"What you interested in?"

"Nothing special. Just wondered."

Leroy used to take speed on the road. Now he has to go
slowly. He needs to be mellow. He leans back against the car
and says, "I'm aiming to build me a log house, soon as I get
time. My wife, though, I don't think she likes the idea."

"Well, let me know when you want me again," Stevie says.
He has a cigarette in his cupped palm, as though sheltering
it from the wind. He takes a long drag, then stomps it on
the asphalt and slouches away.

Stevie's father was two years ahead of Leroy in high school.
Leroy is thirty-four. He married Norma Jean when they were
both eighteen, and their child Randy was born a few months
later, but he died at the age of four months and three days.
He would be about Stevie's age now. Norma Jean and Leroy
were at the drive-in, watching a double feature (*Dr. Strangelove* and *Lover Come Back*), and the baby was sleeping in the

back seat. When the first movie ended, the baby was dead. It was the sudden infant death syndrome. Leroy remembers handing Randy to a nurse at the emergency room, as though he were offering her a large doll as a present. A dead baby feels like a sack of flour. "It just happens sometimes," said the doctor, in what Leroy always recalls as a nonchalant tone. Leroy can hardly remember the child anymore, but he still sees vividly a scene from *Dr. Strangelove* in which the President of the United States was talking in a folksy voice on the hot line to the Soviet premier about the bomber accidentally headed toward Russia. He was in the War Room, and the world map was lit up. Leroy remembers Norma Jean standing catatonically beside him in the hospital and himself thinking: Who is this strange girl? He had forgotten who she was. Now scientists are saying that crib death is caused by a virus. Nobody knows anything, Leroy thinks. The answers are always changing.

When Leroy gets home from the shopping center, Norma Jean's mother, Mabel Beasley, is there. Until this year, Leroy has not realized how much time she spends with Norma Jean. When she visits, she inspects the closets and then the plants, informing Norma Jean when a plant is droopy or yellow. Mabel calls the plants "flowers," although there are never any blooms. She always notices if Norma Jean's laundry is piling up. Mabel is a short, overweight woman whose tight, brown-dyed curls look more like a wig than the actual wig she sometimes wears. Today she has brought Norma Jean an off-white dust ruffle she made for the bed; Mabel works in a custom-upholstery shop.

"This is the tenth one I made this year," Mabel says. "I got started and couldn't stop."

"It's real pretty," says Norma Jean.

"Now we can hide things under the bed," says Leroy, who gets along with his mother-in-law primarily by joking with her. Mabel has never really forgiven him for disgracing her by getting Norma Jean pregnant. When the baby died, she said that fate was mocking her.

"What's that thing?" Mabel says to Leroy in a loud voice,

pointing to a tangle of yarn on a piece of canvas.

Leroy holds it up for Mabel to see. "It's my needlepoint," he explains. "This is a *Star Trek* pillow cover."

"That's what a woman would do," says Mabel. "Great day in the morning!"

"All the big football players on TV do it," he says.

"Why, Leroy, you're always trying to fool me. I don't believe you for one minute. You don't know what to do with yourself—that's the whole trouble. Sewing!"

"I'm aiming to build us a log house," says Leroy. "Soon as my plans come."

"Like *heck* you are," says Norma Jean. She takes Leroy's needlepoint and shoves it into a drawer. "You have to find a job first. Nobody can afford to build now anyway."

Mabel straightens her girdle and says, "I still think before you get tied down y'all ought to take a little run to Shiloh."

"One of these days, Mama," Norma Jean says impatiently.

Mabel is talking about Shiloh, Tennessee. For the past few years, she has been urging Leroy and Norma Jean to visit the Civil War battleground there. Mabel went there on her honeymoon—the only real trip she ever took. Her husband died of a perforated ulcer when Norma Jean was ten, but Mabel, who was accepted into the United Daughters of the Confederacy in 1975, is still preoccupied with going back to Shiloh.

"I've been to kingdom come and back in that truck out yonder," Leroy says to Mabel, "but we never yet set foot in that battleground. Ain't that something? How did I miss it?"

"It's not even that far," Mabel says.

After Mabel leaves, Norma Jean reads to Leroy from a list she has made. "Things you could do," she announces. "You could get a job as a guard at Union Carbide, where they'd let you set on a stool. You could get on at the lumberyard. You could do a little carpenter work, if you want to build so bad. You could—"

"I can't do something where I'd have to stand up all day."

"You ought to try standing up all day behind a cosmetics counter. It's amazing that I have strong feet, coming from two parents that never had strong feet at all." At the moment Norma Jean is holding on to the kitchen counter, raising her knees one at a time as she talks. She is wearing two-pound ankle weights.

"Don't worry," says Leroy. "I'll do something."

"You could truck calves to slaughter for somebody. You wouldn't have to drive any big old truck for that."

"I'm going to build you this house," says Leroy. "I want to make you a real home."

"I don't want to live in any log cabin."

"It's not a cabin. It's a house."

"I don't care. It looks like a cabin."

"You and me together could lift those logs. It's just like lifting weights."

Norma Jean doesn't answer. Under her breath, she is counting. Now she is marching through the kitchen. She is doing goose steps.

Before his accident, when Leroy came home he used to stay in the house with Norma Jean, watching TV in bed and playing cards. She would cook fried chicken, picnic ham, chocolate pie—all his favorites. Now he is home alone much of the time. In the mornings, Norma Jean disappears, leaving a cooling place in the bed. She eats a cereal called Body Buddies, and she leaves the bowl on the table, with the soggy tan balls floating in a milk puddle. He sees things about Norma Jean that he never realized before. When she chops onions, she stares off into a corner, as if she can't bear to look. She puts on her house slippers almost precisely at nine o'clock every evening and nudges her jogging shoes under the couch. She saves bread heels for the birds. Leroy watches the birds at the feeder. He notices the peculiar way goldfinches fly past the window. They close their wings, then fall, then spread their wings to catch and lift themselves. He wonders if they close their eyes when they fall. Norma Jean closes her eyes when they are in bed. She wants the lights turned out. Even then, he is sure she closes her eyes.

He goes for long drives around town. He tends to drive a car rather carelessly. Power steering and an automatic shift make a car feel so small and inconsequential that his body is hardly involved in the driving process. His injured leg stretches out comfortably. Once or twice he has almost hit something, but even the prospect of an accident seems minor in a car. He cruises the new subdivisions, feeling like a criminal rehearsing for a robbery. Norma Jean is probably right about a log house being inappropriate here in the new subdivisions. All the houses look grand and complicated. They depress him.

One day when Leroy comes home from a drive he finds Norma Jean in tears. She is in the kitchen making a potato and mushroom-soup casserole, with grated-cheese topping. She is crying because her mother caught her smoking.

"I didn't hear her coming. I was standing here puffing away pretty as you please," Norma Jean says, wiping her eyes.

"I knew it would happen sooner or later," says Leroy, putting his arm around her.

"She don't know the meaning of the word 'knock,'" says Norma Jean. "It's a wonder she hadn't caught me years ago."

"Think of it this way," Leroy says. "What if she caught me with a joint?"

"You better not let her!" Norma Jean shrieks. "I'm warning you, Leroy Moffitt!"

"I'm just kidding. Here, play me a tune. That'll help you relax."

Norma Jean puts the casserole in the oven and sets the timer. Then she plays a ragtime tune, with horns and banjo, as Leroy lights up a joint and lies on the couch, laughing to himself about Mabel's catching him at it. He thinks of Stevie Hamilton—a doctor's son pushing grass. Everything is funny. The whole town seems crazy and small. He is reminded of Virgil Mathis, a boastful policeman Leroy used to shoot pool with. Virgil recently led a drug bust in a back room at a bowling alley, where he seized ten thousand dollars' worth of marijuana. The newspaper had a picture of him holding up the bags of grass and grinning widely. Right now, Leroy can imagine Virgil breaking down the door and arresting him with a lungful of smoke. Virgil would probably have been alerted to the scene because of all the racket Norma Jean is making. Now she sounds like a hard-rock band. Norma Jean is terrific. When she switches to a Latin-rhythm version of "Sunshine Superman," Leroy hums along. Norma Jean's foot goes up and down, up and down.

"Well, what do you think?" Leroy says, when Norma Jean pauses to search through her music.

"What do I think about what?"

His mind has gone blank. Then he says, "I'll sell my rig and build us a house." That wasn't what he wanted to say. He wanted to know what she thought—what she *really* thought—about them.

"Don't start in on that again," says Norma Jean. She begins playing "Who'll Be the Next in Line?"

Leroy used to tell hitchhikers his whole life story—about his travels, his hometown, the baby. He would end with a question: "Well, what do you think?" It was just a rhetorical question. In time, he had the feeling that he'd been telling the same story over and over to the same hitchhikers. He quit talking to hitchhikers when he realized how his voice sounded—whining and self-pitying, like some teenage-tragedy song. Now Leroy has the sudden impulse to tell Norma Jean about himself, as if he had just met her. They have known each other so long they have forgotten a lot about each other. They could become reacquainted. But when the oven timer goes off and she runs to the kitchen, he forgets why he wants to do this.

The next day, Mabel drops by. It is Saturday and Norma Jean is cleaning. Leroy is studying the plans of his log house, which have finally come in the mail. He has them spread out on the table—big sheets of stiff blue paper, with diagrams and numbers printed in white. While Norma Jean runs the vacuum, Mabel drinks coffee. She sets her coffee cup on a blueprint.

"I'm just waiting for time to pass," she says to Leroy, drumming her fingers on the table.

As soon as Norma Jean switches off the vacuum, Mabel says in a loud voice, "Did you hear about the datsun dog that killed the baby?"

Norma Jean says, "The word is 'dachshund.'"

"They put the dog on trial. It chewed the baby's legs off. The mother was in the next room all the time." She raises her voice. "They thought it was neglect."

Norma Jean is holding her ears. Leroy manages to open the refrigerator and get some Diet Pepsi to offer Mabel. Mabel still has some coffee and she waves away the Pepsi.

"Datsuns are like that," Mabel says. "They're jealous dogs. They'll tear a place to pieces if you don't keep an eye on them."

"You better watch out what you're saying, Mabel," says Leroy.

"Well, facts is facts."

Leroy looks out the window at his rig. It is like a huge piece of furniture gathering dust in the backyard. Pretty soon it will be an antique. He hears the vacuum cleaner. Norma Jean seems to be cleaning the living room rug again.

Later, she says to Leroy, "She just said that about the baby because she caught me smoking. She's trying to pay me back."

"What are you talking about?" Leroy says, nervously shuffling blueprints.

"You know good and well," Norma Jean says. She is sitting in a kitchen chair with her feet up and her arms wrapped around her knees. She looks small and helpless. She says, "The very idea, her bringing up a subject like that! Saying it was neglect."

"She didn't mean that," Leroy says.

"She might not have *thought* she meant it. She always says things like that. You don't know how she goes on."

"But she didn't really mean it. She was just talking."

Leroy opens a king-sized bottle of beer and pours it into two glasses, dividing it carefully. He hands a glass to Norma Jean and she takes it from him mechanically. For a long time, they sit by the kitchen window watching the birds at the feeder.

Something is happening. Norma Jean is going to night school. She has graduated from her six-week body-building course and now she is taking an adult-education course in composition at Paducah Community College. She spends her evenings outlining paragraphs.

"First you have a topic sentence," she explains to Leroy. "Then you divide it up. Your secondary topic has to be connected to your primary topic."

To Leroy, this sounds intimidating. "I never was any good in English," he says.

"It makes a lot of sense."

"What are you doing this for, anyhow?"

She shrugs. "It's something to do." She stands up and lifts her dumbbells a few times.

"Driving a rig, nobody cared about my English."

"I'm not criticizing your English."

Norma Jean used to say, "If I lose ten minutes' sleep, I just drag all day." Now she stays up late, writing compositions. She got a B on her first paper—a how-to theme on soup-based casseroles. Recently Norma Jean has been cooking unusual foods—tacos, lasagna, Bombay chicken. She doesn't play the organ anymore, though her second paper was called "Why Music Is Important to Me." She sits at the kitchen table, concentrating on her outlines, while Leroy plays with his log house plans, practicing with a set of Lincoln Logs. The thought of getting a truckload of notched, numbered logs scares him, and he wants to be prepared. As he and Norma Jean work together at the kitchen table, Leroy has the hopeful thought that they are sharing something, but he knows he is a fool to think this. Norma Jean is miles away. He knows he is going to lose her. Like Mabel, he is just waiting for time to pass.

One day, Mabel is there before Norma Jean gets home from work, and Leroy finds himself confiding in her. Mabel, he realizes, must know Norma Jean better than he does.

"I don't know what's got into that girl," Mabel says. "She used to go to bed with the chickens. Now you say she's up all hours. Plus her a-smoking. I like to died."

"I want to make her this beautiful home," Leroy says, indicating the Lincoln Logs. "I don't think she even wants it. Maybe she was happier with me gone."

"She don't know what to make of you, coming home like this."

"Is that it?"

Mabel takes the roof off his Lincoln Log cabin. "You couldn't get *me* in a log cabin," she says. "I was raised in one. It's no picnic, let me tell you."

"They're different now," says Leroy.

"I tell you what," Mabel says, smiling oddly at Leroy.

"What?"

"Take her on down to Shiloh. Y'all need to get out together, stir a little. Her brain's all balled up over them books."

Leroy can see traces of Norma Jean's features in her mother's face. Mabel's worn face has the texture of crinkled cotton, but suddenly she looks pretty. It occurs to Leroy that Mabel has been hinting all along that she wants them to take her with them to Shiloh.

"Let's all go to Shiloh," he says. "You and me and her. Come Sunday."

Mabel throws up her hands in protest. "Oh, no, not me. Young folks want to be by theirselves."

When Norma Jean comes in with groceries, Leroy says excitedly, "Your mama here's been dying to go to Shiloh for thirty-five years. It's about time we went, don't you think?"

"I'm not going to butt in on anybody's second honeymoon," Mabel says.

"Who's going on a honeymoon, for Christ's sake?" Norma Jean says loudly.

"I never raised no daughter of mine to talk that-a-way," Mabel says.

"You ain't seen nothing yet," says Norma Jean. She starts putting away boxes and cans, slamming cabinet doors.

"There's a log cabin at Shiloh," Mabel says. "It was there

during the battle. There's bullet holes in it."

"When are you going to *shut up* about Shiloh, Mama?" asks Norma Jean.

"I always thought Shiloh was the prettiest place, so full of history," Mabel goes on. "I just hoped y'all could see it once before I die, so you could tell me about it." Later, she whispers to Leroy, "You do what I said. A little change is what she needs."

"Your name means 'the king,' " Norma Jean says to Leroy that evening. He is trying to get her to go to Shiloh, and she is reading a book about another century.

"Well, I reckon I ought to be right proud."

"I guess so."

"Am I still king around here?"

Norma Jean flexes her biceps and feels them for hardness. "I'm not fooling around with anybody, if that's what you mean," she says.

"Would you tell me if you were?"

"I don't know."

"What does *your* name mean?"

"It was Marilyn Monroe's real name."

"No kidding!"

"Norma comes from the Normans. They were invaders," she says. She closes her book and looks hard at Leroy. "I'll go to Shiloh with you if you'll stop staring at me."

On Sunday, Norma Jean packs a picnic and they go to Shiloh. To Leroy's relief, Mabel says she does not want to come with them. Norma Jean drives, and Leroy, sitting beside her, feels like some boring hitchhiker she has picked up. He tries some conversation, but she answers him in monosyllables. At Shiloh, she drives aimlessly through the park, past bluffs and trails and steep ravines. Shiloh is an immense place, and Leroy cannot see it as a battleground. It is not what he expected. He thought it would look like a golf course. Monuments are everywhere, showing through the thick clusters of trees. Norma

Jean passes the log cabin Mabel mentioned. It is surrounded by tourists looking for bullet holes.

"That's not the kind of log house I've got in mind," says Leroy apologetically.

"I know *that.*"

"This is a pretty place. Your mama was right."

"It's O.K.," says Norma Jean. "Well, we've seen it. I hope she's satisfied."

They burst out laughing together.

At the park museum, a movie on Shiloh is shown every half hour, but they decide that they don't want to see it. They buy a souvenir Confederate flag for Mabel, and then they find a picnic spot near the cemetery. Norma Jean has brought a picnic cooler, with pimiento sandwiches, soft drinks, and Yodels. Leroy eats a sandwich and then smokes a joint, hiding it behind the picnic cooler. Norma Jean has quit smoking altogether. She is picking cake crumbs from the cellophane wrapper, like a fussy bird.

Leroy says, "So the boys in gray ended up in Corinth. The Union soldiers zapped 'em finally. April 7, 1862."

They both know that he doesn't know any history. He is just talking about some of the historical plaques they have read. He feels awkward, like a boy on a date with an older girl. They are still just making conversation.

"Corinth is where Mama eloped to," says Norma Jean.

They sit in silence and stare at the cemetery for the Union dead and, beyond, at a tall cluster of trees. Campers are parked nearby, bumper to bumper, and small children in bright clothing are cavorting and squealing. Norma Jean wads up the cake wrapper and squeezes it tightly in her hand. Without looking at Leroy, she says, "I want to leave you."

Leroy takes a bottle of Coke out of the cooler and flips off the cap. He holds the bottle poised near his mouth but cannot remember to take a drink. Finally he says, "No, you don't."

"Yes, I do."

"I won't let you."

"You can't stop me."

"Don't do me that way."

Leroy knows Norma Jean will have her own way. "Didn't I promise to be home from now on?" he says.

"In some ways, a woman prefers a man who wanders," says Norma Jean. "That sounds crazy, I know."

"You're not crazy."

Leroy remembers to drink from his Coke. Then he says, "Yes, you *are* crazy. You and me could start all over again. Right back at the beginning."

"We *have* started all over again," says Norma Jean. "And this is how it turned out."

"What did I do wrong?"

"Nothing."

"Is this one of those women's lib things?" Leroy asks.

"Don't be funny."

The cemetery, a green slope dotted with white markers, looks like a subdivision site. Leroy is trying to comprehend that his marriage is breaking up, but for some reason he is wondering about white slabs in a graveyard.

"Everything was fine till Mama caught me smoking," says Norma Jean, standing up. "That set something off."

"What are you talking about?"

"She won't leave me alone—*you* won't leave me alone." Norma Jean seems to be crying, but she is looking away from him. "I feel eighteen again. I can't face that all over again." She starts walking away. "No, it *wasn't* fine. I don't know what I'm saying. Forget it."

Leroy takes a lungful of smoke and closes his eyes as Norma Jean's words sink in. He tries to focus on the fact that thirty-five hundred soldiers died on the grounds around him. He can only think of that war as a board game with plastic soldiers. Leroy almost smiles, as he compares the Confederates' daring attack on the Union camps and Virgil Mathis's raid on the bowling alley. General Grant, drunk and furious, shoved the Southerners back to Corinth, where Mabel and Jet Beasley were married years later, when Mabel was still thin and good-looking. The next day, Mabel and Jet visited the battleground, and then Norma Jean was born, and then she married Leroy and they had a baby, which they lost, and now Leroy and Norma Jean are here at the same battleground. Leroy knows he is leaving out a lot. He is leaving out the insides of history. History was always just names and dates to him. It occurs to him that building a house out of logs is similarly empty—too simple. And the real inner workings of a marriage, like most of history, have escaped him. Now he sees that building a log house is the dumbest idea he could have had. It was clumsy of him to think Norma Jean would want a log house. It was a crazy idea. He'll have to think of something else, quickly. He will wad the blueprints into tight balls and fling them into the lake. Then he'll get moving again. He opens his eyes. Norma Jean has moved away and is walking through the cemetery, following a serpentine brick path.

Leroy gets up to follow his wife, but his good leg is asleep and his bad leg still hurts him. Norma Jean is far away, walking rapidly toward the bluff by the river, and he tries to hobble toward her. Some children run past him, screaming noisily. Norma Jean has reached the bluff, and she is looking out over the Tennessee River. Now she turns toward Leroy and waves her arms. Is she beckoning to him? She seems to be doing an exercise for her chest muscles. The sky is unusually pale— the color of the dust ruffle Mabel made for their bed.

# The Rookers

Mary Lou Skaggs runs errands for her husband. She hauls lumber, delivers bookshelves, even makes a special trip to town just to exchange flathead screws. Mack will occasionally go out to measure people's kitchens for the cabinets and countertops he makes, but he gets uncomfortable if he has to be away long. And the highway makes him nervous. Increasingly, he stays at home, working in his shop in the basement. They live on a main road between two small Kentucky towns, and the shop sign has been torn down by teenagers so many times that Mack has given up trying to keep it repaired. Mary Lou feels that Mack never charges enough for his work, but she has always helped out—keeping the books, canning and sewing, as well as periodically working for H & R Block—and they have managed to send their youngest child to college. The two older daughters are married, with homes nearby, but Judy is a freshman at Murray State. After she left, Mack became so involved with some experimental woodworking projects that Mary Lou thought he had almost failed to notice that the children had all gone.

For some neighbors, Mack made a dinette booth out of a church pew salvaged from an abandoned country church. The sanding took days. "I'm sanding off layers of hypocrisy," Mack said.

"You sound like that guy that used to stand out on the corner and yell when church let out on Sunday," said Mary Lou. " 'Here come the hyps,' he'd say."

"Who was that?"

"Oh, just some guy in town. That was years ago. He led a crusade against fluoride too."

"Fluoride's O.K. It hardens the teeth."

For their twenty-fifth anniversary, Mack made Mary Lou a round card table from scrap pine, with an old sprocket from a bulldozer as a base. It was connected to the table with a length of lead pipe. "It didn't cost a thing," Mack said. "Just imagination."

The tabletop, a mosaic of wood scraps, was like a crazy quilt, Mary Lou thought. It was heavily varnished with polyurethane, making a slick surface. Mack had spray-painted the sprocket black.

"Do you like it?" he asked.

"Sure."

"No, you don't. I can tell you don't."

"It's real pretty."

"It's not something you would buy in a store," Mack said apologetically.

Mary Lou had never seen a table like it. Automatically, she counted the oddly shaped pieces Mack had fit together for the top. Twenty-one. It seemed that Mack was trying to put together the years of their marriage into a convincing whole and this was as far as he got. Mary Lou is concerned about Mack. He seems embarrassed that they are alone in the house now for the first time in years. When Judy fails to come home on weekends, he paces around restlessly. He has even started reading books and magazines, as if he can somehow keep up with Judy and her studies. Lately he has become obsessed with the weather. He likes to compare the weather with the predictions in the *Old Farmer's Almanac.* He likes it when the *Almanac* is wrong. Anyone else would be rooting for the *Almanac* to be right.

When the women Mary Lou plays Rook with come over, Mack stays in the den watching TV, hardly emerging to say hello. Thelma Crandall, Clausie Dowdy, and Edda Griffin— the Rookers, Mary Lou calls them—are all much older than

Mary Lou, and they are all widows. Mack and Mary Lou married young, and even though they have three grown daughters, they are only in their late forties. Mack says it is unhealthy for her to socialize with senior citizens, but Mary Lou doesn't believe him. It does her good to have some friends.

Mary Lou shows off the new card table when the women arrive one evening. They all come in separate cars, not trusting each other's driving.

"It's set on a bulldozer sprocket," Mary Lou explains.

"How did Mack come up with such an idea?" asks Clausie, admiring the table.

Thelma, the oldest of the group, is reluctant to sit at the table, for fear she will catch her foot in one of the holes at the base.

"Couldn't you cover up the bottom of that table with a rug or something?" asks Edda. "We might catch our feet."

Mary Lou finds an old afghan and drapes it around the bulldozer sprocket, tamping it down carefully in the holes. She gets along with old people, and she feels exhilarated when she is playing cards with her friends. "They tickle me," she told Mack once. "Old people are liable to say anything." Mack said old people gave him the creeps, the way they talked about diseases.

Mary Lou keeps a list of whose turn it is to deal, because they often lose track. When they deal the cards on the new table, the cards shoot across the slick surface. This evening they discuss curtain material, Edda's granddaughter's ovary infection, a place that appeared on Thelma's arm, and the way the climate has changed. All three of the widows live in nice houses in town. When Mary Lou goes to their houses to play Rook, she is impressed by their shag rugs, their matching sets of furniture, their neat kitchens. Their walls are filled with pictures of grandchildren and great-grandchildren. Mary Lou's pictures are scattered around in drawers, and her kitchen is always a mess.

"They're beating the socks off of us," Mary Lou tells Mack

when he watches the game for a moment. Mary Lou is teamed up with Thelma. "I had the bird—that was the only trump I had."

"I haven't had it a time," says Clausie, a peppy little woman with a trim figure.

"I put thirty in the widow and they caught it," Thelma tells Mack.

"The rook's a sign of bad luck," Mack says. "A rook ain't nothing but a crow."

When he returns to the football game he is watching on TV, Edda says with a laugh, "Did y'all hear what Erma Bombeck said? She said any man who watches more than a hundred and sixty-eight football games in one year ought to be declared legally dead."

They all laugh in little bursts and spasms, but Mary Lou says defensively, "Mack doesn't watch that much football. He just watches it because it's on. Usually he has his nose stuck in a book."

"I used to read," says Clausie. "But I got out of the habit."

Later, Mary Lou complains to Mack about his behavior. "You could at least be friendly," she says.

"I like to see you playing cards," says Mack.

"You're changing the subject."

"You light up and you look so pretty."

"I'll say one thing for those old gals. They get out and *go.* They don't hide under a bushel. Like some people I know."

"I don't hide under a bushel."

"You think they're just a bunch of silly old widow women."

"You look beautiful when you're having a good time," says Mack, goosing her and making her jump.

"They're not that old, though," says Mary Lou. "They don't act it. Edda's a great-grandmother, but she's just as spry! She goes to Paducah driving that little Bobcat like she owned the road. And Clausie hasn't got a brain in her head. She's just like a kid—"

But now Mack is absorbed in something on TV, a pudding commercial. Mary Lou has tried to be patient with Mack, thinking that he will grow out of his current phase. Sooner or later, she and Mack will have to face growing older together. Mack says that having a daughter in college makes him feel he has missed something, but Mary Lou has tried to make him see that they could still enjoy life. Before she began playing regularly with the Rookers, she had several ideas for doing things together, now that they were no longer tied down with a family. She suggested bowling, camping, a trip to Opryland. But Mack said he'd rather improve his mind. He has been reading *Shōgun*. He made excuses about the traffic. They had a chance to go on a free weekend to the Paradise Valley Estates, a resort development in the Ozarks. There was no obligation. All they had to do was hear a talk and watch some slides. But Mack hated the idea and said there was a catch. Mack made Mary Lou feel she was pressuring him, and she decided not to bring up these topics for a while. She would wait for him to come out of his shell. But she was disappointed about the free weekend. The resort had swimming, nature trails, horseback riding, golf, fishing, and pontoon boat rentals. The bathrooms had whirlpools.

When the telephone rings at five o'clock one morning, Mary Lou is certain there must be bad news from Judy. As she runs to the kitchen to answer the telephone, her mind runs through dope, suicide, dorm fires. The man on the phone has a loud voice that blares out at her. He makes her guess who he is. He turns out to be Ed Williams, her long-lost brother. Mary Lou is speechless, having concluded several years ago that he must be dead. Ed had gone to Texas for his health, traveling with a woman with a dark complexion and pierced ears. Now he tells Mary Lou he is married to that woman, named Linda, and they are living in California with her two children from a former marriage.

"What do you look like?" asks Mary Lou.

"I'm a beanpole. I have to bend over to make a shadow."

Mary Lou says, "I'm old and fat and ugly. Mack would whip me to hear that. I'm not really, but after nine years, you'd know the difference. It's been nine years, Ed Williams. I could kill you for doing us like that."

"I just finished building me a house, but I don't have a thing I want to put in it except a washer and dryer."

"All the girls are gone. Judy's in college—first one to go. We're proud. She says she's going to make a doctor. Betty and Janie are married, with younguns."

"I've got me a camper and a pickup and a retirement lot," Ed says. "What's Mack up to?"

"Oh, he's so lonesome with all the girls gone that he's acting peculiar."

Disturbed and excited, Mary Lou burns the bacon while she's telling Mack about the call. Mack seems surprised that Ed is still with the same woman.

"How did she get him wrapped around her little finger? Ed would never even stay in one place long enough to get a crop out."

Mary Lou shoves Mack's plate in front of him. "I thought to my *soul* he was dead. When he went out there, he looked terrible. He thought he had TB. But it was just like him not to write or call or say boo."

"Ed always was wild. I bet he was drunk."

Mary Lou sits down to eat. Cautiously, she says, "He wants us to come out and see him."

"Why can't he come here?"

"He's got a family now. He's tied down."

Mack flips through the *Old Farmer's Almanac* as he eats.

Mary Lou says, "We could go out there. We're not tied down."

Mack fastens his finger on a page. "What if Judy wanted to come home? She'd have to stay here by herself."

"You beat all I've ever seen, Mack." Mary Lou smears jelly on her toast and eats a bite. She says, "Ed said he just got to thinking how he wanted to hear from home. He said Christmas was coming up and—you want to know something, Mack? Ed was on my mind all one day last week. And then he calls, just like that. I must have had a premonition. What does the *Farmer's Almanac* say to that?"

Mack points to a weather chart. "It says here we're due for a mild winter—no snow hardly a-tall. But I don't believe it. I believe we're going to have snow before Christmas."

Mack sounds so serious. He sounds like the President delivering a somber message on the economy. Mary Lou doesn't know what to think.

The next evening at Clausie's house, the Rookers are elated over Mary Lou's news, but she doesn't go into details about her brother's bad reputation.

"It sounded just like him," she says. "His voice was just as *clear.*"

Clausie urges Mary Lou to persuade Mack to go to California.

"Oh, we could never afford it," says Mary Lou. "I'm afraid to even bring it up."

"It's awful far," says Thelma. "My oldest girl's daughter went out in May of seventy-three. She left the day school was out."

"Did he say what he was doing?" Edda asks Mary Lou.

"He said he just built him a house and didn't have anything he wanted to put in it but a washer and dryer. Mack's making fun of me for carrying on so, but he never liked Ed anyway. Ed was always a little wild."

For refreshments, Clausie has made lemon chiffon cake and boiled custard. Mary Lou loves being at Clausie's. Her house is like her chiffon cakes, all soft surfaces and pleasant colors, and she has a new factory-waxed Congoleum floor in her kitchen, patterned after a brick wall.

When Clausie clears away the dishes, she pats Mary Lou's hand and says, "Well, maybe your brother will come back home, if you all can't go out. Sounds like his mind's on his family now."

"You and Mack need to go more," says Edda.

"You ought to get Mack out square-dancing!" says Clausie, who belongs to a square-dancing club.

Mary Lou has to laugh, that idea is so farfetched.

"My fiftieth wedding anniversary would have been day before yesterday," says Thelma, whose husband had died the year before.

"It's too bad Otis couldn't have lived just a little longer," says Clausie sympathetically.

"He bought us eight grave plots. Otis wanted me and him to have plenty of room."

The widows compare prices of caskets.

"Law, I wouldn't want to be cremated the way some of them are doing now," says Edda. "To save space."

"Me neither," says Clausie with a whoop. "Did y'all see one of them Russians on television while back? At his funeral there was this horse and buggy pulling the body, and instead of a casket there was this little-bitty vase propped up there. It was real odd looking."

"The very idea!" cries Edda. "Keeping somebody in a vase on the mantel. Somebody might use it for a ashtray."

Clausie and Edda and Thelma are all laughing. Mary Lou shuffles the cards distractedly, the way Mack flips through the *Old Farmer's Almanac,* as if some wisdom might rub off.

"Come on, y'all, let's play," she says.

But the women cannot settle down and concentrate on the game yet. They are still laughing, overflowing with good humor. Mary Lou shuffles the cards endlessly, as though she can never get them exactly right.

Mack hardly watches TV anymore, except when the Rookers are there. He sits in his armchair reading. He belongs to a book club. Since Judy went away to college, he has read *Shōgun, Rage of Angels, The Clowns of God,* and *The Covenant.* He read parts of *Cosmos,* which Mary Lou brought him from the library. He does not believe anything he has read in *Cosmos.* It was not on TV in their part of the country. Now he is struggling along with *The Encyclopedia of Philosophy.*

When he reads that, his face is set in a painful frown.

Mary Lou delivers a gun cabinet to a young couple in a trailer park. How they can afford a gun cabinet, she has no idea. She picks up some sandpaper for Mack. Mack will never make a list. He sends her to town for one or two things at a time. At home, he apologizes for not going on the errand himself. He is rubbing a piece of wood with a rag.

"Look at this," he says excitedly, showing Mary Lou a sketch of some shelves. "I decided what I want to make Judy for Christmas, for a surprise."

The sketch is an intricate design with small compartments.

"Judy called while you were gone," Mack says. "After I talked to her, I got an inspiration. I'm making her this for her dorm room. It's going to have a place here for her turntable, and slots for records. It's called a home entertainment center."

"It's pretty. What did Judy call for?"

"She's coming home tomorrow. Her roommate quit school, and Judy's coming home early to study for her exams next week."

"What happened to her roommate?"

"She wouldn't say. She must be in some kind of trouble, though."

"Is Judy all right?"

"Yeah. After she called, I just got to thinking that I wanted to do something nice for her." Mack is fitting sandpaper onto his sander, using a screwdriver to roll it in. Suddenly he says, "You wouldn't go off and leave me, would you?"

"What makes you say that?"

Mack sets down the sander and takes her by the shoulders, then holds her close to him. He smells like turpentine. "You're always wanting to run around," he says. "You might get ideas."

"Don't worry," says Mary Lou. "I wouldn't think of leaving you." She can't help adding sarcastically, "You'd starve."

"You might go off to find Ed."

"Well, not in that pickup anyway," she says. "The brakes are bad."

When he releases her, he looks happy. He turns on the

sander and runs it across the piece of wood, moving with the grain. When he turns off the sander and begins rubbing away the fine dust with a tack rag, Mary Lou says, "People were always jealous of Ed. The only reason he ever got in trouble was that people picked on him because he carried so much money around with him. People heard he had money, and when he'd pull into town in that rig he drove, the police would think up some excuse to run him in. People were just jealous. Everything he touched turned to money."

The way Mack is rubbing the board with the tack rag makes Mary Lou think of Aladdin and his lamp. He rubs and rubs, nodding when she speaks.

Judy drives a little Chevette she bought with money she earned working at the Burger Chef. She arrives at suppertime the next day with a pizza and a tote bag of books. Mary Lou serves green beans, corn, and slaw with the pizza. She and Mack hover over their daughter. At their insistence, Judy tries to explain what happened to her roommate.

"Stephanie had a crush on this Western Civ professor and she made it into a big thing. Now her boyfriend is giving her a real hard time. He accused her of running around with the teacher, but she didn't. Now he's mad at her, and she just took off to straighten out her head."

"Did she go back home to her mama and daddy?" Mary Lou asks.

Judy shakes her head no, and her hair flies around like a dust mop being shaken. Mary Lou almost expects things to fly out. Judy's hair is curly and flyaway. She has put something on it. Judy is wearing a seashell on a chain around her neck.

"This pizza's cold," says Judy. She won't touch the green beans.

Mack says, "I don't see why she won't stay and finish her tests at least. Now she'll have to pay for a whole extra semester."

"Well, I hope she don't go off the deep end like her mama," says Mary Lou. Judy once told them that Stephanie's mother had had several nervous breakdowns.

"Her daddy don't eat meat a-tall?" asks Mack.

"No. He's a vegetarian."

"And he don't get sick?"

Judy shakes her head again.

After supper, Judy dumps out the contents of her tote bag on the love seat. She has a math book, a science book, something called *A Rhetoric for the Eighties,* and a heavy psychology book. She sits cross-legged on the love seat, explaining quantum mechanics to Mary Lou and Mack. She calls her teacher Bob.

Judy says, "It's not that weird. It's just the study of elementary particles—the littlest things in the world, smaller than atoms. There's some things called photons that disappear if you look for them. Nobody can find them."

"How do they know they're there, then?" asks Mack skeptically.

"Where do they go?" Mary Lou asks.

The seashell bounces between Judy's breasts as she talks excitedly, moving her arms like a cheerleader. She is wearing a plaid flannel shirt with the cuffs rolled back. She says, "If you try to separate them, they disappear. They don't even *exist* except in a group. Bob says this is one of the most *important* discoveries in the history of the world. He says it just *explodes* all the old ideas about physics."

Bob is not the same teacher Stephanie had the crush on. That teacher's name is Tom. Mary Lou has this much straight. Mack is pacing the floor, the way he does sometimes when Judy doesn't come home on the weekend.

"I thought it was philosophy you were taking," he says.

"No, physics."

"Mack's been reading up on philosophy," says Mary Lou. "He thought you were taking philosophy."

"It's similar," Judy says. "In quantum mechanics, there's no final answer. Anything you look at might have a dozen different meanings. Bob says the new physics is discovering what the Eastern mystics have known all along."

Mary Lou is confused. "If these things don't exist, then how do they know about them?"

"They know about them when they're in bunches." Judy

begins writing in her notebook. She looks up and says, "Quantum mechanics is like a statistical study of group behavior."

Abruptly, Mack goes to the basement. Mary Lou picks up her sewing and begins watching *Real People* on TV. She can hear the signs of her husband's existence: the sound of the drill from the shop, then his saw. A spurt of swearing.

The next evening, Judy talks Mary Lou into going to a movie, but Mack says he has work to do. He is busy with the home entertainment center he is building for Judy. Mary Lou is embarrassed to be going to an R-rated movie, but Judy laughs at her. Judy drives her Chevette, and they stop to pick up Clausie, whom Mary Lou has invited.

"Clausie changes with the times," Mary Lou tells her daughter apologetically. "You ought to see the way she gets out and goes. She even square-dances."

Clausie insists on climbing in the back seat because she is small. "I wore pants 'cause I knew y'all would," she says. "I don't wear them when I come to your house, Mary Lou, because I just don't feel right wearing pants around a man."

"I haven't worn a dress since 1980," says Judy.

"This show is going to curl our ears," Mary Lou tells Clausie.

"Oh, Mom," Judy says.

"Is it a dirty movie?" Clausie asks eagerly.

"It's R-rated," says Mary Lou.

"Well, I say live and learn," says Clausie, laughing. "Thelma and Edda would have a fit if they knew what we was up to."

"Mack wouldn't go," says Mary Lou. "He doesn't like to be in the middle of a bunch of women—especially if they're going to say dirty-birds."

"Everybody says those words," says Judy. "They don't mean anything."

The movie is *Stir Crazy*. Mary Lou has to hold her side, she laughs so hard. When the actors cuss, she sinks in her seat, clutching Judy's arm. Judy doesn't even flinch. As she watches the movie, which drags in places, Mary Lou now and then thinks about how her family has scattered. If you break up a group, the individuals could disappear out of existence. She has the unsettling thought that what is happening with Mack is that he is disappearing like that, disconnected from everybody, the way Ed did. On the screen, Gene Wilder is on a mechanical bull, spinning around and around, raising his arm in triumph.

Later, after they drop off Clausie and are driving home, Judy turns on the car radio. Mary Lou is still chuckling over the movie, but Judy seems depressed. She has hardly mentioned her roommate, so Mary Lou asks, "Where'd Stephanie go then, if she didn't go home?"

Judy turns the radio down. "She went to her sister's, in Nashville. Her brother-in-law's a record promoter and they've got this big place with a swimming pool and horses and stuff."

"Well, maybe she can make up with her boyfriend when she cools off."

"I don't think so." Judy turns right at the high school and heads down the highway. She says, "She wants to break up with him, but he won't leave her alone, so she just took off."

Mary Lou sighs. "This day and time, people just do what they please. They just hit the road. Like those guys in the show. And like Ed."

"Stephanie's afraid of Jeff, though, afraid of what he might do."

"What?"

"Oh, I don't know. Just something crazy." Judy turns up the volume of the radio, saying, "Here's a song for you, Mom. It's a dirty song. 'The Horizontal Bop'—get it?"

Mary Lou listens for a moment. "I don't get it," she says, fearing something as abstruse as the photons. In the song, the singer says repeatedly, "Everybody wants to do the Horizontal Bop."

"Oh, I get it," Mary Lou says with a sudden laugh. "I don't dare tell my Rookers about that." A moment later, she says, "But they wouldn't get it. It's the word 'bop.' They probably never heard the word 'bop.'"

Mary Lou feels a little pleased with herself. Bop. Bebop. She's not so old. Her daughter is not so far away. For a brief moment, Mary Lou feels that rush of joy that children experience when they whirl around happily, unconscious of time.

When Mary Lou's friends come to play Rook the following evening, they are curious about Judy's roommate, but Judy won't divulge much. She is curled on the love seat, studying math. Mary Lou explains to the Rookers, "Stephanie comes from a kind of disturbed family. Her mother's had a bunch of nervous breakdowns and her daddy's a vegetarian." Mack has the TV too loud, and it almost seems that the Incredible Hulk is in on the card game. Mary Lou gets Mack to turn down the sound. Later, he turns the TV off and picks up Judy's physics book. As the game goes on, he periodically goes to the telephone and dials the time-and-temperature number. The temperature is dropping, he reports. It is already down to twenty-four. He is hoping for snow, but the Rookers worry about the weather, fearful of driving back in the freezing night air.

When Clausie tells about *Stir Crazy*, Mary Lou tries to describe the scene that cracked her up—Richard Pryor and Gene Wilder dressed up in elaborate feathered costumes. They were supposed to be woodpeckers.

Clausie says, *"I* liked to died when the jailer woke 'em up in the morning, and they was both of 'em trying to use the commode at the same time."

The Rookers keep getting mixed up, missing plays. Thelma plays the wrong color.

"What did you do that for?" asks Edda, her partner tonight. "Trumps is green."

Thelma says, "I'm so bumfuzzled I can't think. I don't know when I've ever listened to such foolishness. Peckerwoods and niggers and a dirty show."

Mary Lou has been thinking of commenting on a new disease she has heard of, in which a person is afflicted by uncontrollable twitching and compulsive swearing, but she realizes that's a bad idea. She jumps up, saying, "Let's stop for refreshments, y'all. I made coconut cake with seven-minute icing."

Mary Lou serves the cake on her good plates, and everyone comments on how moist it is. After finishing her cake and iced tea, Thelma suddenly insists on leaving because of the weather. She says her feet are cold. Mary Lou offers to turn up the heat, but Thelma already has her coat on. She whips out her flashlight and heads for the door. Thelma's Buick sounds like a cement mixer. As they hear it backing out of the driveway, Clausie says, in a confidential tone, "She's mad because we saw that dirty show. The weather, my eye."

"She's real religious," says Edda.

"Well, golly-Bill, I'm as Christian as the next one!" cries Mary Lou. "Them words don't mean anything against religion. I bet Mack just got her stirred up about the temperature."

"Thelma's real old-timey," says Clausie. "She don't have any idea some of the things kids do nowadays."

"Times has changed, that's for sure," says Mary Lou.

Edda says, "Otis spoiled her. He carried her around on a pillow."

Mary Lou takes Mack some cake on a paper plate. He is still reading the physics book.

"We went set," Mary Lou says. "I had the Rook last hand, but it didn't do me any good."

"Thelma fixed your little red wagon, didn't she?" Mack says with a satisfied grin.

"It was your fault, getting her all worked up about the cold. Why don't you play with us—and take Thelma's place?"

"I'm busy studying. I think I've found a mistake in this book." He takes a large bite of cake. "Your coconut is my favorite," he says.

"I'll give you my recipe," Mary Lou snaps, wheeling away.

To Mary Lou's surprise, Judy offers to take Thelma's place and finish the card game. Mary Lou apologizes to her daughter for taking her away from her books, but Judy says she needs a break. Judy wins several hands, trumping with a flourish and grabbing the cards gleefully. Mary Lou is relieved. After Clausie and Edda leave, she feels excited and talkative. She finds herself telling Judy more about Ed, trying to make Judy remember her uncle. Mary Lou finds a box of photographs and shows Judy a picture of him. In the snapshot, he is standing in front of his tractor-trailer truck, holding a can of Hudepohl.

Mary Lou says, "He used to drive these long hauls, and when he'd come back through here, the police would try and pick him up. They heard he had money."

Mack joins Judy on the love seat. He shuffles silently through the pictures, and Mary Lou talks rapidly. "They'd follow him around, just waiting for him to cross that line, to start something. One time he and his first wife, Pauline, went to the show and when they got out they stuck him with a parking ticket. All because he had a record."

Judy and Mack are looking at the pictures together. Mack is studying a picture of himself with Judy, a bald-headed baby clutching a rattle.

"How did he get a record?" asks Judy.

"Wrecks."

"D.W.I.?" asks Judy knowingly. "Driving while intoxicated?"

Mary Lou nods. "Wrecks. A man got killed in one."

"Did they charge him?" Judy asks with sudden eagerness.

"No. It wasn't his fault," Mary Lou says quickly.

"You take after Ed," Mack tells Judy. "You kind of favor him around the eyes."

"He said he was a beanpole," says Mary Lou. "He said he had to bend over to make a shadow. He never had a ounce of fat on his bones."

Judy looks closely at her uncle's picture again, as though trying to memorize it for an exam.

"Wow," she says. "Far out."

Mack, shuffling some of the snapshots into a ragged stack, says to Judy in a plaintive tone, "Your mother wants to leave us and go out to California."

"I never said that," says Mary Lou. "When did I say that?"

Judy is not listening. She is in the kitchen, searching the

refrigerator. "Don't we have any Cokes?" she asks.

"No. We drunk the last one at supper," says Mary Lou, confused.

Judy puts on her jacket. "I'll run out and get some."

"It's freezing out there," says Mack anxiously.

"They're high at the Convenient," Mary Lou calls as Judy goes out the door. "But I guess that's the only place open this late."

Mary Lou sees Mack looking at her as though he is blaming her for Judy's leaving. "What are you looking at me in that tone of voice for?" she demands. "You're always making fun of me. I feel like an old stringling cat."

"Why, I didn't mean to," says Mack, pretending innocence.

"She's gone. Furthermore, she's *grown* and she can go out in the middle of the night if she wants to. She can go to South *America* if she wants to."

Mary Lou puts the cover on the cake stand and runs water in the sink over the cake plates. Before she can say more, Mack has lifted the telephone and is dialing the time-and-temperature number again. He listens, while his mouth drops open, as if in disbelief.

"The temperature's going down a degree every hour," he says in a whisper. "It's down to twenty-one."

Mary Lou suddenly realizes that Mack calls the temperature number because he is afraid to talk on the telephone, and by listening to a recording, he doesn't have to reply. It's his way of pretending that he's involved. He wants it to snow so he won't have to go outside. He is afraid of what might happen. But it occurs to her that what he must really be afraid of is women. Then Mary Lou feels so sick and heavy with her power over him that she wants to cry. She sees the way her husband is standing there, in a frozen pose. Mack looks as though he could stand there all night with the telephone receiver against his ear.

# Detroit Skyline, 1949

When I was nine, my mother took me on a long journey up North, because she wanted me to have a chance to see the tall buildings of Detroit. We lived on a farm in western Kentucky, not far from the U.S. highway that took so many Southerners northward to work in the auto industry just after World War II. We went to visit Aunt Mozelle, Mama's sister, and Uncle Boone Cashon, who had headed north soon after Boone's discharge from the service. They lived in a suburb of Detroit, and my mother had visited them once before. She couldn't get the skyscrapers she had seen out of her mind.

The Brooks bus took all day and all night to get there. On our trip, my mother threw up and a black baby cried all the way. I couldn't sleep for thinking about Detroit. Mama had tried in vain to show me how high the buildings were, pointing at the straight horizon beyond the cornfields. I had the impression that they towered halfway to the moon.

"Don't let the Polacks get you," my father had warned when we left. He had to stay home to milk the cows. My two-year-old brother, Johnny, stayed behind with him.

My aunt and uncle met us in a taxi at the bus station, and before I got a good look at them, they had engulfed me in their arms.

"I wouldn't have knowed you, Peggy Jo," my uncle said. "You was just a little squirt the last time I saw you."

"Don't this beat all?" said Aunt Mozelle. "Boone here could have built us a car by now—and us coming in a taxi."

"We've still got that old plug, but it gets us to town," said Mama.

"How could I build a car?" said Uncle Boone. "All I know is bumpers."

"That's what he does," my aunt said to me. "He puts on bumpers."

"We'll get a car someday soon," Uncle Boone said to his wife.

My uncle was a thin, delicate man with a receding hairline. His speckled skin made me think of the fragile shells of sparrow eggs. My aunt, on the other hand, was stout and tanned, with thick, dark hair draped like wings over her ears. I gazed at my aunt and uncle, trying to match them with the photograph my mother had shown me.

"Peggy's all worked up over seeing the tall buildings," said Mama as we climbed into the taxi. "The cat's got her tongue."

"It has *not!*"

"I'm afraid we've got bad news," said Aunt Mozelle. "The city buses is on strike and there's no way to get into Detroit."

"Don't say it!" cried Mama. "After we come all this way."

"It's trouble with the unions," said Boone. "But they might start up before y'all go back." He patted my knee and said, "Don't worry, littlun."

"The unions is full of reds," Aunt Mozelle whispered to my mother.

"Would it be safe to go?" Mama asked.

"We needn't worry," said Aunt Mozelle.

From the window of the squat yellow taxi, driven by a froglike man who grunted, I scrutinized the strange and vast neighborhoods we were passing through. I had never seen so many houses, all laid out in neat rows. The houses were new, and their pastel colors seemed peaceful and alluring. The sky-scrapers were still as remote to me as the castles in fairy tales, but these houses were real, and they were nestled next to each other in a thrilling intimacy. I knew at once where I wanted to live when I grew up—in a place like this, with neighbors.

My relatives' house, on a treeless new street, had venetian blinds and glossy hardwood floors. The living room carpet had giant pink roses that made me think you could play hopscotch on them. The guest room had knotty-pine paneling and a sweet-smelling cedar closet. Aunt Mozelle had put His and Her towels in our room. They had dogs on them and were pleasurably soft. At home, all of our washrags came out of detergent boxes, and our towels were faded and thin. The house was grand. And I had never seen my mother sparkling so. When she saw the kitchen, she whirled around happily, like a young girl, forgetting her dizziness on the bus. Aunt Mozelle had a toaster, a Mixmaster, an electric stove, and a large electric clock shaped like a rooster. On the wall, copper-bottomed pans gleamed in a row like golden-eyed cats lined up on a fence.

"Ain't it the berries?" my mother said to me. "Didn't I tell you?"

"Sometimes I have to pinch myself," said my aunt.

Just then, the front door slammed and a tall girl with a ponytail bounded into the house, saying "Hey!" in an offhand manner.

"Corn!" I said timidly, which seemed to perplex her, for she stared at me as though I were some odd sort of pet allowed into the house. This was my cousin Betsy Lou, in bluejeans rolled up halfway to her knees.

"Our kinfolks is here," Aunt Mozelle announced.

"Law, you've growed into a beanpole," said Mama to Betsy Lou.

"Welcome to our fair city, and I hope you don't get polio," Betsy Lou said to me.

"Watch what you're saying!" cried her mother. "You'll scare Peggy Jo."

"I imagine it'll be worse this summer than last," said Mama, looking worried.

"If we're stuck here without a car, you won't be any place to catch polio," Aunt Mozelle said, smiling at me.

"Polio spreads at swimming pools," Betsy Lou said.

"Then I'm not going to any swimming pool," I announced flatly.

Aunt Mozelle fussed around in her splendid kitchen, making dinner. I sat at the table, listening to Mama and her sister talk, in a gentle, flowing way, exchanging news, each stopping now and then to smile at the other in disbelief, or to look at me with pride. I couldn't take my eyes off my aunt, because she looked so much like my mother. She was older and heavier, but they had the same wide smile, the same unaffected laughter. They had similar sharp tips on their upper lips, which they filled in with bright red lipstick.

Mama said, "Boone sure is lucky. He's still young and ain't crippled and has a good job."

"Knock on wood," said Aunt Mozelle, rapping the door facing.

They had arranged for me to have a playmate, a girl my age who lived in the neighborhood. At home, in the summertime, I did not play with anyone, for the girls I knew at school lived too far away. Suddenly I found myself watching a chubby girl in a lilac piqué playsuit zoom up and down the sidewalk on roller skates.

"Come on," she said. "It's not hard."

"I'm coming." Betsy Lou had let me have her old skates, but I had trouble fastening them on my Weather-Bird sandals. I had never been on skates. At home there was no sidewalk. I decided to try skating on one foot, like a kid on a scooter, but the skate came loose.

"Put both of them on," said the girl, laughing at me.

Her name was Sharon Belletieri. She had to spell it for me. She said my name over and over until it sounded absurd. "Peggy Peggy Peggy Peggy Peggy." She made my name sound like "piggy."

"Don't you have a permanent?" she asked.

"No," I said, touching my pigtails. "My hair's in plaits 'cause it's summer."

"Har? Oh, you mean *hair?* Like air?" She waved at the air. She was standing there, perfectly balanced on her skates. She pronounced "hair" with two syllables. *Hayer.* I said something like a cross between *herr* and *harr.*

Sharon turned and whizzed down the sidewalk, then skidded to a stop at the corner, twisted around, and faced me.

"Are you going to skate or not?" she asked.

My uncle smoked Old Golds, and he seemed to have excess nervous energy. He was always jumping up from his chair to get something, or to look outside at the thermometer. He had found his name in a newspaper ad recently and had won a free pint of Cunningham's ice cream. My aunt declared that that made him somewhat famous. When I came back that day with the skates, he was sitting on the porch fanning himself with a newspaper. There was a heat wave, he said.

"What did you think of Sharon Belletieri?" he asked.

"She talks funny," I said, sitting down beside him.

"Folks up here all talk funny. I've noticed that too."

Uncle Boone had been a clerk in the war. He told me about the time he had spent in the Pacific theater, sailing around on a battleship, looking for Japs.

"Me and some buddies went to a Pacific island where there was a tribe of people with little tails," he said.

"Don't believe a word he says," said my aunt, who had been listening.

"It's true," said Uncle Boone. "Cross my heart and hope to die." He solemnly crossed his hands on his chest, then looked at his watch and said abruptly to me, "What do you think of Gorgeous George?"

"I don't know."

"How about Howdy Doody?"

"Who's Howdy Doody?"

"This child don't know nothing," he said to my aunt. "She's been raised with a bunch of country hicks."

"He's fooling," said Aunt Mozelle. "Go ahead and show her, Boone, for gosh sakes. Don't keep it a secret."

He was talking about television. I hadn't noticed the set in the living room because it had a sliding cover over the screen. It was a ten-inch table model with an upholstered sound box in a rosewood cabinet.

"We've never seen a television," my mother said.

"This will ruin her," said my aunt. "It's ruined Boone."

Uncle Boone turned on the television set. A wrestling match appeared on the screen, and I could see Gorgeous George flexing his muscles and tossing his curls. The television set resembled our radio. For a long time I was confused, thinking that I would now be able to see all my favorite radio programs.

"It's one of those sets you can look at in normal light and not go blind," my aunt said, to reassure us. "It's called Daylight TV."

"Wait till you see Howdy Doody," said Uncle Boone.

The picture on the television set was not clear. The reception required some imagination, and the pictures frequently dissolved, but I could see Gorgeous George moving across the screen, his curls bouncing. I could see him catch hold of his opponent and wrestle him to the floor, holding him so tight I thought he would choke.

That night, I lay in the cedar-perfumed room, too excited to sleep. I did not know what to expect next. The streetlamps glowed like moons through the venetian blinds, and as I lay there, my guardian angel slowly crept into my mind. In *Uncle Arthur's Bedtime Stories,* there was a picture of a child with his guardian angel hovering over him. It was a man angel, and gigantic, with immense white feathery bird's wings. Probably the boy could never see him because the angel stayed in what drivers of automobiles call a blind spot. I had a feeling that my own guardian angel had accompanied the bus to Michigan and was in the house with me. I imagined him floating above the bus. I knew that my guardian angel was supposed to keep me from harm, but I did not want anyone to know about him. I was very afraid of him. It was a long time before I fell asleep.

In the North, they drank coffee. Aunt Mozelle made a large pot of coffee in the mornings, and she kept it in a Thermos so she could drink coffee throughout the day.

Mama began drinking coffee. "Whew! I'm higher than a kite!" she would say. "I'll be up prowling half the night."

"Little girls shouldn't ought to drink coffee," Uncle Boone said to me more than once. "It turns them black."

"I don't even want any!" I protested. But I did like the enticing smell, which awoke me early in the mornings.

My aunt made waffles with oleomargarine. She kneaded a capsule of yellow dye into the pale margarine.

"It's a law," she told me one morning.

"They don't have that law down home anymore," said Mama. "People's turning to oleo and it's getting so we can't sell butter."

"I guess everybody forgot how it tasted," said Aunt Mozelle.

"I wouldn't be surprised if that business about the dye was a Communist idea," said my uncle. "A buddy of mine at the plant thinks so. He says they want to make it look like butter. The big companies, they're full of reds now."

"That makes sense to me," said Mama. "Anything to hurt the farmer."

It didn't make sense to me. When they talked about reds, all I could imagine was a bunch of little devils in red suits, carrying pitchforks. I wondered if they were what my uncle had seen in the Pacific, since devils had tails. Everything about the North was confusing. Lunetta Jones, for instance, bewildered me. She came for coffee every morning, after my uncle had left in a car pool. Lunetta, a seventh-grade teacher, was from Kentucky, and her parents were old friends of my aunt's, so Mozelle and Boone took a special interest in her welfare. Lunetta's life was tragic, my aunt said. Her sailor-boy husband had died in the war. Lunetta never spoke to me, so I often stared at her unselfconsciously. She resembled one of the Toni twins, except for her horsey teeth. She wore her hair curled tight at the bottom, with a fluffy topknot, and she put hard, precise *g*'s on the ends of words like "talking" and "going," the way both Sharon Belletieri and Betsy Lou did. And she wore elaborate dresses—rayon marquisette dresses with Paris pockets, dresses with tiered tucks, others of tissue chambray, with what she called "taffeta understudies." Sometimes I thought her dresses could carry her away on a frantic ride through the sky, they were so billowy and thin.

"Lunetta's man-crazy," my aunt explained to me. "She's always dressed up in one of them Sunday-go-to-meetin' outfits in case she might come across a man to marry."

Uncle Boone called her thick lipstick "man bait."

The buses remained on strike, and I spent the days in the house. I avoided Sharon Belletieri, preferring to be alone, or to sit entranced before the television set. Sometimes the fading outlines of the characters on the screen were like ghosts. I watched Milton Berle, Morey Amsterdam, *Believe It Or Not, Wax Wackies,* and even *Blind Date.* Judy Splinters, a ventriloquist's dummy with pigtails like mine, was one of my favorites, and I liked the magician Foodini on *Lucky Pup* better than Howdy Doody. Betsy Lou teased me, saying I was too old for those baby shows. She was away most of the time, out on "jelly dates." A jelly date was a Coke date. She had jelly dates with Bob and Jim and Sam all on the same day. She was fond of singing "Let's Take an Old-Fashioned Walk," although one of her boyfriends had a car and she liked to go riding in it more than anything else. Why couldn't he take us to Detroit? I wondered, but I was afraid to ask. I had a sick feeling that we were never going to get to see the buildings of the city.

In the mornings, when there was nothing but snow on television, and the women were gossiping over their coffee in the kitchen, I sat on the enclosed porch and watched the people and the cars pass. During the heat wave, it was breezy there. I sat on the rattan chaise lounge and read Aunt Mozelle's scrapbooks, which I had found on a shelf above the television set. They were filled with brittle newspaper clippings mounted in overlapping rows. The clippings included household hints and cradle notes, but most of the stories were about bizarre occurrences around the world—diseases and kidnappings and disasters. One headline that fascinated me read: TIBETAN STOMACH STOVE DECLARED CANCER CAUSE. The story said that people in Tibet who carry little hot stoves against their abdomens in winter frequently develop cancer from the irritation. I was thankful that I didn't live in a cold climate. Another story was about a boa constrictor that swallowed a horse blanket. And there were a number of strange stories about blue babies. When my aunt found me reading the scrapbooks, she said to me, "Life is amazing. I keep these to remind me of just how strange everything is. And how there are always people worse off." I nodded agreement. The porch was my favorite place. I felt secure there, as I read about these faraway wonders and afflictions. I would look up now and then and imagine I could see the tall buildings of Detroit in the distance.

"This is a two-tone gabardine spectator dress with a low-slung belt in the back," said Lunetta one morning as she turned to model her new dress for us. Lunetta always had official descriptions for her extravagant costumes.

My mother said in a wistful voice, "Law me, that's beautiful. But what would I look like, feeding the chickens in that getup?"

"Just look at them shoes," Aunt Mozelle said.

Lunetta's shoes had butterfly bows and sling heels and open toes. She sat down and tapped her toes as Aunt Mozelle poured coffee for her. She said then, "Is Boone worried about his job now that they caught that red?"

"Well, he is, but he don't let on," said Aunt Mozelle, frowning.

Lunetta seized yesterday's newspaper and spread it out on the table. She pointed at the headlines. I remember the way the adults had murmured over the newspaper the day before. Aunt Mozelle had said, "Don't worry, Boone. You don't work for that company." He had replied, "But the plant is full of sympathizers." Now Lunetta said, "Just think. That man they caught could have given Russia all the plans for the power plant. Nothing's safe. You never know who might turn out to be a spy."

My mother was disturbed. "Everything you all have worked so hard for—and the reds could just come in and take it." She waved her hand at the kitchen. In my mind a strange scene appeared: a band of little red devils marching in with their pitchforks and taking the entire Kelvinator kitchen to hell. Later, it occurred to me that they would take the television set first.

When my uncle came home from work, I greeted him at the door and asked him bluntly, "Are you going to get fired because of the reds?"

He only laughed and twitched my plaits. "No, sugar," he said.

"That don't concern younguns," Aunt Mozelle told me. She said to her husband, "Lunetta was here, spreading ideas."

"Leave it to Lunetta," said Uncle Boone wearily.

That evening they were eager to watch the news on the television set. When the supervisor who had been fired was shown, my uncle said, "I hope they give him what-for."

"He was going to tell Russia about the power plant," I said.

"Hush, Peggy," said Mama.

That evening, I could hear their anxious voices on the porch, as I watched Arthur Godfrey, wrestling, and the barber-shop quartets. It seemed odd to me that my uncle did not want to watch the wrestling. He had told me wrestling was his favorite program.

Sharon Belletieri had a birthday party. Aunt Mozelle took Mama and me to a nearby Woolworth's, where I selected a coloring book for a present. The store was twice the size of ours at home. I also bought a souvenir of my trip—a pair of china dogs, with a label that read "Made in Japan." And my mother bought me a playsuit like Sharon's.

"It's Sanforized. That's good," she said with an air of satisfaction, as she examined seams and labels.

My mother looked pale and tired. At breakfast she had suddenly thrown up, the way she had during our bus trip. "I can't keep anything down this early," she had said. My aunt urged her to drink more coffee, saying it would settle her stomach.

Sharon Belletieri lived with her parents in a famous kind of sanitary house where you couldn't get TB or rheumatic fever because it had no drafts. "You won't have to worry about polio," Betsy Lou had told me. The house had venetian blinds like my aunt's, and there was also a television set, an immense one, on legs. Howdy Doody was on, but no one was watching. I did not know what to say to the children. They all knew each other, and their screams and giggles had a natural continuity, something like the way my mother talked with her sister, and like the splendid houses of the neighborhood, all set so close together.

For her birthday, Sharon's parents gave her a Toni doll that took my breath away. It had a bolero sundress, lace-edged panties and slip, and white shoes and socks—an outfit as fine as any of Lunetta's. It came with a Play Wave, including plastic spin curlers and Toni Creme Rinse. The doll's magic nylon hair was supposed to grow softer in texture the more you gave it permanent waves. Feeling self-conscious in my new playsuit, I sat quietly at the party, longing to give that doll a permanent.

Eventually, even though I had hardly opened my mouth, someone laughed at my accent. I had said the unfortunate word "hair" again, in reference to the doll.

Sharon said, *"She's* from Kentucky."

Growing bold and inspired, I said, "Well, we don't have any reds in Kentucky."

Some of the children laughed, and Sharon took me aside and told me a secret, making me cross my heart and hope to die. "I know who's a red," she told me in a whisper. "My father knows him."

"Who?"

"One of the men your uncle rides with to work. The one who drives the car on Thursdays. He's a red and I can prove it."

Before I could find out more, it was my turn to pin the tail on the donkey. Sharon's mother blindfolded me and spun me around. The children were squealing, and I could feel them shrinking from me. When I took the blindfold off, I was dizzy. I had pinned the donkey's tail on the wallpaper, in the center of a large yellow flower.

That evening Betsy Lou went out with a boy named Sam, the one with the car, and Lunetta came to play canasta with the adults. During *Cavalcade of Stars,* I could hear them in the kitchen, accusing each other of hiding reds, when they meant hearts and diamonds. They laughed so loudly I sometimes missed some of Jack Carter's jokes. The wrestling came on afterward, but my uncle did not notice, so I turned off the television and looked at a magazine. I spent a long time trying to write the last line to a Fab jingle so that I could win a television set and five hundred dollars a month for life. I knew that life in Kentucky would be unbearable without a television.

Between hands, Uncle Boone and Lunetta got into an argument. My uncle claimed there were more reds teaching school than making cars, and Lunetta said it was just the opposite.

"They're firing schoolteachers too," he said to Lunetta.

"Don't look at *me,"* she said. "I signed the loyalty oath."

"Hush your mouth, Boone," said Aunt Mozelle.

"I know who a red is," I said suddenly, coming to the table.

They all looked at me and I explained what Sharon had told me. Too late, I remembered my promise not to tell.

"Don't let anybody hear you say that," said Lunetta. "Your uncle would lose his job. If they even *think* you know somebody that knows somebody, you can get in trouble."

"You better not say anything, hon," said Uncle Boone.

"Peggy, it's past your bedtime," my mother said.

"What did *I* do?"

"Talk gets around," said Lunetta. "There's sympathizers even in the woodwork."

The next day, after a disturbing night in which my guardian angel did nothing to protect me from my terrible secret, I was glum and cranky, and for the first time I refused Aunt Mozelle's waffles.

"Are you burnt out on them?" she asked me.

"No, I just ain't hungry."

"She played too hard at the birthday party," Mama said knowingly to my aunt.

When Lunetta arrived and Mama told her I had played too hard at the birthday party, I burst into tears.

"It's nobody's business if I played too hard," I cried. "Besides," I shrieked at Mama, "you don't feel good at breakfast either. You always say you can't keep anything down."

"Don't be ugly," my mother said sharply. To the others, she said apologetically, "I reckon sooner or later she was bound to show out."

It was Sunday, and the heat wave continued. We all sat on the porch, looking at the Sunday papers. Betsy Lou was reading *Pleasant Valley* by Louis Bromfield. Uncle Boone read the Sunday comics aloud to himself. Actually, he was trying to get my attention, for I sat in a corner, determined to ignore everyone. Uncle Boone read "Abbie an' Slats," "The Gumps," and "Little Orphan Annie." He pretended he was Milton Berle as he read them, but I wouldn't laugh.

Lunetta and Uncle Boone seemed to have forgotten their argument. Lunetta had dressed up for church, but the man she planned to go with had gone to visit his mother's grave instead.

"That man sure did love his mother," she said.

"Why don't you go to church anyway?" asked Betsy Lou. "You're all dressed up."

"I just don't have it in me," said Lunetta. She was wearing a shell-tucked summer shantung dress and raffia T-strap sandals.

"Ain't you hot in that outfit?" asked my aunt. "We're burning up."

"I guess so." Lunetta seemed gloomy and distracted. I almost forgave her for upsetting me about the sympathizers, but then she launched into a complicated story about a baby-sitter who got double-crossed. "This woman baby-sat for her best friend, who was divorced and had two little babies. And come to find out, the friend was going out on dates with the woman's own husband!"

"If that don't beat all," said Mama, her eyes wide. She was drinking her second cup of coffee.

"No telling how long that could have kept up," said my aunt.

"It made a big divorce case," Lunetta said.

"I never saw so many divorce cases," said Mama.

"Would you divorce somebody if you found out they were a Communist?" Lunetta asked.

"I don't know as I would," said Aunt Mozelle. "Depends."

"*I* would," said Mama.

"I probably would," said Lunetta. "How about you, Boone?"

"If I found out Mozelle was a red?" Boone asked, grinning. "I'd probably string her up and tickle her feet till she hollered uncle."

"Oh, Boone," Lunetta said with a laugh. "I know you'd stick up for Mozelle, no matter what."

They sat around that morning talking like this, good-naturedly. In the light of day, the reds were only jokes after all, like the comics. I had decided to eat a bowl of Pep cereal, and "Some Enchanted Evening" was playing on the radio. Suddenly everything changed, as if a black storm had appeared to break the heat wave. My mother gave out a loud whoop and clutched her stomach in pain.

"Where does it hurt?" my aunt cried, grabbing at Mama.

Mama was too much in pain to speak. Her face was distorted, her sharp-pointed lips stretched out like a slingshot. My aunt helped her to the bathroom, and a short while later, my aunt and uncle flew away with her in a taxi. Mama had straightened up enough to say that the pain had subsided, but she looked scared, and the blood had drained from her face. I said nothing to her, not even good-bye.

Betsy Lou, left alone with me, said, "I hope she hasn't got polio."

"Only children get polio," I said, trembling. "She don't have polio."

The telephone rang, and Betsy Lou chattered excitedly, telling one of her boyfriends what had happened. Alone and frightened, I sat on the porch, hugging a fat pile of newspapers and gazing at the street. I could see Sharon Belletieri, skating a block away with two other girls. She was wearing a blue playsuit. She and her friends reminded me of those privileged children in the Peanut Gallery on *Howdy Doody*.

To keep from thinking, I began searching the newspaper for something to put in Aunt Mozelle's scrapbook, but at first nothing seemed so horrible as what had just happened. Some babies had turned blue from a diaper dye, but that story didn't impress me. Then I found an item about a haunted house, and my heart began to race. A priest claimed that mysterious disturbances in a house in Wisconsin were the work of an angelic spirit watching over an eight-year-old boy. Cryptic messages were found on bits of paper in the boy's room. The spirit manifestation had occurred fifteen times. I found my aunt's scissors and cut out the story.

Within two hours, my aunt and uncle returned, with broad smiles on their faces, but I knew they were pretending.

"She's just fine," said Aunt Mozelle. "We'll take you to see her afterwhile, but right now they gave her something to make her sleep and take away the pain."

"She'll get to come home in the morning," said my uncle.

He had brought ice cream, and while he went to the kitchen to dish it out, I showed my aunt the clipping I had found. I helped her put it in her scrapbook.

"Life sure is strange," I said.

"Didn't I tell you?" she said. "Now, don't you worry about your mama, hon. She's going to be all right."

Later that day, my aunt and uncle stood in the corridor
of the hospital while I visited my mother. The hospital was
large and gray and steaming with the heat. Mama lay against
a mound of pillows, smiling weakly.

"*I*'m the one that showed out," she said, looking ashamed.
She took my hand and made me sit on the bed next to her.
"You *were* going to have a little brother or sister," she said.
"But I was mistaken."

"What happened to it?"

"I lost it. That happens sometimes."

When I looked at her blankly, she tried to explain that
there wasn't *really* a baby, as there was when she had Johnny
two years before.

She said, "You know how sometimes one or two of the
chicken eggs don't hatch? The baby chick just won't take hold.
That's what happened."

It occurred to me to ask what the baby's name would
have been.

"I don't know," she said. "I'm trying to tell you there wasn't
really a baby. I didn't know about it, anyway."

"You didn't even know there was a baby?"

"No. I didn't know about it till I lost it."

She tried to laugh, but she was weak, and she seemed as
confused as I was. She squeezed my hand and closed her eyes
for a moment. Then she said, "Boone says the buses will start
up this week. You could go with your aunt to Detroit and
see the big buildings."

"Without you?"

"The doctor said I should rest up before we go back. But
you go ahead. Mozelle will take you." She smiled at me sleepily.
"I wanted to go so bad—just to see those big fancy store windows. And I wanted to see your face when you saw the city."

That evening, *Toast of the Town* was on television, and
then Fred Waring, and *Garroway at Large.* I was lost among
the screen phantoms—the magic acts, puppets, jokes, clowns,

dancers, singers, wisecracking announcers. My aunt and uncle laughed uproariously. Uncle Boone was drinking beer, something I had not seen him do, and the room stank with the smoke of his Old Golds. Now and then I was aware of all of us sitting there together, laughing in the dim light from the television, while my mother was in the hospital. Even Betsy Lou was watching with us. Later, I went to the guest room and sat on the large bed, trying to concentrate on finishing the Fab jingle.

> Here's to a fabulous life with Fab
> There's no soap scum to make wash drab
> Your clothes get cleaner—whiter, too—

I heard my aunt calling to me excitedly. I was missing something on the television screen. I had left because the news was on.

"Pictures of Detroit!" she cried. "Come quick. You can see the big buildings."

I raced into the living room in time to see some faint, dark shapes, hiding behind the snow, like a forest in winter, and then the image faded into the snow.

"Mozelle can take you into Detroit in a day or two," my uncle said. "The buses is starting up again."

"I don't want to go," I said.

"You don't want to miss the chance," said my aunt.

"Yes, I do."

That night, alone in the pine-and-cedar room, I saw everything clearly, like the sharpened images that floated on the television screen. My mother had said an egg didn't hatch, but I knew better. The reds had stolen the baby. They took things. They were after my aunt's copper-bottomed pans. They stole the butter. They wanted my uncle's job. They were invisible, like the guardian angel, although they might wear disguises. You didn't know who might be a red. You never knew when you might lose a baby that you didn't know you had. I understood it all. I hadn't trusted my guardian angel, and so he had failed to protect me. During the night, I hit upon a last line to the Fab jingle, but when I awoke I saw how silly and inappropriate it was. It was going over and over in my mind: *Red soap makes the world go round.*

On the bus home a few days later, I slept with my head in my mother's lap, and she dozed with her head propped against my seat back. She was no longer sick, but we were both tired and we swayed, unresisting, with the rhythms of the bus. When the bus stopped in Fort Wayne, Indiana, at midnight, I suddenly woke up, and at the sight of an unfamiliar place, I felt—with a new surge of clarity—the mystery of travel, the vastness of the world, the strangeness of life. My own life was a curiosity, an item for a scrapbook. I wondered what my mother would tell my father about the baby she had lost. She had been holding me tightly against her stomach as though she feared she might lose me too.

I had refused to let them take me into Detroit. At the bus station, Aunt Mozelle had hugged me and said, "Maybe next time you come we can go to Detroit."

"If there *is* a next time," Mama said. "This may be her only chance, but she had to be contrary."

"I didn't want to miss *Wax Wackies* and *Judy Splinters*," I said, protesting.

"We'll have a car next time you come," said my uncle. "If they don't fire everybody," he added with a laugh.

"If that happens, y'all can always come back to Kentucky and help us get a crop out," Mama told him.

The next afternoon, we got off the bus on the highway at the intersection with our road. Our house was half a mile away. The bus driver got our suitcases out of the bus for us, and then drove on down the highway. My father was supposed to meet us, but he was not there.

"I better not carry this suitcase," said Mama. "My insides might drop."

We left our suitcases in a ditch and started walking, expecting to meet Daddy on the way.

My mother said, "You don't remember this, but when you

was two years old I went to Jackson, Tennessee, for two weeks to see Mozelle and Boone—back before Boone was called over-seas?—and when I come back the bus driver let me off here and I come walking down the road to the house carrying my suitcase. You was playing in the yard and you saw me walk up and you didn't recognize me. For the longest time, you didn't know who I was. I never *will* forget how funny you looked."

"They won't recognize us," I said solemnly. "Daddy and Johnny."

As we got to the top of the hill, we could see that our little white house was still there. The tin roof of the barn was barely visible through the tall oak trees.

# Offerings

Sandra's maternal grandmother died of childbed fever at the age of twenty-six. Mama was four. After Sandra was born, Mama developed an infection but was afraid to see the doctor. It would go away, she insisted. The infection disappeared, but a few years later inexplicable pains pierced her like needles. Blushing with shame, and regretting her choice of polka-dotted panties, she learned the worst. It was lucky they caught it in time, the doctor said. During the operation, Mama was semi-conscious, with a spinal anesthetic, and she could hear the surgeons discussing a basketball game. Through blurred eyes, she could see a red expanse below her waist. It resembled the Red Sea parting, she said.

Sandra grows vegetables and counts her cats. It is late summer and her woodpile is low. She should find time to insulate the attic and to fix the leak in the basement. Her husband is gone. Jerry is in Louisville, working at a K Mart. Sandra has stayed behind, reluctant to spend her weekends with him watching go-go dancers in smoky bars. In the garden, Sandra loads a bucket with tomatoes and picks some dill, a cucumber, a handful of beans. The dead bird is on a stump, untouched since yesterday. When she rescued the bird from the cat, it seemed only stunned, and she put it on a table out on the porch, to let it recover. The bird had a spotted breast, a pink throat, and black-and-gray wings—a flicker, she thought. Its curved beak reminded her of Heckle and Jeckle. A while later, it tried to flap its wings, while gasping and contorting its body, and she decided to put it outside. As she opened the door,

the dog rushed out eagerly ahead of her, and the bird died
in her hand. Its head went limp.

Sandra never dusts. Only now, with her mother and grandmother coming to visit, does she notice that cobwebs are strung
across corners of the ceiling in the living room. Later, with a
perverse delight, she sees a fly go by, actually trailing a wisp
of cat hair and dust. Her grandmother always told her to dust
under her bed, so the dust bunnies would not multiply and
take over, as she would say, like wandering Jew among the
flowers.

Grandmother Stamper is her father's mother. Mama is
bringing her all the way from Paducah to see where Sandra
is living now. They aren't going to tell Grandmother about
the separation. Mama insisted about that. Mama has never told
Grandmother about her own hysterectomy. She will not even
smoke in front of Grandmother Stamper. For twenty-five years,
Mama has sneaked smokes whenever her mother-in-law is
around.

Stamper is not Grandmother's most familiar name. After
Sandra's grandfather, Bob Turnbow, died, Grandmother
moved to Paducah, and later she married Joe Stamper, who
owned a shoestore there. Now she lives in a small apartment
on a city street, and—as she likes to say, laughing—has more
shoes than she has places to go. Sandra's grandfather had a
slow, wasting illness—Parkinson's disease. For five years,
Grandmother waited on him, feeding him with a spoon, changing the bed, and trying her best to look after their dying farm.
Sandra remembers a thin, twisted man, his face shaking, saying,
"She's a good woman. She lights up the fires in the sky."

"I declare, Sandy Lee, you have moved plumb out into
the wilderness," says Grandmother.

In her white pants suit, Sandra's grandmother looks like
a waitress. The dog pokes at her crotch as she picks her way
down the stone path to the porch. Sandra has not mowed in
three weeks. The mower is broken, and there are little bushes
of ragweed all over the yard.

"See how beautiful it is," says Mama. "It's just as pretty

as a picture." She waves at a hillside of wild apple trees and weeds, with a patch of woods at the top. A long-haired calico cat sits under an overgrown lilac bush, also admiring the view.

"You need you some goats on that hill," says Grandmother.

Sandra tells them about the raccoon she saw as she came home one night. At first, she thought it was a porcupine. It was very large, with slow, methodical movements. She followed it as far as she could with her headlights. It climbed a bank with grasping little hands. It occurs to Sandra that porcupines have quills like those thin pencils *Time* magazine sends with its subscription offers.

"Did you ever find out what went with your little white cat?" Mama asks as they go inside.

"No. I think maybe he got shot," Sandra says. "There's been somebody shooting people's cats around here ever since spring." The screen door bangs behind her.

The oven is not dependable, and supper is delayed. Grandmother is restless, walking around the kitchen, pretending not to see the dirty linoleum, the rusty, splotched sink, the peeling wallpaper. She puzzles over the bunches of dill and parsley hanging in the window. Mama has explained about the night shift and overtime, but when Sandra sees Grandmother examining the row of outdoor shoes on the porch and, later, the hunting rifle on the wall, she realizes that Grandmother is looking for Jerry. Jerry took his hunting boots with him, and Sandra has a feeling he may come back for the rifle soon.

It's the cats' suppertime, and they sing a chorus at Sandra's feet. She talks to them and gives them chicken broth and Cat Chow. She goes outside to shoo in the ducks for the night, but tonight they will not leave the pond. She will have to return later. If the ducks are not shut in their pen, the fox may kill them, one by one, in a fit—amazed at how easy it is. A bat circles above the barn. The ducks are splashing. A bird Sandra can't identify calls a mournful good night.

"Those silly ducks wouldn't come in," she says, setting the table. Her mother and grandmother stand around and watch her with starved looks.

"I'm collecting duck expressions," she goes on. " 'Lucky

duck,' 'duck your head,' 'set your ducks in a row,' 'a sitting duck.' I see where they all come from now."

"Have a rubber duck," says Mama. "Or a duck fit."

"Duck soup," says Grandmother.

"Duck soup?" Sandra says. "What does that mean?"

"It means something is real easy," says Grandmother. "Easy as pie."

"It was an old picture show too," Mama says. "The name of the show was *Duck Soup.*"

They eat on the porch, and the moths come visiting, flapping against the screen. A few mosquitoes squeeze through and whine about their heads. Grandmother's fork jerks; the corn slips from her hand. Sandra notices that her dishes don't match. Mama and Grandmother exclaim over the meal, praising the tomatoes, the fresh corn. Grandmother takes another piece of chicken. "It has such a crispy crust!" she says.

Sandra will not admit the chicken is crisp. It is not even brown, she says to herself.

"How did you do that?" Grandmother wants to know.

"I boiled it first. It's faster."

"I never heard of doing it that way," Grandmother says.

"You'll have to try that, Ethel," says Mama.

Sandra flips a bug off her plate.

Her grandmother sneezes. "It's the ragweed," she says apologetically. "It's the time of the year for it. Doesn't it make you sneeze?"

"No," says Sandra.

"It never used to do you that way," Mama says.

"I know," says Grandmother. "I helped hay many a time when I was young. I can't remember it bothering me none."

The dog is barking. Sandra calls him into the house. He wants to greet the visitors, but she tells him to go to his bed, under the divan, and he obeys.

Sandra sits down at the table again and presses Grandmother to talk about the past, to tell about the farm Sandra can barely remember. She recalls the dizzying porch swing, a dog with a bushy tail, the daisy-edged field of corn, and a litter of squirming kittens like a deep pile of mated socks in a drawer. She wants to know about the trees. She remembers the fruit trees and the gigantic walnuts, with their sweeping arms and their hard, green balls that sometimes hit her on the head. She also remembers the day the trees came down.

"The peaches made such a mess on the grass you couldn't walk," her grandmother explains. "And there were so many cherries I couldn't pick them all. I had three peach trees taken down and one cherry tree."

"That was when your granddaddy was so bad," Mama says to Sandra. "She had to watch him night and day and turn him ever' so often. He didn't even know who she was."

"I just couldn't have all those in the yard anymore," says Grandmother. "I couldn't keep up with them. But the walnut trees were the worst. Those squirrels would get the nuts and roll them all over the porch and sometimes I'd step on one and fall down. Them old squirrels would snarl at me and chatter. Law me."

"Bessie Grissom had a tree taken down last week," says Mama. "She thought it would fall on the house, it was so old. A tornado might set down."

"How much did she have to pay?" asks Grandmother.

"A hundred dollars."

"When I had all them walnut trees taken down back then, it cost me sixty dollars. That just goes to show you."

Sandra serves instant butterscotch pudding for dessert. Grandmother eats greedily, telling Sandra that butterscotch is her favorite. She clashes her spoon as she cleans the dish. Sandra does not eat any dessert. She is thinking how she would like to have a bourbon-and-Coke. She might conceal it in a coffee cup. But she would not be able to explain why she was drinking coffee at night.

After supper, when Grandmother is in the bathroom, Mama says she will wash the dishes, but Sandra refuses.

"Do you hear anything from Jerry?" Mama asks.

Sandra shrugs. "No. He'd better not waltz back in here. I'm through waiting on him." In a sharp whisper, she says,

"I don't know how long I can keep up that night-shift lie."

"But she's been through so much," Mama says. "She thinks the world of you, Sandra."

"I know."

"She thinks Jerry hung the moon."

"I tell you, if he so much as walks through that door—"

"I love those cosmos you planted," Mama says. "They're the prettiest I've ever seen. I'd give anything if I could get mine to do like that."

"They're volunteers. I didn't do a thing."

"You didn't?"

"I didn't thin them either. I just hated to thin them."

"I know what you mean," says Mama. "It always broke my heart to thin corn. But you learn."

A movie, *That's Entertainment!*, is on TV. Sandra stands in the doorway to watch Fred Astaire dancing with Eleanor Powell, who is as loose as a rag doll. She is wearing a little-girl dress with squared shoulders.

"Fred Astaire is the limberest thing I ever saw," says Mama.

"I remember his sister Adele," says Grandmother. "She could really dance."

"Her name was Estelle," says Mama.

"Estelle Astaire?" says Sandra. For some reason, she remembers a girl she knew in grade school named Sandy Beach.

Sandra makes tomato sauce, and they offer to help, but she tells them to relax and watch the movie. As she scalds tomatoes and presses hot pulp through a food mill, she listens to the singing and tap-dancing from the next room. She comes to the doorway to watch Gene Kelly do his famous "Singin' in the Rain" number. His suit is soaked, and he jumps into puddles with both feet, like a child. A policeman scowls at his antics. Grandmother laughs. When the sauce boils down, Sandra pours it into bowls to cool. She sees bowls of blood lined up on the counter. Sandra watches Esther Williams dive through a ring of fire and splash in the center of a star formed by women, with spread legs, lying on their backs in the water.

During a commercial, Sandra asks her mother if she wants to come to the barn with her, to help with the ducks. The dog bounds out the door with them, happy at this unexpected excursion. Out in the yard, Mama lights a cigarette.

"Finally!" Mama says with a sigh. "That feels good."

Two cats, Blackie and Bubbles, join them. Sandra wonders if Bubbles remembers the mole she caught yesterday. The mole had a star-shaped nose, which Bubbles ate first, like a delicacy.

The ducks are not in the barn, and Sandra and her mother walk down a narrow path through the weeds to the pond. The pond is quiet as they approach. Then they can make out patches of white on the dark water. The ducks hear them and begin diving, fleeing to the far shore in panic.

"There's no way to drive ducks in from a pond," Mama says.

"Sometimes they just take a notion to stay out here all night," says Sandra.

They stand side by side at the edge of the pond while Mama smokes. The sounds of evening are at their fullest now, and lightning bugs wink frantically. Sometimes Sandra has heard foxes at night, their menacing yaps echoing on the hillside. Once, she saw three fox pups playing in the full moon, like dancers in a spotlight. And just last week she heard a baby screaming in terror. It was the sound of a wildcat—a thrill she listens for every night now. It occurs to her that she would not mind if the wildcat took her ducks. They are her offering.

Mama throws her cigarette in the pond, and a duck splashes. The night is peaceful, and Sandra thinks of the thousands of large golden garden spiders hidden in the field. In the early morning the dew shines on their trampolines, and she can imagine bouncing with an excited spring from web to web, all the way up the hill to the woods.

# Still Life
# with Watermelon

For several weeks now, Louise Milsap has been painting pictures of watermelons. The first one she tried looked like a dark-green basketball floating on an algae-covered pond. Too much green, she realized. She began varying the backgrounds, and sometimes now she throws in unusual decorative objects—a few candles, a soap dish, a pair of wire pliers. She tried including other fruits, but the size of the melons among apples and grapes made them appear odd and unnatural. When she saw a photograph of a cornucopia in a magazine, she imagined a huge watermelon stuck in its mouth.

Louise's housemate, Peggy Wilson, insists that a rich collector from Paducah named Herman Priddle will buy the pictures. Peggy and her husband, Jerry, had rented an apartment from him, but Jerry ran away with Priddle's mistress and now Peggy lives with Louise. Peggy told her, "That man's whole house is full of them stupid watermelons." When Peggy said he would pay a fortune for anything with a watermelon in it, Louise bought a set of paints.

Peggy said, "He's got this one cute picture of these two little colored twins eating a slice of watermelon. One at each end, like bookends. I bet he paid at least thirty dollars for it."

Louise has lost her job at Kroger's supermarket, and she lies to the unemployment office about seeking a new job. Instead, she spends all day painting on small canvas boards in her canning room. Her husband, Tom, is in Texas with Jim Yates, a carpenter who worked for him. A month before, Tom suddenly left his business and went out West to work on Jim's uncle's ranch. Louise used to like Tom's impulsiveness. He would call up a radio program and dedicate love songs to her, knowing it both embarrassed and pleased her to hear her name on the radio. Tom never cared about public opinion. Before he went to Texas, he bought a cowboy hat from Sam's Surplus. He left in his pickup, his "General Contracting" sign still painted on the door, and he didn't say when he would return. Louise said to him, "If you're going to be a born-again cowboy, I guess you'll want to get yourself all bunged up on one of them bull machines."

"That ain't necessarily what I'm aiming to do," he said.

"Go ahead. *See* if I care."

Louise, always a practical person, is determined to get along without Tom. She should look for a job, but she doesn't want to. She paints a dozen pictures in a row. She feels less and less practical. For two dollars and eighty-nine cents she buys a watermelon at Kroger's and paints a picture of it. It is a long, slender melon the color of a tobacco worm, with zigzag stripes. She went to Kroger's from force of habit, and then felt embarrassed to be seen at her old checkout lane.

"Old man Priddle would give you a hundred dollars for that," says Peggy, glancing at the painting when she comes home from work. Louise is just finishing the clouds in the background. Clouds had been a last-minute inspiration.

Peggy inserts a Dixieland tape into Louise's tape deck and opens a beer. Beer makes Peggy giggly, but Dixieland puts her in a sad mood because her husband once promised to take her to New Orleans to hear Al Hirt in person. Louise stands there with her paintbrush, waiting to see what will happen.

Peggy says, "He's got this big velvet tapestry on his wall? It's one big, solid watermelon that must have weighed a ton." Laughing, she stretches her arms to show the size. The beer can tilts, about to spill. Three slugs of beer and Peggy is already giggly.

Louise needs Peggy's rent money, but having her around

is like having a grown child who refuses to leave home. Peggy reads Harlequin romances and watches TV simultaneously. She pays attention when the minister on *The 700 Club* gives advice on budgets. "People just aren't *smart* about the way they use credit cards," she informs Louise. This is shop talk from her job in customer services at the K Mart. Peggy keeps promising to call Herman Priddle, to make an appointment for Louise to take her paintings to Paducah, but Peggy has a thing about using the telephone. She doesn't want to tie up the line in case her husband tries to call. She frowns impatiently when Louise is on the telephone. One good thing about living with Peggy—she does all the cooking. Sometimes she pours beer into the spaghetti sauce—"to give it a little whang," she says.

"You shouldn't listen to that tape," Louise says to Peggy later. The music is getting to Peggy by now. She sits in a cross-legged, meditative pose, the beer can balanced in her palm.

"I just don't know what he sees in a woman who's twenty years older than him," says Peggy. "With a face-lift."

"How long can it last, anyhow?"

"Till she needs another face-lift, I reckon."

"Well, that can't be long. I read they don't last," says Louise.

"That woman's so big and strong, she could skin a mule one-handed," says Peggy, lifting her beer.

Louise puts away her paints and then props the new picture against a chair. Looking at the melon, she can feel its weight and imagine just exactly how ripe it is.

While she paints, Louise has time to reflect on their situation: two women with little in common whose husbands are away. Both men left unconscionably. Sudden yearnings. One thought he could be a cowboy (Tom had never been on a horse); the other fell for an older woman. Louise cannot understand either compulsion. The fact that she cannot helps her not to care.

She tried to reason with Tom—about how boyish his notion was and how disastrous it would be to leave his business. Jim

Yates had lived in Denver one summer, and in every conversation he found a way to mention Colorado and how pure the air was there. Tom believed everything Jim said. "You can't just take off and expect to pick up your business where you left it when you get back," Louise argued. "There's plenty of guys waiting to horn in. It takes *years* to get where you've got." That was Louise being reasonable. At first Tom wanted her to go with him, but she wouldn't dream of moving so far away from home. He accused her of being afraid to try new things, and over a period of weeks her resistance turned to anger. Eventually Louise, to her own astonishment, threw a Corning Ware Petite Pan at Tom and made his ear bleed. He and Jim took off two days later. The day they left, Tom was wearing a T-shirt that read: "You better get in line now 'cause I get better-looking every day." Who did he think he was?

Peggy does not like to be reminded of the watermelon collector, and Louise has to probe for information. Peggy and her husband, Jerry ("Flathead") Wilson, had gone to live in Paducah, forty miles away, and had had trouble finding work and a place to live, but an elderly man, Herman Priddle, offered them three identical bedrooms on the third floor of his house. "It was a mansion," Peggy told Louise. Then Priddle hired Jerry to convert two of the rooms into a bathroom and a kitchen. Peggy laid vinyl tiles and painted the walls. The old man, fascinated, watched them work. He let Peggy and Jerry watch his TV and he invited them to eat with him. His mistress, a beautician named Eddy Gail Moses, slept with him three nights a week, and while she was there she made enough hamburger-and-macaroni casseroles to last him the rest of the week. She lived with her father, who disapproved of her behavior, despite her age.

Before Peggy knew what was happening, her husband had become infatuated with the woman, and he abruptly went to live with her and her father, leaving Peggy with Herman Priddle. Although Peggy grew suspicious of the way he looked at her, she and Priddle consoled each other for a while. Peggy started making the casseroles he was used to, and she stayed in Paducah for a few months, working at a pit barbecue stand. Gradually, Peggy told Louise, the old man began collecting pictures of watermelons. He looked for them in flea markets, at antique shops, and in catalogs; and he put ads in trade papers. When he hung one of the pictures in her bedroom, Peggy moved out. The watermelon was sliced lengthwise and it resembled a lecherous grin, she said, shuddering.

"Peggy's still in shock from the way Jerry treated her," Louise tells Tom in a letter one evening. She writes him in care of a tourist home in Amarillo, Texas. She intends to write only perfunctory replies to his postcards so he will know she is alive, but she finds herself being more expressive than she ever was in the four years they were face to face. Hitting him seemed to release something in her, but she won't apologize. She won't beg him to come back. He doesn't know she has lost her job. And if he saw her paintings, he would laugh.

When Louise seals the letter, Peggy says to her, "Did I tell you I heard Jim Yates is queer?"

"No."

"Debbie Potts said that at work. She used to know Jim Yates back in high school."

"Well, I don't believe it. He's too overbearing."

"Debbie Potts has been to Europe," says Peggy, looking up from the kitchen counter, where she is making supper. "Did you know that?"

"Hooray for her."

"That don't mean she's an expert on anything," Peggy says apologetically. "I'm sure she don't know what she's talking about."

"For crying out loud."

"I'm sorry, Louise. I'm always putting my big foot in it. But you know, a lot of guys are coming right out now and saying they're gay? It's amazing." She laughs wildly. "They sure wouldn't be much use where it counts, would they? At least Flathead ran off with a woman—knock on wood." Peggy taps a wooden spoon against the counter.

"How can you love a guy called Flathead?" says Louise, irritated. Apparently Jerry Wilson's nickname has nothing to do with his appearance. Louise has read that the Flathead Indians used to tie rocks to their heads to flatten them—why, she cannot imagine.

Peggy says, "It's just what I know him by. I never thought about it."

Peggy is making a casserole, probably one of Eddy Gail Moses's recipes. The Dixieland tape is playing full blast. Peggy says, "The real reason he run off with that floozy was she babied him."

"I wouldn't baby a man if my life depended on it," says Louise.

She rummages around for a stamp. Too late, she wonders if she should have told Tom about the trouble with the air conditioner. He will think she is hinting for him to come home. Tom was always helpful around the house. He helped choose the kitchen curtains, saying that a print of butterflies she wanted was too busy and suggesting a solid color. She always admired him for that. It was so perceptive of him to say the curtains were busy. But that didn't mean anything abnormal. In fact, after he started hanging out with Jim Yates, Tom grew less attentive to such details. He and Jim Yates had a Space Invaders competition going at Patsy's Dairy Whip, and sometimes they stayed there until midnight. Jim, who hit six thousand long before Tom, several times had his name on the machine as high scorer of the day. Once Tom brought Jim over for supper, and Louise disliked the way Jim took charge, comparing her tacos to the ones he'd had in Denver and insisting that she get up and grate more cheese. It seemed to Louise that he was still playing Space Invaders. Tom didn't notice. The night, weeks later, when Louise threw the Corning Ware at Tom, she knew she was trying to get his attention.

Late one evening, Peggy tells Louise that she saw her husband at the K Mart. He didn't realize that Peggy worked there. "He turned all shades when he saw me," Peggy says. "But I wasn't surprised. I had a premonition."

Peggy believes in dreams and coincidences. The night before she saw him, she had read a romance story about a complicated adoption proceeding. Louise doesn't get the connection
and Peggy is too drunk to explain. She and Jerry have been
out drinking, talking things over. Louise notices that Peggy
already has a spot on her new pants suit, which she managed
to buy even though she owes Louise for groceries.

"Would you take him back?" Louise wants to know.

"If he's good." Peggy laughs loudly. "He's coming over
again one day next week. He had to get back to Paducah tonight."

"Is he still with that woman?"

"He *said* he wasn't." Peggy closes her eyes and does a
dance step. Then she says exuberantly, "Everything Flathead
touches turns to money. He cashed this check at the K Mart
for fifty dollars. He sold a used hot-water heater and made a
twenty-dollar profit on it. Imagine that."

When Peggy sees Louise polishing her toenails, she says
abruptly, "Your second toe is longer than your big toe. That
means you dominate your husband."

"Where'd you get that idea?"

"Didn't you know that? Everybody knows that."

Louise says, "Are any of them stories you read ever about
women who beat up their husbands?"

Peggy laughs. "What an idea!"

Louise is thinking of Tom's humiliation the night she struck
him with the dish. Suddenly in her memory is a vague impression that the lights flickered, the way it was said the electricity
used to do on certain midnights when the electric chair was
being used at the state penitentiary, not far away.

If Peggy goes back to her husband, Louise will have to
earn some extra money. It dawns on her that the paintings
are an absurd idea. Childish. For a few days she stays out of
the canning room, afraid to look at the pictures. Halfheartedly
she reads the want ads. They say: salesclerk, short-order cook,
secretarial assistant, salesclerk.

On the day she is scheduled to sign up for her weekly

unemployment check, Louise arranges the paintings in the living room, intending to decide whether to continue with them. The pictures are startling. Some of the first ones appear to be optical illusions—watermelons disappearing like black holes into vacant skies. The later pictures are more credible— one watermelon is on a table before a paned window, with the light making little windows on the surface of the fruit; another, split in half, is balanced against a coffee percolator. Louise pretends she's a woman from Mars and the paintings are the first things she sees on earth. They aren't bad, but the backgrounds worry her. They don't match the melons. Why would a watermelon be placed against a blue sky? One water- melon on a flowered tablecloth resembles a blimp that has landed in a petunia bed. Even the sliced melons are unrealistic. The red is wrong—too pale, like a tongue. Tom sent her a picture postcard of the Painted Desert, but Louise suspects the colors in *that* picture are too brilliant. No desert could look like that.

On her way to the unemployment office, Louise picks up a set of acrylics on discount at Big-D. Acrylics are far more economical than oils. In the car, Louise, pleased by the prospect of the fresh tubes of paint, examines the colors: scarlet, cobalt blue, Prussian blue, aquamarine, emerald, yellow ochre, or- ange, white, black. She doesn't really need green. The discov- ery that yellow and blue make green still astonishes her; when she mixes them, she feels like a magician. As she drives toward the unemployment office she wonders recklessly if the green of the trees along the street could be broken down by some scientific process into their true colors.

At the unemployment office the line is long and the build- ing stuffy. The whole place seems wound up. A fat woman standing behind Louise says, "One time it got so hot here I passed out, and not a soul would help. They didn't want to lose their place in line. Look at 'em. Lined up like cows at a slaughterhouse. Ever notice how cows follow along, nose to tail?"

"Elephants have a cute way of doing that," says Louise,

in high spirits. "They grab the next one's tail with their trunk."

"Grab," the woman says. "That's all people want to do. Just grab." She reaches inside her blouse and yanks her bra strap back onto her shoulder. She has yellow hair and blue eyes. She could turn green if she doesn't watch out, Louise thinks. The line moves slowly. No one faints.

When Louise arrives at home, Peggy's husband is there, and he and Peggy are piling her possessions into his van. Peggy has happy feet, like Steve Martin on TV. She is moving to Paducah with Jerry. Calmly Louise pours a glass of iced tea and watches the ice cubes crack.

"I already up and quit work," Peggy calls to Louise from her bedroom.

"I got us a place in a big apartment complex," says Jerry with an air of satisfaction.

"It's got a swimming pool," says Peggy, appearing with an armload of clothes on hangers.

"I saved twenty dollars a month by getting one without a dishwasher," says Jerry. "I'm going to put one in myself."

Peggy's husband is tall and muscular, with a sparse mustache that a teenager might grow. He looks amazingly like one of the Sha Na Na, the one in the sleeveless black T-shirt. Louise notices that he can't keep his hands off his wife. He holds on to her hips, her elbows, as she tries to pack.

"Tell what else you promised," Peggy says.

"You mean about going to New Orleans?" Jerry says.

"Yeah."

Louise says, "Well, don't you go off without setting me up with that watermelon man. I was counting on you."

"I'll give him a call tomorrow," says Peggy.

"Could you do it right now, before I lose track of y'all?"

Louise's sharp tone works. Peggy pulls away from Jerry and goes to the telephone.

While she is trying to find the number, she says, "I hate to mention it, Louise, but I gave you a whole month's rent and it's only been a week. Do you think . . . ?"

While Peggy is on the telephone, Louise writes a check

for seventy-five dollars. She writes boldly and decisively, with enlarged numbers. Her new bank balance is twelve dollars and eleven cents. If Flathead Wilson were *her* husband, she would show him the road.

"He said come over Tuesday afternoon," says Peggy, taking the check. "I just know he's going to love your pictures. He sounded thrilled."

After Peggy and Jerry leave, Louise notices the mail, which Peggy has left on a lamp table—a circular, the water-and-light bill, and a letter from Tom, postmarked ten days before. Louise laughs with relief when she reads that Jim Yates went to Mexico City with a woman he met in Amarillo. Jim plans to work in adobe construction. "Can you imagine going to Mexico to work?" Tom writes. "Usually it's the other way around."

Happily Louise plays a Glen Campbell tape and washes the dishes Peggy has left. Peggy gave Louise all her cooking utensils—the cracked enamel pans and scratched Teflon. "Flathead's going to buy me all new," she said. Louise wishes Peggy hadn't left before hearing the news from Tom. But she's glad to be alone at last. While Glen Campbell sings longingly of Galveston, Louise for the first time imagines Tom doing chores on a ranch. Something like housework, no doubt, except out of doors.

She paints through the weekend, staying up late, eating TV dinners at random. It thrills her to step back from a picture and watch the sea of green turn into a watermelon. She loves the way the acrylics dry so easily; they are convenient, like Perma-Press clothing. After finishing several pictures, she discovers a trick about backgrounds: If she makes them hazier, the watermelons stand out in contrast, look less like balloons floating in space. With the new paints, she hits upon the right mix for the red interiors, and now the watermelon slices look good enough to eat.

On the day of Louise's appointment with Herman Priddle, Tom suddenly walks in the door. Louise freezes. She's standing in the center of the living room, as though she had been standing there all during his absence, waiting for his return. She can tell how time has passed by the way his jeans have faded. His hair has grown shaggy and he has a deep tan.

"Surprise!" he says with a grin. "I'm home."

Louise manages to say, "What are you doing back here?"

"And why ain't you at work?" Tom says.

"Laid off."

"What's going on here?" he asks, seeing the pictures.

Suddenly Louise is ashamed of them. She feels confused. "You picked a *fine* time to show up," she says. She tries to explain about the paintings. Her explanation makes no sense.

For a long time Tom studies her pictures, squatting to see the ones on the floor. His jeans strain at the seams. He reaches out to touch one picture, as though for a moment he thought the watermelon might be real. Louise begins taking the paintings to her car, snatching them from under his gaze. He follows her, carrying some of the paintings.

Tom says, "I couldn't wait to get back home."

"You didn't have to go off like that."

"I've been thinking things over."

"So have I." She slams the rear hatch door of her car. "Where's the pickup?"

"Totaled it north of Amarillo."

"What? I thought all the roads were flat and straight out there."

He shrugs. "I reckon they are."

"Where'd you get that junk heap?" she asks. The car he has brought home is a rusted-out hulk.

"In Amarillo. It was the best I could do—cost me two hundred dollars. But it drives good."

He opens the door of his car and takes out a McDonald's sack from the front seat. "I brought you a Big Mac," he says.

Later, when he insists on driving her in her car to Paducah, Louise doesn't try to stop him. She sits still and glum beside him, like a child being escorted to a school recital. On the way, she says, "That postcard you sent of the Painted Desert

was mailed in Amarillo. I thought the Painted Desert was in
Arizona."

"I didn't mail it till I got back to Amarillo."

"I thought maybe you hadn't even been there."

"Yes, I was."

"I thought maybe you sent it just to impress me."

"Why would I do that?"

"So I wouldn't think the West was just dull, open spaces."

"Well, it wasn't. And I did go to the Painted Desert."

"What else did you do out there?"

"Different things."

"Look—John Wayne's dead. Don't think you have to be
the strong, silent type just 'cause you went out West."

Louise wants to know about the colors of the Painted Desert, but she can't bring herself to ask Tom about them. Tom
is driving the car with his forearms loosely draped over the
wheel and his elbows sticking out. He drives so casually. Louise
imagines him driving all the way to Texas like this, as if he
had nothing better to do.

"I did a lot of driving around," Tom says finally, after smoking a cigarette all the way down. "Just to see what there was
to see."

"Sounds fascinating." Louise doesn't know why she wants
to give him such a hard time. She realizes that she is shaking
at the thought of him wrecking his pickup, alone in some empty
landscape. The ear she hit is facing her—no sign of damage.
His hair is growing over it and she can't really see where she
hit him. His sideburn, shaped like the outline of Italy, juts out
onto his jaw. Tom is home and she doesn't know what that
means.

Herman Priddle's house has a turret, a large bay window,
and a wraparound porch, which a woman is sweeping.

"Would you say that's a mansion?" Louise asks Tom.

"Not really."

"Peggy said it was."

Louise makes Tom wait in the car while she walks up to

the house. She thinks the woman on the porch must be Eddy Gail Moses, but she turns out to be Priddle's niece. She has on a turquoise pants suit and wears her hair up in sculptured curls. When Louise inquires, the woman says, "Uncle Herman's in the hospital. He had a stroke a-Sunday and he's real bad, but they pulled him off the critical list today."

"I brought some pictures for him to see," says Louise nervously.

"Watermelons, I bet," says the woman, eyeing Louise.

"He was supposed to buy my pictures."

"Well, the thing of it *is*—what are we to do with the ones he's got? He'll have to be moved. He can't stay by hisself in this big old place." The woman opens the door. "Look at these things."

Louise follows her into the dim room cluttered with antiques. The sight of all the watermelons in the room is stunning. The walls are filled, and other paintings are on the floor, leaning against the wall. Louise stands and stares while the woman chatters on. There are so many approaches Louise has not thought of—close-ups, groupings, unusual perspectives, floral accompaniments. All her own pictures are so prim and tidy. The collection includes oils, drawings, watercolors, even a needlepoint chair cover and a china souvenir plate. The tapestry Peggy described is a zeppelin floating above the piano. Louise has the feeling that she is witnessing something secret and forbidden, something of historical importance. She is barely aware that Tom has entered and is talking to Herman Priddle's niece. Louise feels foolish. In sixth grade the teacher had once pointed out to the class how well Louise could draw, and now—as if acting at last on the basis of that praise—Louise has spent two months concocting an elaborate surprise for an eccentric stranger. What could she have been thinking of?

"Looks like somebody's crazy about watermelons," Tom is saying politely.

"They won't bring a thing at auction," the woman replies with a laugh. In a hushed voice then, she says, "He sure had me fooled. He was here by hisself so much I didn't know what-all was going on. Now it seems like he was always collecting these things. It suited him. Do you ever have people do you that way? You think things are one way and then they get turned around and you lose track of how they used to be?"

"I know what you mean," says Tom, nodding with enthusiasm.

On the way home Louise is in tears. Tom, perplexed, tries to console her, telling her that her pictures are as good as any of the old man's watermelons.

"Don't worry about him," he says, holding her hand. "It won't matter that you lost your job. I thought I'd go see about getting a small-business loan to get started again. We'll get straightened out somehow."

Louise, crying, cannot reply. She doesn't feel like arguing.

"I didn't even know you could draw," Tom says.

"I'm not going to paint any more watermelons," she says.

"You won't have to."

Louise blows her nose and dries her eyes. Tom's knuckles are tapping a tune against the steering wheel and he seems to be driving automatically. His mind could be somewhere else, like someone in an out-of-body experience. But Louise is the one who has been off on a crazy adventure. She knows now that she painted the watermelons out of spite, as if to prove to Tom that she could do something as wild as what he was doing. She lost her head during the past weekend when she was alone, feeling the glow of independence. Gazing at the white highway line, she tries to imagine the next steps: eating supper with Tom, going to bed together, returning to old routines. Something about the conflicting impulses of men and women has gotten twisted around, she feels. She had preached the idea of staying home, but it occurs to her now that perhaps the meaning of home grows out of the fear of open spaces. In some people that fear is so intense that it is a disease, Louise has read.

At the house, Louise reaches the door first, and she turns to see Tom coming up the walk. His face is in shadow against the afternoon sun. His features aren't painted in; she wouldn't recognize him. Beyond him is a vacant lot—a field of weeds and low bushes shaped like cupcakes. Now, for the first time, Louise sees the subtle colors—amber, yellow, and deep shades of purple—leaping out of that landscape. The empty field is broad and hazy and dancing with light, but it fades away for a moment when Tom reaches the doorway and his face thrusts out from the shadow. He looks scared. But then he grins slowly. The coastline of Italy wobbles a little, retreats.

# Old Things

Cleo Watkins makes invisible, overlapping rings on the table with her cup as she talks.

"The kids just got off to school and I'm still in one piece," she says. "Last night we was up till all hours watching that special and my eyes is pasted together this morning. After the weekend we've been through, now everybody's going off and I'll be so lonesome all day!"

Cleo puts her elbow on the kitchen table and switches the receiver to the other ear. Her friend Rita Jean Wiggins says she had trouble getting her car started yesterday in time for church; it flooded and she had to let it sit for a while. Rita Jean is worried sick about her cat Dexter and is going to take him to the vet again. As Cleo listens, she notices that Tom Brokaw is introducing a guest who is going to talk about men as single parents. Cleo doesn't know whether to listen to Tom or Rita Jean. For a minute she loses the train of Rita Jean's story.

"Just a minute, I better turn this television down." Cleo crosses the kitchen and lowers the volume. "This house is such a mess," says Cleo, sitting down again. "And you don't know how embarrassing it all is—Linda's car here all the time, the kids going in and out. She's making an old woman out of me."

"Did she bring much from home?" Rita Jean asks.

"Mostly things the kids needed, and a lot of her clothes," Cleo says, watching the faces move on the television screen. "I told her wasn't no use carrying all that over here, they'd be going back before long, but she wouldn't listen. You can't walk here."

Rita Jean's voice is sympathetic. "I'm sure she'll get straightened out with Bob in no time."

"I don't know. Looks like she's moved in. She went to trade day out here at the stockyard, and she come back with the awfulest conglomeration you ever saw."

"What all did she get?"

"A rocking chair she's going to refinish, and a milk glass lamp, and some kind of whatnot, and a big grabbag—a box of junk you buy for a dollar and then there might be one thing in it you want. I never saw such par'phenalin."

"Was there anything in it she could use?" asks Rita Jean. Rita Jean, who has no children, is always intensely concerned about Cleo's family.

"She found a wood spoon she said was antique."

"People are antique-crazy."

"You're telling me." Cleo has spent years trying to get rid of things she has collected. After her husband died, she moved to town, to a little brick house with a dishwasher and wall-to-wall carpet. Cleo's two sons haven't mentioned it, but Linda says it's awful that Cleo has gotten rid of every reminder of Jake. There is nothing but the picture album left. All his suits were given away, and the rest of his things boxed up and sold. She gave away all his handkerchiefs, neatly washed and ironed. They were monogrammed with the initials RJW, for Robert Jacob Watkins. And now somebody with totally different initials is carrying them around and blowing his nose on them. Linda reminds her of this every so often but Cleo isn't sorry. She doesn't want to live in the past.

After talking to Rita Jean, Cleo cleans the house with unusual attention. The kids have scattered their things everywhere. Cleo hangs up Tammy's clothes and puts Davey's toys in the trunk Linda has brought. The trunk is yellow enamel with thin black swirls that make it look old. Linda has antiqued it.

Cleo pins patterns down on the length of material laid

on the table. She is cutting out a set of cheerleader outfits that have to be done by next week. The cheerleader outfits are red and gray, made like bib overalls, with shorts. Everything is double seams, and the bibs have pockets with flaps.

"Get down from there, Prissy-Tail!" The cat has attacked the flimsy pattern and torn it. "You know you're not supposed to be on Mama's sewing." Cleo waves the scissors at Prissy-Tail, who scampers onto Cleo's shoulder. Cleo sets her down on a pillow, saying, "I can't cut out with you dancing on my shoulder." Prissy-Tail struts around on the divan, purring.

"I could tell you things that would sizzle your tailfeathers," Cleo says.

Cleo backs in the front door, pulling the storm door shut with her foot. On TV there is a wild west shoot-out, and the radio is blaring out an accompanying song with a heavy, driving beat. Tammy is talking on the telephone.

"What do you mean, what do I mean? Oh, you know what I mean. Anyway, we're at my grandmother's and my mother's going out tonight—Davey, quit it!—that was my little brother. He's a meanie. I just stuck my tongue out at him. Anyway, do you think he'll ask you or what? Unh-huh. That's what I thought."

Cleo stands in the hallway, adjusting to the sounds. Tammy's patter on the phone is meaningless to her. Linda had never done that. Linda had been such a quiet child. She hears Tammy speaking in a knowing tone.

"You know what April told Kevin? I nearly died! Kevin was going to ask her for her homework? And he said to her could she meet him at the Dairy Queen and she said she might and she might not, and he said to her could she carry him because his car was broke down? And she said he had legs, he could walk! I think he's mad at her."

"Watch out, Tammy, I'm coming through," says Cleo. Davey has returned to the television, and Tammy is sprawled out in the kitchen doorway. Tammy is wearing ripped bluejeans and a velour pullover with stripes down the sleeves. Tammy bends her knees so half the doorway is clear, and Cleo squeezes by, balancing the groceries on her hip.

Tammy hangs up and pokes into the grocery sack. "Chicken! Not again!"

"Chicken was ninety-nine cents a pound," says Cleo. "You better be glad you're where there's food on the table, kid."

"Ick! All that yellow fat."

"The yellower a chicken is, the better it is. That's how you tell when they're good. If they're blue they're not any 'count. Or if they've got spots."

"Oooh!" Tammy makes a twisted face. "Why can't you just buy it already fried?"

"Hah! We're lucky we don't have to pull the feathers off. I used to kill chickens, you know. Whack their heads off, dip 'em in boiling water, pick off the feathers. I'd like to see you pick a chicken!"

Cleo reaches around Tammy and hugs her. Tammy squeals. "Hey, why don't we just eat the cat?"

"Now you're going to hurt somebody's feelings," says Cleo, as Tammy squirms away from her.

Tammy prances out of the room and the noises return. The television; the radio; the buzz of the electric clock; the whir of the furnace making its claim for attention. The kids never hear the noises. Kids never seem to care about anything anymore, Cleo thinks. Tammy had a complete toy kitchen, with a stove and refrigerator, when she was five, and she didn't care anything about it. It cost a fortune. Linda's children always make Cleo feel old.

"I'm old enough to be a grandmother," Rita Jean said early in their acquaintance. Rita Jean had lost her husband too.

"I think of you as a spring chicken," Cleo told her.

"You're not that much older than me. Louise Brown is two years younger than me, and she's a grandmother. Imagine, thirty-five and a grandmother."

"That makes me feel old."

"I feel old," said Rita Jean. "To think that the war could be that long ago."

Rita Jean's husband was twenty-one when he left for Vietnam. It was early in the war and nobody thought it would turn out so bad. She has a portrait on her dresser of a young man she hardly knew, a child almost. Now Rita Jean is old enough to be the mother of a boy like that.

Cleo told Rita Jean she could still get married and have a baby. She could start all over again.

"If anybody would have me," said Rita Jean.

"You don't try."

"Sometimes I think I'm just waiting to get into Senior Citizens."

"Listen to yourself," said Cleo. "That's the most ridiculous thing I ever heard. Why, *I'm* not but fifty-two."

"They say that's the prime of life," said Rita Jean.

"Where are you going, Mama? Tell me where you're going." Davey is pulling at Linda's belt.

"Oh, Davey, look. You're going to mess up Mama's outfit. I told you seven times, Shirley and me's going to Paducah to hear some music. It's not anything you're interested in, so don't be saying you want to go too."

Linda has washed her hair and put on a new pants suit, a tangerine color. Cleo knows Linda cannot afford it, but Linda always has to have the best.

Tammy, sitting with her legs propped up on the back of the divan, says, with mock surprise, "You mean you're going to miss *Charlie's Angels?* You ain't *never* missed *Charlie's Angels!*"

"Them younguns want you to stay home," Cleo says as Linda combs her hair. It is wet and falls in skinny black ringlets.

"I can't see what difference it makes." Linda lights a cigarette.

"These children need a daddy around."

"You're full of prunes if you think I'm going back to Bob!" Linda says, turning on the blow dryer. She raises her voice. "I don't feel like hanging around the same house with somebody that can go for three hours without saying a word. He might as well not be there."

"Hush. The children might hear you."

Linda works on her hair, holding out damp strands and brushing them under with the dryer to style them. Cleo admires the way her daughter keeps up her appearance. She can't imagine Bob would ever look at another woman when he has Linda. Cleo cannot believe Bob has mistreated Linda. It is just as though she has been told some wild tale about outer space, like something on a TV show.

Cleo says, "I bet he's just held in and held in till he's tight as a tick. People do that. I know you—impatient. Listen. A man takes care of a woman. But it works the other way round too. If he thinks you're not giving him enough loving, he'll draw up—just like a morning glory at evening. You think he's not paying any attention to you, but maybe you've been too busy for him."

Cleo knows Linda thinks she is silly. Daughters never believe their mothers. "You have to remember to give each other some loving," she says, her confidence fading. "Don't take each other for granted."

"Bob's no morning glory." Linda puts on lip gloss and works her lips together.

"You'll be wondering how to buy them kids fine things. You'll be off on your own, girl."

Linda says nothing. She examines her face in the mirror and picks at a speck on her cheek.

Davey gets his lessons on the floor in front of the television. He is learning a new kind of arithmetic Cleo has never heard of. Later, Cleo watches *Charlie's Angels* with Tammy, and after Tammy goes to bed, she watches the *10 O'Clock Report*. She tells herself that she has to wait up to unlock the doors for Linda. She has put a chain on the door, because young people are going wild, breaking in on defenseless older women. Cleo is afraid Linda's friend Shirley is a bad influence. Shirley had to get married and didn't finish school. Now she is divorced. She even let her husband have her kids, while she went gallivanting around. Cleo cannot imagine a mother giving her kids away. Shirley's husband moved to Alabama with the kids, and

Shirley sees them only occasionally. On TV, Johnny Carson keeps breaking into the funny dance he does when a joke flops. Cleo usually gets a kick out of that, but it doesn't seem funny this time, with him repeating it so much. Johnny has been divorced twice, but now he is happily married. He is the stay-at-home type, she has read.

Cleo is well into the *Tomorrow* show, which is a disturbing discussion of teenage alcoholism, when Linda returns. Linda's cheeks are glowing and she looks happy.

"I thought Duke Ellington was dead," says Cleo, when Linda tells her about the concert.

"He is. But his brother leads the band. He directs the band like this." Linda makes her hands dive in fishlike movements. "He danced around, with his back to the audience, swaying along in a trance. He had on this dark pink suit the exact same color of Miss Imogene's panties that time in fifth grade—when she fell off the desk?"

Cleo groans. Everything seems to distress her, she notices. She is afraid Linda has been drinking.

"And the band had this great singer!" Linda goes on. "She wore a tight skullcap with sequins on it? And a brown tuxedo, and she sounded for all the world like Ella Fitzgerald. Boy, was she sexy. She had a real deep voice, but she could go real high at times."

Linda unscrews the top of a quart of Coke and pours herself a glass. She drinks the Coke thirstily. "I wouldn't be explaining all this to you if you had gone. I tried to get you to go with me."

"And leave the kids here?" Cleo turns off the TV.

"Shirley had on the darlingest outfit. It had these pleats—what do you want, Davey?"

Davey is trailing a quilt into the living room. "I couldn't sleep," he whines. "The big girls was going to get me."

"He means Charlie's Angels," says Cleo. "We were watching them and they kept him awake."

"He's had a bad dream. Here, hon." Linda hugs Davey and takes him back to bed.

"I worked myself to death yesterday getting this house in shape and it looks like a cyclone hit it," Cleo says to Rita Jean on the telephone the next morning. "First, tell me how's Dexter."

Cleo listens to Rita Jean's account of Dexter's trip to the vet. "He said there's nothing to do now but wait. He's not suffering any, and the vet said it would be all right if I keep him at home. He's asleep most of the time. He's the pitifulest thing."

Rita Jean's cat is thirteen. After the news came from Vietnam, Rita Jean got a cat and then another cat when the first one got run over. The present cat she has kept in the house all its life.

"The one thing about cats," says Cleo, trying to sound comforting, "is that there's more where that one come from. You'll grieve, but you'll get over it and get you another cat."

"I guess so."

Cleo tells about Linda's night out. "She was dolled up so pretty, she looked like she was going out on a date. It made me feel so funny. She had on a new pants suit. The kids didn't want her to go, either. They know something's wrong. They never miss a thing."

"Kids don't miss much," Rita Jean agrees.

"And how in the world does she think they can afford to keep on like they've been doing? But I think they'll get back together."

"Surely they will."

"Knock on wood." Cleo has to stretch to reach the door facing. She is getting a headache. Absently, she watches the *Today* credits roll by as Rita Jean tells about her brother's trip out West. He tried to get her to go along, but she couldn't think of closing her house up and she wouldn't leave Dexter. "They went to the Grand Canyon and Yosemite and a bunch of other places," Rita Jean says. "You should see the load of pictures they took. They must of takened a bushel."

"It must be something to be able to take off like that,"

Cleo says. "I never had the chance when we lived on the farm, but now there are too many maniacs on the road." Cleo sips her coffee, knowing it will aggravate her headache. "The way things are going around here, I think maybe I ought to go out West. I think I'll just get me a wig and go running around!" Cleo laughs at herself, but a pain jabs at her temple. Rita Jean laughs, and Cleo goes on, "I thinks Linda's going to have it out with Bob finally. They're going to meet over at the lake one day next week. It wasn't none of my business, but I tried to tell her she ought to simmer down and think it over."

"I think they'll patch it up, Cleo. I really do."

"That Bob Isbell was always the best thing!" Cleo leans back in her chair, almost dreamily. "I tell you, girl, I couldn't have survived if it hadn't been for him when Jake passed away. He was here every hour; he seen to it that we all got to where we was going; he took care of the house here and then went back and took care of their house. He was even washing dishes. Davey was little-bitty then. Of course, none of us could think straight and we didn't see right then all he was doing, but don't you know we appreciated it. I never will forget how good he was."

"He always was good to the kids."

"They had to pinch them pennies, but those kids never did without. He makes good at the lumberyard, and with what Linda brings in from the K Mart, they're pretty well off. That house is just as fine as can be—and Linda walks off and leaves it! You just can't tell me he done her that way, the way she said. And she don't seem to care!"

"She's keeping it in."

"I keep halfway expecting Bob to pull in the driveway, but he hasn't called or said boo to the kids or anything. I don't want to run them out, but I'll be glad when they get this thing worked out! They're tearing up jack! There's always something a-going. A washing machine or the dishwasher. The television, of course. I never saw so many dishes as these younguns can mess up. I never aimed to be feeding Coxey's Army! And they just strow like you've never seen. Right through the middle of the living room. Here comes one dropping this and that, and then right behind here comes the other one. Prissy-Tail's got her tail tied up in knots with all the combustion here!"

Cleo stands up. She has to get an aspirin. "Well, I'll let you get back to your doodling!"

When Cleo starts toward the refrigerator to get ice water, Prissy-Tail bounds straight out of the living room and beats her to the refrigerator.

"You're going to throw me down," she cries.

She gives Prissy-Tail some milk and takes two aspirins. Phil Donahue is talking to former dope addicts. Cleo turns off the TV and finishes her coffee. She looks around at all the extra objects that have accumulated. A tennis racket. Orange-and-blue-striped shoes. Bluejeans in heaps like rag dolls. Tammy's snapshots scattered around on the divan and end tables. A collapsible plaid suitcase. Tote bags with dirty clothes streaming out the tops. Davey's Star Wars toys and his red computer toy that resembles a Princess phone. Tammy's Minute Maker camera. Cleo has forgotten how to move effortlessly through the clutter children make. She pours more coffee and looks at the mail. She looks at a mail-order catalog which specializes in household gadgets. She is impressed with the number of things you can buy to help you organize things, items such as plastic pockets for grocery coupons and accessory chests for closets. She spends a long time then studying the luxurious compartments of a Winnebago in a magazine ad. She imagines traveling out West in it, doing her cooking in the tiny kitchen, but she can't think why she would be going out West by herself.

The cheerleaders' outfits are taking a week. Everything has to be done over. Cleo puts zippers in upside down, allows too much on seams, has to cut plackets out twice. The cheerleaders come over for a fitting and everything is the wrong size. Cleo tells the cheerleaders, "I'm just like a wiggleworm in hot ashes." In comparison to the overalls, the blouses are easy, but she has trouble with the interfacing.

"You don't charge enough," Linda tells her. "You should charge twenty-five dollars apiece for those things."

"People here won't pay that much," Cleo says.

Linda is in and out. The kids visit Bob at home during the weekend. It is more peaceful, but it makes Cleo worry. She is almost glad when they return Sunday evening, carrying tote bags of clothes and playthings. Bob has taken them out for pizza every meal, and they turn up their noses at what she has on the table—fried channel cat and hush puppies. Linda doesn't eat either. She is going out with Shirley. Cleo gives Prissy-Tail more fish than she can eat.

"Smile, Grandma."

"Well, hurry up," Cleo says, her body poised as if about to take off and fly. "I can't hold like this all day."

"Just a minute." Tammy moves the camera around. It looks like the mask on a space suit. "Say cheese!"

Cleo holds her smile, which is growing halfhearted and strained. The camera clicks, and the flashbulb flares. Together, they watch the picture take shape. Like the dawn, it grows in intensity until finally Cleo's features appear. The Cleo in the picture stands there vacantly, like a scared cat.

"I look terrible," says Cleo.

"You look old, Grandma."

On the cheerleader outfits, Cleo is down to finger work. As she whips the facings, she imagines Bob alone in the big ranch house. What would a man do in a house like that by himself? Linda had left him late one night and brought Tammy and Davey over, right in the middle of *The Tonight Show* (John Davidson was the guest host). The children were half asleep. Cleo imagines them groggy and senseless, one day hooked on dope.

The cheerleader outfits are finished. There are some flaws, Cleo knows, where she has had to take out and put in again so many times, but she tells herself that only somebody who sews will notice them. She pulls out bright blue basting thread. She does some wash, finishes this week's *Family Circle* and cuts out a hamburger casserole recipe she thinks the kids might like. She throws away the *Family Circle* and the old *TV Guide*. She carries out trash. Then she straightens up her sewing corner and sorts her threads. She collects Tammy's scattered pictures and puts them in a pile. As she tries to find a box they will fit in, she accidentally steps on the cat's tail. "Oh, I'm sorry!" she cries, shocked. Prissy-Tail hides under the couch. Cleo can't find a box the right size.

When the cheerleaders try on their new outfits, Cleo spots bits of blue basting thread she has missed. Embarrassed, she pulls out the threads. She knows the cheerleaders will go to the ball game and someone will see blue basting thread sticking out.

Later, thinking she will go to the show if there is a decent one on, Cleo drives to the shopping center. There isn't. An invasion from outer space and Jane Fonda. Cleo parks and goes to the K Mart. She waves at Linda, who is busy with a long line of people at her register. Cleo walks around the store and finds a picture album with plastic pockets for Tammy. She will pay for it with some of the money she collected from the cheerleaders. Davey will want something too, but she doesn't know what to buy that he will like. After rejecting all the toys she sees, she buys a striped turtleneck sweater on sale. The album and sweater are roughly the same price. She doesn't see Linda when she goes through the checkout line.

Cleo sits in the parking lot of the shopping center for a long time and then she goes home and makes the hamburger recipe.

"You all go on about your cats like they was babies," says Linda. Linda is sanding a rocking chair, which is upside down on newspapers in the hall.

"They're a heap sight less trouble," says Cleo, who is dusting. Rita Jean has called to say Dexter is home from the hospital, but there isn't much hope.

"Stop fanning doors, Tammy," Linda says. "Grandma's got a present for you."

Cleo brings out the picture album and the sweater.

"Now I want you to keep all them pictures in this," she tells Tammy. "Here, squirt," she says to Davey. "Here's something else for me to pick up."

The children take the presents wordlessly, examining them. Tammy turns the pages and pokes her fingers into the picture pockets. Davey rips the plastic wrapper off the sweater and holds it up. "It fits!" he says.

Davey turns on the television and Tammy sits on the divan, turning the empty pages of the picture album.

"You didn't have to do that," says Linda to Cleo.

"I'm just keeping up with the times," Cleo says. "Spend, spend, spend."

"Nothing wrong with keeping up with the times," says Linda.

"I see you are. With all that old-timey stuff you're collecting. Explain that."

"Everybody's going back to old-timey stuff. Furniture like yours is out of style."

"Then maybe one day it'll be antique. If I live that long." Cleo pokes the dusting broom at the ceiling.

"We're getting on your nerves," says Linda. "We're going to be getting out before long."

"I hope you mean going back home where you belong. Not that I mean to kick you out. You know what I mean."

"We're going back home, all right," Linda says. "This is the big night—I'm going to meet Bob at Kenlake. I'm going to have it out with him. I can't wait." She wipes the rocker with a rag and turns it right side up. "There, I think that's enough. What a job. If I could just find a twin to it. Tammy, turn that radio down; you're bothering Grandma."

Cleo has to sit down. She is out of breath. The broom falls to the floor as she sinks onto the divan. "I'm not sixteen anymore," she says. "I give out too quick."

"Mama, there's not a thing wrong with you. You just don't do anything with yourself."

"What do you mean?"

"Look at you; you're still a young woman. You could go to school, make a nurse or something. That Mrs. Smith over yonder is sixty-eight and flies an airplane. By herself too."

"I can see me doing that." Cleo clutches a needlepoint pillow. Tammy and Davey are arguing, sounding like wild Indians, but the racket is losing its definition around her. She finds it hard to pick out individual sounds. It is just a racket, something like a prolonged, steady snore—with lots of tuneful snorts and snuffles and puffs. Jake used to snore like that, but she could always tug the covers or kick at him gently and he would stop.

"Rita Jean said I was in the prime of life," says Cleo.

"Rita Jean should talk. Look at her. She petted that cat to death, if you ask me. And I never heard anything so ridiculous as her not wanting to go out West when she had the chance! I'd be gone in a minute!"

"People can't just have everything they want, all the time," Cleo says.

"I'm not mad at you, Mama. But people don't have to do what they don't want to as much now as they used to."

"I should know that," Cleo says. "It's all over television. You make me feel awful."

"I don't mean to. It's for your own good."

Prissy-Tail jumps up on the divan and Cleo grabs her. She squirms up onto Cleo's shoulder.

"You sure are lucky, Prissy-Tail, that you don't have to worry," Cleo says.

Linda pulls the rocker through the doorway into the living room. It scrapes the paint on the door facing.

Cleo is behind on supper. She is making a blackberry cobbler and she is confused about the timing. The children's favorite show comes on before supper is ready. They take their plates into the living room. *Mork and Mindy* is the one thing

Tammy and Davey agree on. Cleo fills her plate and watches it with them. It isn't one of her regular stories, and it seems strange to her. Mork is from outer space and drinks through his finger. Otherwise, he is like a human being. Cleo finds his nonstop wisecracks hard to follow. Also, he wears galluses and sleeps hanging upside down. Jake used to wear galluses, Cleo thinks suddenly. Mork lives with Mindy, but Davey and Tammy seem to think nothing of it. Cleo is pleased that they eat the hamburger casserole without complaining. During the commercial she gets them large helpings of hot blackberry cobbler.

In the light she sees that Tammy is wearing blue eye shadow. "It makes you look holler-eyed," Cleo tells her, but Tammy shrugs.

When Tammy and Davey are asleep, Cleo gets out her family picture album. It has few pictures, compared to the way people take pictures nowadays, she thinks. The little black corners are coming loose, and some of the pictures are lying at crazy angles. She tries to put them back in place, knowing they won't stay. She looks through the pictures of her parents' wedding trip to Biloxi. Her parents look so young. Her mother looks like Linda in the picture. She is wearing a long baggy dress in style at the time. Cleo's father is a slim, dark-haired man in the picture. He is smiling. He always smiled. Cleo's parents are both dead. She turns the pages to her own honeymoon pictures. One, in which she and Jake look like children, was taken by a stranger in front of the Jefferson Davis monument. She looks carefully at Jake's face, realizing that the memory of the snapshots is more real than the memory of his actual face. As she turns the pages she sees herself and Jake get slightly older. A picture of Linda shows a stubborn child with bangs.

Cleo looks at a picture of Jake on the tractor. He is grinning into the sun. That was Jake when he was happy. He was a quiet man. Cleo studies a picture taken the year he died, and she wonders suddenly if Jake had ever cheated on her. He could have that time he went to the state fair, she thinks. When he returned he acted strangely, bringing back a red ribbon he had won, and talking in a peculiar way about the future

of the family farm. Jake would never forgive her for selling
the farm. It was surely her way of cheating on him, she thinks
uncomfortably, but she never would have thought of divorcing
him, just as she has not been able later to think of remarrying.

On the last pages of the album she sees a surprise, a picture
she does not recognize at first. It is dim figures on a television
screen. Then she remembers. Tammy took pictures of *Charlie's
Angels* the night Linda missed it.

"Here, Mama, that's you." Tammy had pointed to the dark-
haired actress, whose face was no bigger than a pencil eraser
and hard to make out.

"Just give me her money and I'll do without her looks,"
Linda had replied.

Tammy has put this picture in Cleo's family album. Cleo
cannot think why Tammy would do this. Then she sees on
the next page that Tammy has also put in the picture she
took of Cleo. The picture is the last one in the scrapbook.
Again, Cleo sees herself, looking scared and old.


"The roof fell in," Cleo tells Rita Jean the next day. "Linda
says she's not going back to Bob. She says she wants a separation
and he's agreed to move out. Them children will be packed
from pillar to post. I didn't sleep a wink all night last night."

Cleo is at Rita Jean's. Cleo has driven over, skipping the
*Today* show and her morning phone conversation. Now she
feels more comfortable at Rita Jean's than at home. The house
is brightly decorated with handmade objects. Rita belongs to
a mail-order craft club which sends a kit every month. She
has made a new embroidered wall hanging of an Arizona sunset. Cleo admires it and says, as she gazes at a whipstitch, "What
I don't understand is how my daughter can carry on like she
does. She chirps like a bird!"

"I just don't know," says Rita Jean. "Don't look at this
mess," she says as she leads Cleo to the back room, where
Dexter is sleeping in a box. "The vet said there's not a thing
wrong with him. He's just wearing out. He said keep him warm,
have food for him whenever he wants it, and pet him and

talk to him. It might be that I kept him in too long and he's just pined away. Do you think that was right, to keep him in like that all this time?"

"If you had let him out he would have just got run over," says Cleo. She strokes Dexter and he stirs slightly. His fur is dull and thin.

"I'll just have to accept it," says Rita Jean.

"Maybe it will be good for you," says Cleo, more harshly than she intends. "I've about decided there's no use trying to hang on to anything. You just lose it all in the end. You might as well just not care."

"Don't talk that way, Cleo."

"I must be getting old." Cleo laughs. "I'm saying what I think more. Or younger, one. Old people and children—they always say what they think."

Over coffee, Cleo talks Rita Jean into going to trade day at the stockyard.

"Linda said we've got to get out, keep up with the times," Cleo says. "Just what I need—more junk. But it's the style."

"Maybe it will take our minds off of everything," says Rita Jean, getting her scarf.

Most of the traders at the stockyard are farmers who trade in secondhand goods on the side. Cleo is shocked to realize this, though she knows nobody can make a living on a farm these days. She recognizes some of the farmers, behind their folding tables of dusty old objects. Even at the time of Jake's death, feeding the cows was costing almost as much as the milk brought. She cannot imagine Jake in a camper, peddling some old junk from the barn. That would kill him if the heart attack hadn't.

Cleo and Rita Jean drift from table to table, touching Depression glass, crystal goblets, cracked china, cast-off egg beaters and mixers, rusted farm implements, and greasy wooden boxes stuffed with buttons and papers.

"I never saw so much old stuff," says Cleo.

"Look at this," says Rita Jean, pointing to a box of plastic jump ropes. "These aren't old."

They look at hand-tooled leather belts and billfolds, made by prisoners. And paintings of bright scenes on black velvet— bullfights and skylines and sunsets. A man in a cowboy hat displays the paintings from a fancy camper called a Sports Coach.

"He must have come from far away," says Rita Jean.

"I used to have a set of these." Cleo holds a tiny crystal salt shaker, without the pepper. There is a syrup holder to match.

"You could spend all day here," says Rita Jean, looking around like a lost child.

Cleo doesn't hear her. All of a sudden her blood is rushing to her head and her stomach is churning. She is looking at a miniature Early American whatnot, right in front of her. It is imitation mahogany. She holds it, touching it, turning it, amazed.

"If it had been a snake it would have bit me!" cries Cleo, astonished. But Rita Jean is intent on examining a set of enamel canisters with cat decals on them and doesn't notice.

The whatnot cannot be the same one. Cleo cannot remember what happened to the little whatnot that sat on the dresser, the box in which Jake kept his stamps, his receipts, and his bankbook.

This whatnot has a door held in place by a wooden button, and on the top, like books on a shelf, is a series of tiny boxes, with sliding covers like match boxes. The little boxes have names: Book Plates, Mending Tape, Gummed Patches, Rubber Bands, Gummed Labels, Mailing Labels. There are pictures on the spines of the boxes, together forming a scene—an old-fashioned train running through a meadow past a river, with black smoke trailing across three of the boxes and meeting a distant mountain. A steamboat is in the background. The curved track extends from the first box to the last. The scene is faded green and yellow, and there are lacy ferns and a tree in the foreground. The boxes are a simple picture puzzle to put in order. Cleo's children played with the puzzle when they were small, but her grandchildren were never interested in it. It cannot be the very same whatnot, she thinks.

"I'm going to buy this!" Cleo says.

"That's high," says Rita Jean, fingering the price sticker. The whatnot is three dollars.

Cleo looks at the train. Two of the pictures are out of order, and she rearranges them so that the caboose is at the end. For a moment she can see the train gliding silently through the pleasant scene, as quietly as someone dreaming, and she can imagine her family aboard the train as it crosses a fertile valley—like the place down by the creek that Jake loved—on its way out West. On the train, her well-behaved sons and their children are looking out the windows, and Linda and Bob are driving the train, guiding the cowcatcher down the track, while Tammy and Davey patiently count telephone poles and watch the passing scenery. Cleo is following unafraid in the caboose, as the train passes through the golden meadow and they all wave at the future and smile perfect smiles.

# Drawing Names

On Christmas Day, Carolyn Sisson went early to her parents' house to help her mother with the dinner. Carolyn had been divorced two years before, and last Christmas, coming alone, she felt uncomfortable. This year she had invited her lover, Kent Ballard, to join the family gathering. She had even brought him a present to put under the tree, so he wouldn't feel left out. Kent was planning to drive over from Kentucky Lake by noon. He had gone there to inspect his boat because of an ice storm earlier in the week. He felt compelled to visit his boat on the holiday, Carolyn thought, as if it were a sad old relative in a retirement home.

"We're having baked ham instead of turkey," Mom said. "Your daddy never did like ham baked, but whoever heard of fried ham on Christmas? We have that all year round and I'm burnt out on it."

"I love baked ham," said Carolyn.

"Does Kent like it baked?"

"I'm sure he does." Carolyn placed her gifts under the tree. The number of packages seemed unusually small.

"It don't seem like Christmas with drawed names," said Mom.

"Your star's about to fall off." Carolyn straightened the silver ornament at the tip of the tree.

"I didn't decorate as much as I wanted to. I'm slowing down. Getting old, I guess." Mom had not combed her hair and she was wearing a workshirt and tennis shoes.

"You always try to do too much on Christmas, Mom."

Carolyn knew the agreement to draw names had bothered her mother. But the four daughters were grown, and two had children. Sixteen people were expected today. Carolyn herself could not afford to buy fifteen presents on her salary as a clerk at J. C. Penney's, and her parents' small farm had not been profitable in years.

Carolyn's father appeared in the kitchen and he hugged her so tightly she squealed in protest.

"That's all I can afford this year," he said, laughing.

As he took a piece of candy from a dish on the counter, Carolyn teased him. "You'd better watch your calories today."

"Oh, not on Christmas!"

It made Carolyn sad to see her handsome father getting older. He was a shy man, awkward with his daughters, and Carolyn knew he had been deeply disappointed over her failed marriage, although he had never said so. Now he asked, "Who bought these 'toes'?"

He would no longer say "nigger toes," the old name for the chocolate-covered creams.

"Hattie Smoot brought those over," said Mom. "I made a pants suit for her last week," she said to Carolyn. "The one that had stomach bypass?"

"When PeeWee McClain had that, it didn't work and they had to fix him back like he was," said Dad. He offered Carolyn a piece of candy, but she shook her head no.

Mom said, "I made Hattie a dress back last spring for her boy's graduation, and she couldn't even find a pattern big enough. I had to 'low a foot. But after that bypass, she's down to a size twenty."

"I think we'll all need a stomach bypass after we eat this feast you're fixing," said Carolyn.

"Where's Kent?" Dad asked abruptly.

"He went to see about his boat. He said he'd be here."

Carolyn looked at the clock. She felt uneasy about inviting Kent. Everyone would be scrutinizing him, as if he were some new character on a soap opera. Kent, who drove a truck for the Kentucky Loose-Leaf Floor, was a part-time student at

Murray State. He was majoring in accounting. When Carolyn started going with him early in the summer, they went sailing on his boat, which had "Joyce" painted on it. Later he painted over the name, insisting he didn't love Joyce anymore—she was a dietician who was always criticizing what he ate—but he had never said he loved Carolyn. She did not know if she loved him. Each seemed to be waiting for the other to say it first.

While Carolyn helped her mother in the kitchen, Dad went to get her grandfather, her mother's father. Pappy, who had been disabled by a stroke, was cared for by a live-in housekeeper who had gone home to her own family for the day. Carolyn diced apples and pears for fruit salad while her mother shaped sweet potato balls with marshmallow centers and rolled them in crushed cornflakes. On TV in the living room, *Days of Our Lives* was beginning, but the Christmas tree blocked their view of the television set.

"Whose name did you draw, Mom?" Carolyn asked, as she began seeding the grapes.

"Jim's."

"You put Jim's name in the hat?"

Mom nodded. Jim Walsh was the man Carolyn's youngest sister, Laura Jean, was living with in St. Louis. Laura Jean was going to an interior decorating school, and Jim was a textiles salesman she had met in a class. "I made him a shirt," Mom said.

"I'm surprised at you."

"Well, what was I to do?"

"I'm just surprised." Carolyn ate a grape and spit out the seeds. "Emily Post says the couple should be offered the same room when they visit."

"You know we'd never stand for that. I don't think your dad's ever got over her stacking up with that guy."

"You mean shacking up."

"Same thing." Mom dropped the potato masher, and the metal rattled on the floor. "Oh, I'm in such a tizzy," she said.

As the family began to arrive, the noise of the TV played

against the greetings, the slam of the storm door, the outside wind rushing in. Carolyn's older sisters, Peggy and Iris, with their husbands and children, were arriving all at once, and suddenly the house seemed small. Peggy's children Stevie and Cheryl, without even removing their jackets, became involved in a basketball game on TV. In his lap, Stevie had a Merlin electronic toy, which beeped randomly. Iris and Ray's children, Deedee and Jonathan, went outside to look for cats.

In the living room, Peggy jiggled her baby, Lisa, on her hip and said, "You need you one of these, Carolyn."

"Where can I get one?" said Carolyn, rather sharply.

Peggy grinned. "At the gittin' place, I reckon."

Peggy's critical tone was familiar. She was the only sister who had had a real wedding. Her husband, Cecil, had a Gulf franchise, and they owned a motor cruiser, a pickup truck, a camper, a station wagon, and a new brick colonial home. Whenever Carolyn went to visit Peggy, she felt apologetic for not having a man who would buy her all these things, but she never seemed to be attracted to anyone steady or ambitious. She had been wondering how Kent would get along with the men of the family. Cecil and Ray were standing in a corner talking about gas mileage. Cecil, who was shorter than Peggy and was going bald, always worked on Dad's truck for free, and Ray usually agreed with Dad on politics to avoid an argument. Ray had an impressive government job in Frankfort. He had coordinated a ribbon-cutting ceremony when the toll road opened. What would Kent have to say to them? She could imagine him insisting that everyone go outside later to watch the sunset. Her father would think that was ridiculous. No one ever did that on a farm, but it was the sort of thing Kent would think of. Yet she knew that spontaneity was what she liked in him.

Deedee and Jonathan, who were ten and six, came inside then and immediately began shaking the presents under the tree. All the children were wearing new jeans and cowboy shirts, Carolyn noticed.

"Why are y'all so quiet?" she asked. "I thought kids whooped and hollered on Christmas."

"They've been up since *four*," said Iris. She took a cigarette from her purse and accepted a light from Cecil. Exhaling smoke, she said to Carolyn, "We heard Kent was coming." Before Carolyn could reply, Iris scolded the children for shaking the packages. She seemed nervous.

"He's supposed to be here by noon," said Carolyn.

"There's somebody now. I hear a car."

"It might be Dad, with Pappy."

It was Laura Jean, showing off Jim Walsh as though he were a splendid Christmas gift she had just received.

"Let me kiss everybody!" she cried, as the women rushed toward her. Laura Jean had not been home in four months.

"Merry Christmas!" Jim said in a booming, official-sounding voice, something like a TV announcer, Carolyn thought. He embraced all the women and then, with a theatrical gesture, he handed Mom a bottle of Rebel Yell bourbon and a carton of boiled custard which he took from a shopping bag. The bourbon was in a decorative Christmas box.

Mom threw up her hands. "Oh, no, I'm afraid I'll be a alky-holic."

"Oh, that's ridiculous, Mom," said Laura Jean, taking Jim's coat. "A couple of drinks a day are good for your heart."

Jim insisted on getting coffee cups from a kitchen cabinet and mixing some boiled custard and bourbon. When he handed a cup to Mom, she puckered up her face.

"Law, don't let the preacher in," she said, taking a sip. "Boy, that sends my blood pressure up."

Carolyn waved away the drink Jim offered her. "I don't start this early in the day," she said, feeling confused.

Jim was a large, dark-haired man with a neat little beard, like a bird's nest cupped on his chin. He had a Northern accent. When he hugged her, Carolyn caught a whiff of cologne, something sweet, like chocolate syrup. Last summer, when Laura Jean brought him home for the first time, she had made a point of kissing and hugging him in front of everyone. Dad had virtually ignored him. Now Carolyn saw that Jim was telling Cecil that he always bought Gulf gas. Red-faced, Ray accepted a cup of boiled custard. Carolyn fled to the kitchen and began grating cheese for potatoes au gratin. She dreaded Kent's arrival.

When Dad arrived with Pappy, Cecil and Jim helped set up the wheelchair in a corner. Afterward, Dad and Jim shook hands, and Dad refused Jim's offer of bourbon. From the kitchen, Carolyn could see Dad hugging Laura Jean, not letting go. She went into the living room to greet her grandfather.

"They roll me in this buggy too fast," he said when she kissed his forehead.

Carolyn hoped he wouldn't notice the bottle of bourbon, but she knew he never missed anything. He was so deaf people had given up talking to him. Now the children tiptoed around him, looking at him with awe. Somehow, Carolyn expected the children to notice that she was alone, like Pappy.

At ten minutes of one, the telephone rang. Peggy answered and handed the receiver to Carolyn. "It's Kent," she said.

Kent had not left the lake yet. "I just got here an hour ago," he told Carolyn. "I had to take my sister over to my mother's."

"Is the boat O.K.?"

"Yeah. Just a little scraped paint. I'll be ready to go in a little while." He hesitated, as though waiting for assurance that the invitation was real.

"This whole gang's ready to eat," Carolyn said. "Can't you hurry?" She should have remembered the way he tended to get sidetracked. Once it took them three hours to get to Paducah, because he kept stopping at antique shops.

After she hung up the telephone, her mother asked, "Should I put the rolls in to brown yet?"

"Wait just a little. He's just now leaving the lake."

"When's this Kent feller coming?" asked Dad impatiently, as he peered into the kitchen. "It's time to eat."

"He's on his way," said Carolyn.

"Did you tell him we don't wait for stragglers?"

"No."

"When the plate rattles, we eat."

"I know."

"Did you tell him that?"

"No, I didn't!" cried Carolyn, irritated.

When they were alone in the kitchen, Carolyn's mother said to her, "Your dad's not his self today. He's fit to be tied about Laura Jean bringing that guy down here again. And him bringing that whiskey."

"That was uncalled for," Carolyn agreed. She had noticed that Mom had set her cup of boiled custard in the refrigerator.

"Besides, he's not too happy about that Kent Ballard you're running around with."

"What's it to him?"

"You know how he always was. He don't think anybody's good enough for one of his little girls, and he's afraid you'll get mistreated again. He don't think Kent's very dependable."

"I guess Kent's proving Dad's point."

Carolyn's sister Iris had dark brown eyes, unique in the family. When Carolyn was small, she tried to say "Iris's eyes" once and called them "Irish eyes," confusing them with a song their mother sometimes sang, "When Irish Eyes Are Smiling." Thereafter, they always teased Iris about her smiling Irish eyes. Today Iris was not smiling. Carolyn found her in a bedroom smoking, holding an ashtray in her hand.

"I drew your name," Carolyn told her. "I got you something I wanted myself."

"Well, if I don't want it, I guess I'll have to give it to you."

"What's wrong with you today?"

"Ray and me's getting a separation," said Iris.

"Really?" Carolyn was startled by the note of glee in her response. Actually, she told herself later, it was because she was glad her sister, whom she saw infrequently, had confided in her.

"The thing of it is, I had to beg him to come today, for Mom and Dad's sake. It'll kill them. Don't let on, will you?"

"I won't. What are you going to do?"

"I don't know. He's already moved out."

"Are you going to stay in Frankfort?"

"I don't know. I have to work things out."

Mom stuck her head in the door. "Well, is Kent coming or not?"

"He *said* he'd be here," said Carolyn.

"Your dad's about to have a duck with a rubber tail. He can't stand to wait on a meal."

"Well, let's go ahead, then. Kent can eat when he gets here."

When Mom left, Iris said, "Aren't you and Kent getting along?"

"I don't know. He said he'd come today, but I have a feeling he doesn't really want to."

"To hell with men." Iris laughed and stubbed out her cigarette. "Just look at us—didn't we turn out awful? First your divorce. Now me. And Laura Jean bringing that guy down. Daddy can't stand him. Did you see the look he gave him?"

"Laura Jean's got a lot more nerve than I've got," said Carolyn, nodding. "I could wring Kent's neck for being late. Well, none of us can do anything right—except Peggy."

"Daddy's precious little angel," said Iris mockingly. "Come on, we'd better get in there and help."

While Mom went to change her blouse and put on lipstick, the sisters brought the food into the dining room. Two tables had been put together. Peggy cut the ham with an electric knife, and Carolyn filled the iced tea glasses.

"Pappy gets buttermilk and Stevie gets Coke," Peggy directed her.

"I know," said Carolyn, almost snapping.

As the family sat down, Carolyn realized that no one ever asked Pappy to "turn thanks" anymore at holiday dinners. He was sitting there expectantly, as if waiting to be asked. Mom cut up his ham into small bits. Carolyn waited for a car to drive up, the phone to ring. The TV was still on.

"Y'all dig in," said Mom. "Jim? Make sure you try some

of these dressed eggs like I fix."

"I thought your new boyfriend was coming," said Cecil to Carolyn.

"So did I!" said Laura Jean. "That's what you wrote me."

Everyone looked at Carolyn as she explained. She looked away.

"You're looking at that pitiful tree," Mom said to her. "I just know it don't show up good from the road."

"No, it looks fine." No one had really noticed the tree. Carolyn seemed to be seeing it for the first time in years— broken red plastic reindeer, Styrofoam snowmen with crumbling top hats, silver walnuts which she remembered painting when she was about twelve.

Dad began telling a joke about some monks who had taken a vow of silence. At each Christmas dinner, he said, one monk was allowed to speak.

"Looks like your vocal cords would rust out," said Cheryl.

"Shut up, Cheryl. Granddaddy's trying to tell something," said Cecil.

"So the first year it was the first monk's turn to talk, and you know what he said? He said, 'These taters is lumpy.' "

When several people laughed, Stevie asked, "Is that the joke?"

Carolyn was baffled. Her father had never told a joke at the table in his life. He sat at the head of the table, looking out past the family at the cornfield through the picture window.

"Pay attention now," he said. "The second year Christmas rolled around again and it was the second monk's turn to say something. He said, 'You know, I think you're right. The taters *is* lumpy.' "

Laura Jean and Jim laughed loudly.

"Reach me some light-bread," said Pappy. Mom passed the dish around the table to him.

"And so the third year," Dad continued, "the third monk got to say something. What he said"—Dad was suddenly overcome with mirth—"what he said was, 'If y'all don't shut up arguing about them taters, I'm going to leave this place!' "

After the laughter died, Mom said, "Can you imagine any-body not a-talking all year long?"

"That's the way monks are, Mom," said Laura Jean. "Monks are economical with everything. They're not wasteful, not even with words."

"The Trappist Monks are really an outstanding group," said Jim. "And they make excellent bread. No preservatives."

Cecil and Peggy stared at Jim.

"You're not eating, Dad," said Carolyn. She was sitting between him and the place set for Kent. The effort at telling the joke seemed to have taken her father's appetite.

"He ruined his dinner on nigger toes," said Mom.

"Dottie Barlow got a Barbie doll for Christmas and it's black," Cheryl said.

"Dottie Barlow ain't black, is she?" asked Cecil.

"No."

"That's funny," said Peggy. "Why would they give her a black Barbie doll?"

"She just wanted it."

Abruptly, Dad left the table, pushing back his plate. He sat down in the recliner chair in front of the TV. The Blue–Gray game was beginning, and Cecil and Ray were hurriedly finishing in order to join him. Carolyn took out second helpings of ham and jello salad, feeling as though she were eating for Kent in his absence. Jim was taking seconds of everything, complimenting Mom. Mom apologized for not having fancy napkins. Then Laura Jean described a photography course she had taken. She had been photographing close-ups of car parts—fenders, headlights, mud flaps.

"That sounds goofy," said one of the children, Deedee.

Suddenly Pappy spoke. "Use to, the menfolks would eat first, and the children separate. The womenfolks would eat last, in the kitchen."

"You know what I could do with you all, don't you?" said Mom, shaking her fist at him. "I could set up a plank out in the field for y'all to eat on." She laughed.

"Times are different now, Pappy," said Iris loudly. "We're just as good as the men."

"She gets that from television," said Ray, with an apologetic laugh.

Carolyn noticed Ray's glance at Iris. Just then Iris matter-of-factly plucked an eyelash from Ray's cheek. It was as though she had momentarily forgotten about the separation.

Later, after the gifts were opened, Jim helped clear the tables. Kent still had not come. The baby slept, and Laura Jean, Jim, Peggy, and Mom played a Star Trek board game at the dining room table, while Carolyn and Iris played Battlestar Galactica with Cheryl and Deedee. The other men were quietly engrossed in the football game, a blur of sounds. No one had mentioned Kent's absence, but after the children had distributed the gifts, Carolyn refused to tell them what was in the lone package left under the tree. It was the most extravagantly wrapped of all the presents, with an immense ribbon, not a stick-on bow. An icicle had dropped on it, and it reminded Carolyn of an abandoned float, like something from a parade.

At a quarter to three, Kent telephoned. He was still at the lake. "The gas stations are all closed," he said. "I couldn't get any gas."

"We already ate and opened the presents," said Carolyn.

"Here I am, stranded. Not a thing I can do about it."

Kent's voice was shaky and muffled, and Carolyn suspected he had been drinking. She did not know what to say, in front of the family. She chattered idly, while she played with a ribbon from a package. The baby was awake, turning dials and knobs on a Busy Box. On TV, the Blues picked up six yards on an end sweep. Carolyn fixed her eyes on the tilted star at the top of the tree. Kent was saying something about Santa Claus.

"They wanted me to play Santy at Mama's house for the littluns. I said—you know what I said? 'Bah, humbug!' Did I ever tell you what I've got against Christmas?"

"Maybe not." Carolyn's back stiffened against the wall.

"When I was little bitty, Santa Claus came to town. I was about five. I was all fired up to go see Santy, and Mama took me, but we were late, and he was about to leave. I had to run across the courthouse square to get to him. He was giving away suckers, so I ran as hard as I could. He was climbing up on the fire engine—are you listening?"

"Unh-huh." Carolyn was watching her mother, who was folding Christmas paper to save for next year.

Kent said, "I reached up and pulled at his old red pants leg, and he looked down at me, and you know what he said?"

"No—what?"

"He said, 'Piss off, kid.' "

"Really?"

"Would I lie to you?"

"I don't know."

"Do you want to hear the rest of my hard-luck story?"

"Not now."

"Oh, I forgot this was long distance. I'll call you tomorrow. Maybe I'll go paint the boat. That's what I'll do! I'll go paint it right this minute."

After Carolyn hung up the telephone, her mother said, "I think my Oriental casserole was a failure. I used the wrong kind of mushroom soup. It called for cream of mushroom and I used golden mushroom."

"Won't you *ever* learn, Mom?" cried Carolyn. "You always cook too much. You make *such* a big deal—"

Mom said, "What happened with Kent this time?"

"He couldn't get gas. He forgot the gas stations were closed."

"Jim and Laura Jean didn't have any trouble getting gas," said Peggy, looking up from the game.

"We tanked up yesterday," said Laura Jean.

"Of course you did," said Carolyn distractedly. "You always think ahead."

"It's your time," Cheryl said, handing Carolyn the Battlestar Galactica toy. "I did lousy."

"Not as lousy as I did," said Iris.

Carolyn tried to concentrate on shooting enemy missiles, raining through space. Her sisters seemed far away, like the spaceships. She was aware of the men watching football, their hands in action as they followed an exciting play. Even though Pappy had fallen asleep, with his blanket in his lap he looked like a king on a throne. Carolyn thought of the quiet accommodation her father had made to his father-in-law, just as Cecil and Ray had done with Dad, and her ex-husband had tried to do once. But Cecil had bought his way in, and now Ray was getting out. Kent had stayed away. Jim, the newcomer, was with the women, playing Star Trek as if his life depended upon it. Carolyn was glad now that Kent had not come. The story he told made her angry, and his pity for his childhood made her think of something Pappy had often said: "Christmas is for children." Earlier, she had listened in amazement while Cheryl listed on her fingers the gifts she had received that morning: a watch, a stereo, a nightgown, hot curls, perfume, candles, a sweater, a calculator, a jewelry box, a ring. Now Carolyn saw Kent's boat as his toy, more important than the family obligations of the holiday.

Mom was saying, "I wanted to make a Christmas tablecloth out of red checks with green fringe. You wouldn't think knit would do for a tablecloth, but Hattie Smoot has the prettiest one."

"You can do incredible things with knit," said Jim with sudden enthusiasm. The shirt Mom had made him was bonded knit.

"Who's Hattie Smoot?" asked Laura Jean. She was caressing the back of Jim's neck, as though soothing his nerves.

Carolyn laughed when her mother began telling Jim and Laura Jean about Hattie Smoot's operation. Jim listened attentively, leaning forward with his elbows on the table, and asked eager questions, his eyes as alert as Pappy's.

"Is she telling a joke?" Cheryl asked Carolyn.

"No. I'm not laughing at you, Mom," Carolyn said, touching her mother's hand. She felt relieved that the anticipation of Christmas had ended. Still laughing, she said, "Pour me some of that Rebel Yell, Jim. It's about time."

"I'm with you," Jim said, jumping up.

In the kitchen, Carolyn located a clean spoon while Jim washed some cups. Carolyn couldn't find the cup Mom had left in the refrigerator. As she took out the carton of boiled custard, Jim said, "It must be a very difficult day for you."

Carolyn was startled. His tone was unexpectedly kind, genuine. She was struck suddenly by what he must know about her, because of his intimacy with her sister. She knew nothing about him. When he smiled, she saw a gold cap on a molar, shining like a Christmas ornament. She managed to say, "It can't be any picnic for you either. Kent didn't want to put up with us."

"Too bad he couldn't get gas."

"I don't think he wanted to get gas."

"Then you're better off without him." When Jim looked at her, Carolyn felt that he must be examining her resemblances to Laura Jean. He said, "I think your family's great."

Carolyn laughed nervously. "We're hard on you. God, you're brave to come down here like this."

"Well, Laura Jean's worth it."

They took the boiled custard and cups into the dining room. As Carolyn sat down, her nephew Jonathan begged her to tell what was in the gift left under the tree.

"I can't tell," she said.

"Why not?"

"I'm saving it till next year, in case I draw some man's name."

"I hope it's mine," said Jonathan.

Jim stirred bourbon into three cups of boiled custard, then gave one to Carolyn and one to Laura Jean. The others had declined. Then he leaned back in his chair—more relaxed now—and squeezed Laura Jean's hand. Carolyn wondered what they said to each other when they were alone in St. Louis. She knew with certainty that they would not be economical with words, like the monks in the story. She longed to be with them, to hear what they would say. She noticed her mother picking at a hangnail, quietly ignoring the bourbon. Looking at the bottle's gift box, which showed an old-fashioned scene, children on sleds in the snow, Carolyn thought of Kent's boat again. She felt she was in that snowy scene now with Laura Jean and Jim, sailing in Kent's boat into the winter breeze, into falling snow. She thought of how silent it was out on the lake, as though the whiteness of the snow were the absence of sound.

"Cheers!" she said to Jim, lifting her cup.

# The Climber

The former astronaut claims that walking on the moon was nothing, compared to walking with Jesus. Walking with Jesus is forever, but the moon visit was just three days. The preacher emcee, trailing the long cord of his microphone, moves with slow-motion bounces, as though trying to get the feel of the astronaut's walk on the moon. The preacher has on a pink plaid jacket, and because the TV color isn't tuned properly, his face is the same bright shade.

Dolores has the Christian channel on only for the music. She likes to think she is impervious to evangelists. She usually laughs at the way they talk so urgently, even happily, about the end of the world. But today the show sends a chill through her. After the astronaut leaves, a missions specialist describes the "gap of unbelief" that can only be bridged by Jesus Christ. The gap of unbelief sounds threatening, like the missile gap.

"Quit it, Petey. You're giving me the heebie-jeebies," Dolores says. She refrains from kicking at the little boy from down the street, who is underfoot. She is arranging dogwood blossoms in a vase and Petey is repeating "Fuzzy Duck" in a monotone. Petey is nine, and he wears a strange little sweatsuit with the arms and legs cut off and the edges hanging in shreds.

"Jesus is a vampire," says Petey.

"Where'd you get that idea?"

"My brother said so."

"How does he know?"

"He studied it. In a book."

"I've heard a lot of things, but I never heard that."

Petey slams the door and charges down the driveway on his bicycle, making hot-rod sounds. He rides an old bicycle with a banana seat, a hand-me-down from his older brother, who is in jail for breaking into an insurance agency and stealing three calculators. In Dolores's opinion, their mother is an alcoholic who lets her kids run wild.

Petey has been hanging around this morning to see the tree cut down. A tree service is coming to saw down the tall tulip tree near the corner of the house. Dolores's husband, Glenn, is having the tree cut down to make room for a workshop he plans to build. He has been stripping furniture, and he wants to begin making picnic tables to sell. But the tree cutting was scheduled for an inopportune time. It confuses Dolores. Later in the morning, she has an appointment with a gynecologist, and she is frightened. When the doctor she saw at the clinic two days earlier examined the lump in her breast, he advised seeing a specialist immediately. The lump has been there for several months, and it seems to change shape and move around. Dolores kept thinking it would go away. Then, after her friend Dusty Bivens urged her to see a doctor, Dolores became alarmed. Dusty had read an article in *Ladies' Home Journal* about breast examinations. Dusty keeps up with medical news. She has had a D & C, a hysterectomy, and a gall bladder attack. She has to avoid spicy and greasy foods. Dolores has noticed that whenever women get together, they talk about diseases. Men never do. This is probably why Dolores is hesitant to tell Glenn about seeing the doctor. She has not mentioned the lump to him, the way sometimes women don't tell their husbands they are pregnant until it has been confirmed by a doctor. They save the news for a special time. This is a scene Dolores has frequently seen in the movies, but she never knew anyone who did that. She had always told Glenn when she suspected she was pregnant. Now their three children are grown and married.

Of course, Glenn would be perfectly reasonable, pointing out the way Dusty tends to overreact. Once, when an earthquake was predicted for western Kentucky, where they live,

Dusty went on an impromptu vacation with her children. They went to a dude ranch in Arizona, and Dusty took her new set of Teflon II pans with her. Dusty has a fearful nature, but she often does bold things, like taking off for the dude ranch, or enrolling in beauty school at the age of thirty-seven. She has even had an affair.

Near the house are three oaks, two maples, and an ash tree. The tulip tree, at the southeast corner, is the tallest, probably over eighty feet high. It is filled with plump green buds, resembling the pods in a movie about body snatchers Dolores saw on TV. Earlier in the week, when Jerry McClain from Jerry's Tree Service said he would have to bring his climber out to bring the tree down, Dolores thought he was referring to some sort of machine, like a cherry picker.

"He means a guy who climbs trees," Glenn explained to her later.

"I thought you sawed a tree down at the bottom."

"No. It might fall on the house. They have to cut it down in sections and let 'em down on ropes."

"Do you really have to cut it down?"

"Even if it wasn't for the workshop, we're lucky a twister hasn't knocked that tree down on us."

"But your timing's way off," said Dolores. "That tree's about to bloom. Can't you even let it get through with its blooming?"

Now Glenn is in the front yard with his father, Boyce Mullins, waiting for the tree crew to arrive. Boyce had tried to dissuade Glenn from hiring the expensive tree service, but Glenn hadn't listened. Dolores turns the volume of the TV up. A trio of sexy girls is singing a disco spiritual, "I've Never Had Love Like This Before." There are no words to the song beyond the title, which they sing repeatedly. Dolores turns on the leftover breakfast coffee. She considers calling Dusty, but it is too early. Dusty has night classes in Paducah, and she sleeps late.

Dolores takes a cup of coffee to the front porch and offers it to her father-in-law.

"I reckon you're here to put your two cents' worth in, Boyce," she says, handing him the mug.

"Did you put sugar in it?"

"I stuck my finger in it. That sweetened it. Of course I put sugar in it. You think after all these years I don't know how you take it?"

"My son here thinks he's got to pay a fancy price to hire experts," says Boyce, tasting his coffee.

"We've been round and round on this," Glenn says to Dolores.

"I'd help out, but my herny's too bad," Boyce says. Boyce wears a truss and walks oddly—holding in the device that holds him in.

"It's O.K.," says Glenn. "These guys know what they're doing."

"You wouldn't need them experts. Me and you could bring that thing down."

"We should have done it years ago," says Glenn. "The roots are eating into the foundation."

"I never heard you complain about that tree before," says Dolores.

Glenn laughs in a way that embarrasses her, as though he were apologizing to his father for his wife's sentimentality. The night before, when she couldn't sleep, Glenn asked her why she had been so touchy recently.

"Maybe you're going through the change," he suggested.

"How is that possible?" she wanted to know. "I'm not but forty-one."

"My sister-in-law's cousin went through it at the age of twenty-eight. Nobody could stand to be around her."

"That makes her a freak," said Dolores. "I'm not going through any change. Besides, the change comes later nowadays than it used to."

Glenn fell asleep soon after, and he did not know that

Dolores lay there and cried until she could feel the tears run down on her breasts.

Petey turns in the driveway on his bicycle, racing just ahead of the tree service truck.

"That kid's just begging for trouble," Dolores says.

Two men are in the truck, and two others follow in a van. The word JERRY'S on the door of the truck is painted in fancy lettering, with the Y drawn as a tree, its branches and roots curving around the name.

One of the men wears a T-shirt that says CELESTIAL SEASONINGS, MORNING THUNDER. He hunkers against a maple tree and pokes sprigs of Chattanooga Chew Chew into his mouth.

"That's the climber," Glenn says to Dolores.

The other men begin unloading equipment—shiny red chain saws, orange hard-hats, long poles with forked ends. While Glenn talks to the men, Dolores crosses the yard to watch the climber. He takes one look up the tulip tree, gauging its height, then begins to shinny up. He has a coil of rope and a leather harness with him. He has long hair and a bristly mustache.

"He's climbing without spikes," one of the men says to Dolores.

"He climbs like a monkey, sure as you're born," says Boyce, with an admiring whistle.

"You just wish you could get up there with him," says Dolores.

"Don't I, though?" says Boyce, grinning. "Remember the time me and my brother Emmett cut down that dead pine? That thing split in two and we thought it was coming after us both. We run ever which of a way." Boyce laughs in little gasps.

The climber is high in the branches, near the top of the tree. The leaves jiggle and dance. Then he lets down a rope and hauls up a chain saw, which bumps against the trunk as it ascends. Dolores can see elbows sticking out of the leaves, and she glimpses the climber's T-shirt, a bright red and blue, a stranded kite. She has a crick in her neck from looking up.

Dolores warns Petey to get his bike out of the driveway. "It'll get smashed." She adds, "So will you if you don't watch out."

Petey bares his teeth, pretending he has fangs. "I'm the baby Jesus," he says.

"And I'm the devil," says Dolores.

A sound splits the air. The climber has begun to saw. A small branch floats down through the leaves. It is tied to the rope.

"Kindling wood," says Boyce.

"We'll put it all in the chipper," says Jerry McClain, the man in charge of the crew.

Glenn is helping the crew with the rope, and Boyce has settled down in an aluminum folding chair under a maple tree. He is relaxing with his cigar, just as though he has come to watch the trotters at the fair.

"He's a free-lance climber," one of the crew members says to Dolores. "I would have done it, but I saw that tree and said, 'No, *sir*.' That tree's something else. You couldn't get me up that sucker. You never know what poplars will do, that high. They're funny trees."

The telephone is ringing in the kitchen, and Dolores runs inside to snatch it up on the fourth ring. It is Tammy, her newly married daughter, calling to ask about a weskit she is cutting out.

"I lost part of the pattern," Tammy says. "And I have to cut the facings out by guess. Do you cut them on the bias?"

"I don't know what weskit you're talking about."

"You made me one with rickrack once, remember?"

"There's this guy up a tree and he's all the way to the top—that tulip tree? Glenn's got some men out here and they're cutting the tree down. I can't think straight."

"Which tree? I don't know trees by name."

"The one at the corner of the house."

"Oh. Well, I'll let you go if you're busy. I wanted to get

this thing together before Jimmy comes in for dinner."

"Cut it on the bias," says Dolores impulsively. Her daughter calls her every day, to ask something obvious.

After hanging up, Dolores pours herself some coffee. She looks in the refrigerator at a chicken carcass and half a meat loaf. It occurs to her that Boyce and Glenn might like some cake and iced tea later, but she does not have time to bake a cake before her appointment. She does not know what kind to make anyway. She puts in a load of wash, but she doesn't have enough dirty clothes for a full load, so she sets the water level at low. She straightened up the house earlier, as if preparing for company. Now there is nothing to do. Her mother always said worriers made the best housekeepers. The Oak Ridge Boys are singing "Elvira" on the radio. The Oak Ridge Boys used to be a gospel quartet when Dolores was a child. Now, inexplicably, they are a group of young men with blow-dried hair, singing country-rock songs about love.

From the porch steps, she watches the climber saw off a branch. It gets caught in some leaves as it falls, and the men steer the branch down with the rope. Glenn dashes around the yard, pulling at one end of the rope. High in the tree, the climber is hanging in his leather sling.

"He don't even use spikes," says Petey. "Gah!"

When the branch reaches the ground, Glenn unties it and tosses it in the driveway near the truck.

Dolores watches the men work until the tip of the trunk is denuded. It sways slightly, like a sailboat ready to come about. The climber steadies himself, adjusts his straps, then swings his right leg over a limb and straddles it.

"He's going to dehorn that thing,"says Boyce.

"I can't stand this anymore," says Dolores.

She telephones Dusty.

"Aren't you scared?" Dusty asks when Dolores describes what is going on. "Why don't you come over here where it's safe?"

"It's not like you think. This guy's slicing it off, a piece at a time." Dolores hears the chain saw pause, then the swish of branches, the shouts of the men. "He looks like a hippie," she says.

"You don't see many of them anymore."

"He chews tobacco too."

"Is he cute?"

"Not bad. You should come over *here*."

"I don't know if I could kiss somebody that chewed tobacco." Dusty laughs. "Did I tell you what that high-tone husband of mine says to me?"

"No, what?"

"He said he'll take me back—on condition."

"What?"

"If I quit beauty school."

"You don't want to do that."

"He thinks he's got it *over* me," Dusty says. "He thinks I'm bound to come crawling back to him because I was so bad."

Dusty's marriage broke up over a college student Dusty ran around with for a while. Dusty, who was fifteen years older than the boy, thought there was no age problem until he graduated and hitchhiked to California with a backpack.

Dolores says, "Well, wish me luck. I see the doctor at eleven."

"Girl, I don't envy you."

"I can't eat a thing."

"You better eat."

"I ate half a Breakfast Bar."

"I want you to call me the minute you get back."

"I will."

"I'm glad you're going through with it," Dusty says. "That specialist is new at the clinic, and this town has needed somebody like that for the longest time."

Dolores hears the chain saw start and stop. She hears a tree trunk breaking. She says, her voice tightening, "If I die, I want you to look in on Glenn. He won't be able to take care of himself. He'll be so helpless and—"

"I'm not listening," says Dusty. "I won't let you talk like that."

The work has been going on for two hours. Dolores has watched intermittently as the climber stripped the branches and sectioned the tree. He sat casually in his leather sling, rared back like a woodpecker, sawing with one hand and smoking a cigarette with the other. Now that he is lower in the tree, where the trunk is thicker, he has abandoned the use of the rope. He lets the sections fall to the ground. Dolores holds on to Glenn as a large piece splits loose from the tree. The force of the fall strips large patches of the bark off, and the ground actually shakes.

"Isn't he amazing?" Glenn asks.

"Amazing," she says. She feels goosebumps on her arms.

The crew tosses small branches into the chipper, which sucks them up like a vacuum cleaner, grinding them instantaneously. The chips fly into the truckbed. When the machine's noise dies down, the men remove their hard-hats, which have earpieces like the headphones on a stereo.

The young man who was afraid to climb the tree says to Dolores, "Lloyd up yonder, he won't wear mufflers. He don't wear a safety shield."

"Or spikes either," says Dolores.

Later, when the climber touches ground, his legs bent like a horseman's, he sits down under a large oak and smokes a cigarette in silence. He is drinking water from a plastic jug. Sweat mats his hair. He seems like a temperamental actor collecting himself offstage after a performance. The other men are cutting the final section of the tree, down to a low stump. Dolores stands on a thin log, waiting for it to roll, balancing herself and remembering how as a little girl she pretended to fly when she jumped off a log. It is twenty minutes to eleven.

"If I had a saw I'd cut down all them little trees," says Petey, flinging a rope at one of the quince bushes.

"No, you wouldn't, little buddy," says Glenn.

"My brother would," says Petey. "He'd do anything. He ate a cricket."

Petey lassos a branch of the apple tree. Glenn looks up and sees Dolores. He asks, "Are you going somewhere? You have on your lipstick."

"I have to go to town."

"Oh. Well, take your time. I've got a lot of cleaning up to do."

Glenn joins the other men, who are putting their tools in the truck. The yard is scattered with the large limp leaves and pods from the tree. The broad leaves look like hands. Dolores thinks of the way Phil Donahue holds hands with the women in his audience who stand up to ask questions. He clutches them by one hand, half supporting them as they stand nervously before the microphone. It is a steadying, caring grasp. Dolores picks apart one of the green pods to find the hidden bloom. Inside are skinny petals. She counts them as she pinches them off. The men drive away, the climber riding in the chipper truck.

As she lies under a paper sheet on a cushioned table, with her breasts flattened, Dolores thinks about the climber and the nonchalant way he took risks, as though to fall would be incidental. For Dolores, the risk is going to the doctor, for fear of his diagnosis. Some part of her still believes that what you don't know won't hurt you. The doctor's name is Dr. Knight, and he has cold hands. Dolores stares into a corner of the room, the way she is told to do when she visits the optometrist. The doctor's thick glasses, his mint breath, his stethoscope, hover over her. His examination is swift, his fingers drumming her breasts rapidly. Then he presses hard against her nipple.

"It hurts," says Dolores.

"That's good. That's a good sign."

Dr. Knight does not speak again until she is dressed, sitting before him in his office. The clinic is new, but his office holds more magazines than Dolores remembers ever seeing.

"I waited too long to see about this," she says apologetically. "I kept thinking it would go away."

In a tone like an anchorman delivering the news on TV, Dr. Knight says, "You have fibrocystic disease. A thickening of the breast tissue. It's very common in women your age, especially women who haven't had children for a long time."

"Is that cancer?"

"No."

"Do you have to operate?"

"No. It's only a thickening of tissue. Sometimes it's painful. If it were cancer, it probably wouldn't hurt." For several minutes, Dr. Knight explains her disease. Dolores sits on the edge of her chair, but she does not really piece together in her mind what he is saying. She watches the dimple in his chin move in and out, like a tuck in a piece of heavy material. He gives her a pamphlet titled "How to Examine Your Breasts."

"I won't prescribe anything now," Dr. Knight says. "But my recommendation is that you strictly avoid all caffeine. That includes coffee, tea, cola, and chocolate."

On a prescription pad, he lists the items. At Dolores's request, he writes down the name of her disease. She folds the list and puts it inside the pamphlet.

The doctor says, "I want to check you again in three months. Maybe I'll need to order an X-ray. But there's no need to be alarmed."

As she drives home, Dolores feels confused, surprised that her sense of relief feels so peculiar. There is nothing momentous in what she has been through. Nothing important has happened that morning. A tree has been cut down; her daughter has cut out a weskit; the doctor has made a routine examination; Dolores has forgotten to make lunch. She stops at a grocery and buys bread, baloney, mustard, and on impulse, a watermelon from Georgia. The doctor's words linger in her mind. "Fibrocystic disease." She likes the sound of it. She could talk about this the way Dusty talks about her gall bladder. Dusty has to resist fried chicken; Dolores will have to resist chocolate cake. Somehow, this is a welcome guide for living, something certain—particular and silly. Yet somehow she feels cheated. She wonders what it would take to make a person want to walk with the Lord, a feeling that would be greater than walking on the moon.

At home she trips over the yellow extension cord Glenn has trailed through the kitchen and almost drops the watermelon. Glenn takes the watermelon from her and bends to kiss her. He asks, "Are you still mad at me for cutting down the tree?"

"I wasn't mad at you," she says. "I don't care how many trees you cut down."

"You sound funny. What's wrong?"

"I'll tell you later." Dolores nods at Petey, who has followed the watermelon into the house.

Glenn goes outside, and the electric chain saw roars. Dolores slaps sandwiches together. Bread, mustard, baloney. With quick sawing motions, she slices the watermelon and then thrusts a chunk at Petey.

"Here, smarty, feed your face," she says.

With an energetic twist in her walk, she goes to call Glenn and Boyce in to eat. Her husband is rolling a log into a growing woodpile, a neatly organized grouping, like an abstract sculpture. Dolores hardly recognizes the leaf-littered yard, the twigs flung everywhere, the pile of wood chips at the end of the driveway, the raw sections of the tree strewn around. Her eyes rest on a familiar quince bush in front of the house. It flowers in the spring, but sometimes in the fall a turn of the weather, or perhaps a rush of desire, will make the bush bloom again, briefly, with a few carmine flowers—scattered, but unmistakably bright.

# Residents
# and Transients

Since my husband went away to work in Louisville, I have, to my surprise, taken a lover. Stephen went ahead to start his new job and find us a suitable house. I'm to follow later. He works for one of those companies that require frequent transfers, and I agreed to that arrangement in the beginning, but now I do not want to go to Louisville. I do not want to go anywhere.

Larry is our dentist. When I saw him in the post office earlier in the summer, I didn't recognize him at first, without his smock and drills. But then we exchanged words—"Hot enough for you?" or something like that—and afterward I started to notice his blue Ford Ranger XII passing on the road beyond the fields. We are about the same age, and he grew up in this area, just as I did, but I was away for eight years, pursuing higher learning. I came back to Kentucky three years ago because my parents were in poor health. Now they have moved to Florida, but I have stayed here, wondering why I ever went away.

Soon after I returned, I met Stephen, and we were married within a year. He is one of those Yankees who are moving into this region with increasing frequency, a fact which disturbs the native residents. I would not have called Stephen a Yankee. I'm very much an outsider myself, though I've tried to fit in since I've been back. I only say this because I overhear the skeptical and desperate remarks, as though the town were being invaded. The schoolchildren are saying "you guys" now and smoking dope. I can image a classroom of bashful country hicks, listening to some new kid blithely talking in a Northern brogue about his year in Europe. Such influences are making people jittery. Most people around here would rather die than leave town, but there are a few here who think Churchill Downs in Louisville would be the grandest place in the world to be. They are dreamers, I could tell them.

"I can't imagine living on a *street* again," I said to my husband. I complained for weeks about living with *houses* within view. I need cornfields. When my parents left for Florida, Stephen and I moved into their old farmhouse, to take care of it for them. I love its stateliness, the way it rises up from the fields like a patch of mutant jimsonweeds. I'm fond of the old white wood siding, the sagging outbuildings. But the house will be sold this winter, after the corn is picked, and by then I will have to go to Louisville. I promised my parents I would handle the household auction because I knew my mother could not bear to be involved. She told me many times about a widow who had sold off her belongings and afterward stayed alone in the empty house until she had to be dragged away. Within a year, she died of cancer. Mother said to me, "Heartbreak brings on cancer." She went away to Florida, leaving everything the way it was, as though she had only gone shopping.

The cats came with the farm. When Stephen and I appeared, the cats gradually moved from the barn to the house. They seem to be my responsibility, like some sins I have committed, like illegitimate children. The cats are Pete, Donald, Roger, Mike, Judy, Brenda, Ellen, and Patsy. Reciting their names for Larry, my lover of three weeks, I feel foolish. Larry had asked, "Can you remember all their names?"

"What kind of question is that?" I ask, reminded of my husband's new job. Stephen travels to cities throughout the South, demonstrating word-processing machines, fancy typewriters that cost thousands of dollars and can remember what you type. It doesn't take a brain like that to remember eight cats.

"No two are alike," I say to Larry helplessly.

We are in the canning kitchen, an airy back porch which I use for the cats. It has a sink where I wash their bowls and cabinets where I keep their food. The canning kitchen was my mother's pride. There, she processed her green beans twenty minutes in a pressure canner, and her tomato juice fifteen minutes in a water bath. Now my mother lives in a mobile home. In her letters she tells me all the prices of the foods she buys.

From the canning kitchen, Larry and I have a good view of the cornfields. A cross-breeze makes this the coolest and most pleasant place to be. The house is in the center of the cornfields, and a dirt lane leads out to the road, about half a mile away. The cats wander down the fence rows, patroling the borders. I feed them Friskies and vacuum their pillows. I ignore the rabbits they bring me. Larry strokes a cat with one hand and my hair with the other. He says he has never known anyone like me. He calls me Mary Sue instead of Mary. No one has called me Mary Sue since I was a kid.

Larry started coming out to the house soon after I had a six-month checkup. I can't remember what signals passed between us, but it was suddenly appropriate that he drop by. When I saw his truck out on the road that day, I knew it would turn up my lane. The truck has a chrome streak on it that makes it look like a rocket, and on the doors it has flames painted.

"I brought you some ice cream," he said.

"I didn't know dentists made house calls. What kind of ice cream is it?"

"I thought you'd like choc-o-mint."

"You're right."

"I know you have a sweet tooth."

"You're just trying to give me cavities, so you can charge me thirty dollars a tooth."

I opened the screen door to get dishes. One cat went in and another went out. The changing of the guard. Larry and I sat on the porch and ate ice cream and watched crows in the corn. The corn had shot up after a recent rain.

"You shouldn't go to Louisville," said Larry. "This part of Kentucky is the prettiest. I wouldn't trade it for anything."

"I never used to think that. Boy, I couldn't wait to get out!" The ice cream was thrillingly cold. I wondered if Larry envied me. Compared to him, I was a world traveler. I had lived in a commune in Aspen, backpacked through the Rockies, and worked on the National Limited as one of the first female porters. When Larry was in high school, he was known as a hell-raiser, so the whole town was amazed when he became a dentist, married, and settled down. Now he was divorced.

Larry and I sat on the porch for an interminable time on that sultry day, each waiting for some external sign—a sudden shift in the weather, a sound, an event of some kind—to bring our bodies together. Finally, it was something I said about my new filling. He leaped up to look in my mouth.

"You should have let me take X-rays," he said.

"I told you I don't believe in all that radiation."

"The amount is teensy," said Larry, holding my jaw. A mouth is a word processor, I thought suddenly, as I tried to speak.

"Besides," he said, "I always use the lead apron to catch any fragmentation."

"What are you talking about?" I cried, jerking loose. I imagined splintering X-rays zinging around the room. Larry patted me on the knee.

"I should put on some music," I said. He followed me inside.

Stephen is on the phone. It is 3:00 P.M. and I am eating supper—pork and beans, cottage cheese and dill pickles. My routines are cockeyed since he left.

"I found us a house!" he says excitedly. His voice is so familiar I can almost see him, and I realize that I miss him. "I want you to come up here this weekend and take a look at it," he says.

"Do I have to?" My mouth is full of pork and beans.

"I can't buy it unless you see it first."

"I don't care what it looks like."

"Sure you do. But you'll like it. It's a three-bedroom brick with a two-car garage, finished basement, dining alcove, patio—"

"Does it have a canning kitchen?" I want to know.

Stephen laughs. "No, but it has a rec room."

I quake at the thought of a rec room. I tell Stephen, "I know this is crazy, but I think we'll have to set up a kennel in back for the cats, to keep them out of traffic."

I tell Stephen about the New Jersey veterinarian I saw on a talk show who keeps an African lioness, an ocelot, and three margays in his yard in the suburbs. They all have the run of his house. "Cats aren't that hard to get along with," the vet said.

"Aren't you carrying this a little far?" Stephen asks, sounding worried. He doesn't suspect how far I might be carrying things. I have managed to swallow the last trace of the food, as if it were guilt.

"What do *you* think?" I ask abruptly.

"I don't know what to think," he says.

I fall silent. I am holding Ellen, the cat who had a vaginal infection not long ago. The vet X-rayed her and found she was pregnant. She lost the kittens, because of the X-ray, but the miscarriage was incomplete, and she developed a rare infection called pyometra and had to be spayed. I wrote every detail of this to my parents, thinking they would care, but they did not mention it in their letters. Their minds are on the condominium they are planning to buy when this farm is sold. Now Stephen is talking about our investments and telling me things to do at the bank. When we buy a house, we will have to get a complicated mortgage.

"The thing about owning real estate outright," he says, "is that one's assets aren't liquid."

"Daddy always taught me to avoid debt."

"That's not the way it works anymore."

"He's going to pay cash for his condo."

"That's ridiculous."

Not long ago, Stephen and I sat before an investment counselor, who told us, without cracking a smile, "You want to select
an investment posture that will maximize your potential." I
had him confused with a marriage counselor, some kind of
weird sex therapist. Now I think of water streaming in the
dentist's bowl. When I was a child, the water in a dentist's
bowl ran continuously. Larry's bowl has a shut-off button to
save water. Stephen is talking about flexibility and fluid assets.
It occurs to me that wordprocessing, all one word, is also a
runny sound. How many billion words a day could one of Stephen's machines process without forgetting? How many pecks
of pickled peppers can Peter Piper pick? You don't *pick* pickled
peppers, I want to say to Stephen defiantly, as if he has asked
this question. Peppers can't be pickled till *after* they're picked,
I want to say, as if I have a point to make.

Larry is here almost daily. He comes over after he finishes
overhauling mouths for the day. I tease him about this peculiar-
ity of his profession. Sometimes I pretend to be afraid of him.
I won't let him near my mouth. I clamp my teeth shut and
grin widely, fighting off imaginary drills. Larry is gap-toothed.
He should have had braces, I say. Too late now, he says. Cats
march up and down the bed purring while we are in it. Larry
does not seem to notice. I'm accustomed to the cats. Cats,
I'm aware, like to be involved in anything that's going on.
Pete has a hobby of chasing butterflies. When he loses sight
of one, he searches the air, wailing pathetically, as though abandoned. Brenda plays with paper clips. She likes the way she
can hook a paper clip so simply with one claw. She attacks
spiders in the same way. Their legs draw up and she drops
them.

I see Larry watching the cats, but he rarely comments
on them. Today he notices Brenda's odd eyes. One is blue
and one is yellow. I show him her paper clip trick. We are
in the canning kitchen and the daylight is fading.

"Do you want another drink?" asks Larry.

"No."

"You're getting one anyway."

We are drinking Bloody Marys, made with my mother's canned tomato juice. There are rows of jars in the basement. She would be mortified to know what I am doing, in her house, with her tomato juice.

Larry brings me a drink and a soggy grilled cheese sandwich.

"You'd think a dentist would make something dainty and precise," I say. "Jello molds, maybe, the way you make false teeth."

We laugh. He thinks I am being funny.

The other day he took me up in a single-engine Cessna. We circled west Kentucky, looking at the land, and when we flew over the farm I felt I was in a creaky hay wagon, skimming just above the fields. I thought of the Dylan Thomas poem with the dream about the birds flying along with the stacks of hay. I could see eighty acres of corn and pasture, neat green squares. I am nearly thirty years old. I have two men, eight cats, no cavities. One day I was counting the cats and I absentmindedly counted myself.

Larry and I are playing Monopoly in the parlor, which is full of doilies and trinkets on whatnots. Every day I notice something that I must save for my mother. I'm sure Larry wishes we were at his house, a modern brick home in a good section of town, five doors down from a U.S. congressman. Larry gets up from the card table and mixes another Bloody Mary for me. I've been buying hotels left and right, against the advice of my investment counselor. I own all the utilities. I shuffle my paper money and it feels like dried corn shucks. I wonder if there is a new board game involving money market funds.

"When my grandmother was alive, my father used to bury her savings in the yard, in order to avoid inheritance taxes," I say as Larry hands me the drink.

He laughs. He always laughs, whatever I say. His lips are

like parentheses, enclosing compliments.

"In the last ten years of her life she saved ten thousand dollars from her social security checks."

"That's incredible." He looks doubtful, as though I have made up a story to amuse him. "Maybe there's still money buried in your yard."

"Maybe. My grandmother was very frugal. She wouldn't let go of *anything*."

"Some people are like that."

Larry wears a cloudy expression of love. Everything about me that I find dreary he finds intriguing. He moves his silvery token (a flatiron) around the board so carefully, like a child learning to cross the street. Outside, a cat is yowling. I do not recognize it as one of mine. There is nothing so mournful as the yowling of a homeless cat. When a stray appears, the cats sit around, fascinated, while it eats, and then later, just when it starts to feel secure, they gang up on it and chase it away.

"This place is full of junk that no one could throw away," I say distractedly. I have just been sent to jail. I'm thinking of the boxes in the attic, the rusted tools in the barn. In a cabinet in the canning kitchen I found some Bag Balm, antiseptic salve to soften cows' udders. Once I used teat extenders to feed a sick kitten. The cows are gone, but I feel their presence like ghosts. "I've been reading up on cats," I say suddenly. The vodka is making me plunge into something I know I cannot explain. "I don't want you to think I'm this crazy cat freak with a mattress full of money."

"Of course I don't." Larry lands on Virginia Avenue and proceeds to negotiate a complicated transaction.

"In the wild, there are two kinds of cat populations," I tell him when he finishes his move. "Residents and transients. Some stay put, in their fixed home ranges, and others are on the move. They don't have real homes. Everybody always thought that the ones who establish the territories are the most successful—like the capitalists who get ahold of Park Place." (I'm eyeing my opportunities on the board.) "They are the strongest, while the transients are the bums, the losers."

"Is that right? I didn't know that." Larry looks genuinely surprised. I think he is surprised at how far the subject itself extends. He is such a specialist. Teeth.

I continue bravely. "The thing is—this is what the scientists are wondering about now—it may be that the transients are the superior ones after all, with the greatest curiosity and most intelligence. They can't decide."

"That's interesting." The Bloody Marys are making Larry seem very satisfied. He is the most relaxed man I've ever known. "None of that is true of domestic cats," Larry is saying. "They're all screwed up."

"I bet somewhere there are some who are footloose and fancy free," I say, not believing it. I buy two hotels on Park Place and almost go broke. I think of living in Louisville. Stephen said the house he wants to buy is not far from Iroquois Park. I'm reminded of Indians. When certain Indians got tired of living in a place—when they used up the soil, or the garbage pile got too high—they moved on to the next place.

It is a hot summer night, and Larry and I are driving back from Paducah. We went out to eat and then we saw a movie. We are rather careless about being seen together in public. Before we left the house, I brushed my teeth twice and used dental floss. On the way, Larry told me of a patient who was a hemophiliac and couldn't floss. Working on his teeth was very risky.

We ate at a place where you choose your food from pictures on a wall, then wait at a numbered table for the food to appear. On another wall was a framed arrangement of farm tools against red felt. Other objects—saw handles, scythes, pulleys— were mounted on wood like fish trophies. I could hardly eat for looking at the tools. I was wondering what my father's old tit-cups and dehorning shears would look like on the wall of a restaurant. Larry was unusually quiet during the meal. His reticence exaggerated his customary gentleness. He even ate french fries cautiously.

On the way home, the air is rushing through the truck. My elbow is propped in the window, feeling the cooling air like water. I think of the pickup truck as a train, swishing through the night.

Larry says then, "Do you want me to stop coming out to see you?"

"What makes you ask that?"

"I don't have to be an Einstein to tell that you're bored with me."

"I don't know. I still don't want to go to Louisville, though."

"I don't want you to go. I wish you would just stay here and we would be together."

"I wish it could be that way," I say, trembling slightly. "I wish that was right."

We round a curve. The night is black. The yellow line in the road is faded. In the other lane I suddenly see a rabbit move. It is hopping in place, the way runners will run in place. Its forelegs are frantically working, but its rear end has been smashed and it cannot get out of the road.

By the time we reach home I have become hysterical. Larry has his arms around me, trying to soothe me, but I cannot speak intelligibly and I push him away. In my mind, the rabbit is a tape loop that crowds out everything else.

Inside the house, the phone rings and Larry answers. I can tell from his expression that it is Stephen calling. It was crazy to let Larry answer the phone. I was not thinking. I will have to swear on a stack of cats that nothing is going on. When Larry hands me the phone I am incoherent. Stephen is saying something nonchalant, with a sly question in his voice. Sitting on the floor, I'm rubbing my feet vigorously. "Listen," I say in a tone of great urgency. "I'm coming to Louisville— to see that house. There's this guy here who'll give me a ride in his truck—"

Stephen is annoyed with me. He seems not to have heard what I said, for he is launching into a speech about my anxiety.

"Those attachments to a place are so provincial," he says.

"People live all their lives in one place," I argue frantically.

"What's wrong with that?"

"You've got to be flexible," he says breezily. "That kind of romantic emotion is just like flag-waving. It leads to nationalism, fascism—you name it; the very worst kinds of instincts. Listen, Mary, you've got to be more open to the way things are."

Stephen is processing words. He makes me think of liquidity, investment postures. I see him floppy as a Raggedy Andy, loose as a goose. I see what I am shredding in my hand as I listen. It is Monopoly money.

After I hang up, I rush outside. Larry is discreetly staying behind. Standing in the porch light, I listen to katydids announce the harvest. It is the kind of night, mellow and languid, when you can hear corn growing. I see a cat's flaming eyes coming up the lane to the house. One eye is green and one is red, like a traffic light. It is Brenda, my odd-eyed cat. Her blue eye shines red and her yellow eye shines green. In a moment I realize that I am waiting for the light to change.

# The Retreat

Georgeann has put off packing for the annual church retreat. "There's plenty of time," she tells Shelby when he bugs her about it. "I can't do things that far ahead."

"Don't you want to go?" he asks her one evening. "You used to love to go."

"I wish they'd do something different just once. Something besides pray and yak at each other." Georgeann is basting facings on a child's choir robe, and she looks at him testily as she bites off a thread.

Shelby says, "You've been looking peaked lately. I believe you've got low blood."

"There's nothing wrong with me."

"I think you better get a checkup before we go. Call Dr. Armstrong in the morning."

When Georgeann married Shelby Pickett, her mother warned her about the disadvantages of marrying a preacher. Reformed juvenile delinquents are always the worst kind of preachers, her mother said—just like former drug addicts in their zealousness. Shelby was never that bad, though. In high school, when Georgeann first knew him, he was on probation for stealing four cases of Sun-Drop Cola and a ham from Kroger's. There was something charismatic about him even then, although he frightened her at first with his gloomy countenance—a sort of James Dean brooding—and his tendency to contradict whatever the teachers said. But she admired the way he argued so smoothly and professionally in debate class. He always had a smart answer that left his opponent speechless.

He was the type of person who could get away with anything. Georgeann thought he seemed a little dangerous—he was always staring people down, as though he held a deep grudge—but when she started going out with him, at the end of her senior year, she was surprised to discover how serious he was. He had spent a month studying the life of Winston Churchill. It wasn't even a class assignment. No one she knew would have thought of doing that. When the date of the senior prom approached, Shelby said he couldn't take her because he didn't believe in dancing. Georgeann suspected that he was just embarrassed and shy. On a Friday night, when her parents were away at the movies, she put on a Kinks album and tried to get him to loosen up, to get in shape for the prom. It was then that he told her of his ambition to be a preacher. Georgeann was so moved by his sense of atonement and his commitment to the calling—he had received the call while hauling hay for an uncle—that she knew she would marry him. On the night of the prom, they went instead to the Burger King, and he showed her the literature on the seminary while she ate a Double Whopper and french fries.

The ministry is not a full-time calling, Georgeann discovered. The pay is too low. While Shelby attended seminary, he also went to night school to learn a trade, and Georgeann supported him by working at Kroger's—the same one her husband had robbed. Georgeann had wanted to go to college, but they were never able to afford for her to go.

Now they have two children, Tamara and Jason. During the week, Shelby is an electrician, working out of his van. In ten years of marriage, they have served in three different churches. Shelby dislikes the rotation system and longs for a church he can call his own. He says he wants to grow with a church, so that he knows the people and doesn't have to preach only the funerals of strangers. He wants to perform the marriages of people he knew as children. Shelby lives by many little rules, some of which come out of nowhere. For instance, for years he has rubbed baking soda onto his gums after brushing his teeth, but he cannot remember who taught him to do this, or exactly why. Shelby comes from a broken home, so he wants things to last. But the small country churches in western Kentucky are dying, as people move to town or simply lose interest in the church. The membership at the Grace United Methodist Church is seventy-five, but attendance varies between thirty and seventy. The day it snowed this past winter, only three people came. Shelby was so depressed afterward that he couldn't eat Sunday dinner. He was particularly upset because he had prepared a special sermon aimed at Hoyt Jenkins, who somebody said had begun drinking, but Hoyt did not appear. Shelby had to deliver the sermon anyway, on the evils of alcohol, to old Mr. and Mrs. Elbert Flood and Miss Addie Stone, the president of the WCTU chapter.

"Even the best people need a little reinforcement," Shelby said halfheartedly to Georgeann.

She said, "Why didn't you just save that sermon? You work yourself half to death. With only three people there, you could have just talked to them, like a conversation. You didn't have to waste a big sermon like that."

"The church isn't for just a conversation," said Shelby.

The music was interesting that snowy day. Georgeann plays the piano at church. As she played, she listened to the voices singing—Shelby booming out like Bert Parks; the weak, shaky voices of the Floods; and Miss Stone, with a surprisingly clear and pretty little voice. She sounded like a folk singer. Georgeann wanted to hear more, so she abruptly switched hymns and played "Joy to the World," which she knew the Floods would have trouble with. Miss Stone sang out, high above Shelby's voice. Later, Shelby was annoyed that Georgeann changed the program because he liked the church bulletins that she typed and mimeographed each week for the Sunday service to be an accurate record of what went on that day. Georgeann made corrections in the bulletin and filed it away in Shelby's study. She penciled in a note: "Three people showed up." She even listed their names. Writing this, Georgeann felt peculiar, as though a gear had shifted inside her.

Even then, back in the winter, Shelby had been looking forward to the retreat, talking about it like a little boy anticipating summer camp.

Georgeann has been feeling disoriented. She can't think about the packing for the retreat. She's not finished with the choir robes for Jason and Tamara, who sing in the youth choir. On the Sunday before the retreat, Georgeann realizes that it is communion Sunday and she has forgotten to buy grape juice. She has to race into town at the last minute. It is overpriced at the Kwik-Pik, but that is the only place open on Sunday. Waiting in line, she discovers that she still has hair clips in her hair. As she stands there, she watches two teenage boys — in their everyday jeans and poplin jackets—playing an electronic video game. One boy is pressing buttons, his fingers working rapidly and a look of rapture on his face. The other boy is watching and murmuring "Gah!" Georgeann holds her hand out automatically for the change when the salesgirl rings up the grape juice. She stands by the door a few minutes, watching the boys. The machine makes tom-tom sounds, and blips fly across the TV screen. When she gets to the church, she is so nervous that she sloshes the grape juice while pouring it into the tray of tiny communion glasses. Two of the glasses are missing because she broke them last month while washing them after communion service. She has forgotten to order replacements. Shelby will notice, but she will say that it doesn't matter, because there won't be that many people at church anyway.

"You spilled some," says Tamara.

"You forgot to let us have some," Jason says, taking one of the tiny glasses and holding it out. Tamara takes one of the glasses too. This is something they do every communion Sunday.

"I'm in a hurry," says Georgeann. "This isn't a tea party."

They are still holding the glasses out for her.

"Do you want one too?" Jason asks.

"No. I don't have time."

Both children look disappointed, but they drink the sip of grape juice, and Tamara takes the glasses to wash them.

"Hurry," says Georgeann.

Shelby doesn't mention the missing glasses. But over Sunday dinner, they quarrel about her going to a funeral he has to preach that afternoon. Georgeann insists that she is not going.

"Who is he?" Tamara wants to know.

Shelby says, "No one you know. Hush."

Jason says, "I'll go with you. I like to go to funerals."

"I'm not going," says Georgeann. "They give me nightmares, and I didn't even know the guy."

Shelby glares at her icily for talking like this in front of the children. He agrees to go alone and promises Jason he can go to the next one. Today the children are going to Georgeann's sister's to play with their cousins. "You don't want to disappoint Jeff and Lisa, do you?" Shelby asks Jason.

As he is getting ready to leave, Shelby asks Georgeann, "Is there something about the way I preach funerals that bothers you?"

"No. Your preaching's fine. I like the weddings. And the piano and everything. But just count me out when it comes to funerals." Georgeann suddenly bangs a skillet in the sink. "Why do I have to tell you that ten times a year?"

They quarrel infrequently, but after they do, Georgeann always does something spiteful. Today, while Shelby and the kids are away, she cleans out the henhouse. It gives her pleasure to put on her jeans and shovel manure in a cart. She wheels it to the garden, not caring who sees. People drive by and she waves. There's the preacher's wife cleaning out her henhouse on Sunday, they are probably saying. Georgeann puts down new straw in the henhouse and gathers the eggs. She sees a hen looking droopy in a corner. "Perk up," she says. "You look like you've got low blood." After she finishes with the chore, she sits down to read the Sunday papers, feeling relieved that she is alone and can relax. She gets very sleepy, but in a few minutes she has to get up and change clothes. She is getting itchy under the waistband, probably from chicken mites.

She turns the radio on and finds a country music station.

When Shelby comes in, with the children, she is asleep on the couch. They tiptoe around her and she pretends to sleep on. "Sunday is a day of rest," Shelby is saying to the children. "For everybody but preachers, that is." Shelby turns off the radio.

"Not for me," says Jason. "That's my day to play catch with Jeff."

When Georgeann gets up, Shelby gives her a hug, one of his proper Sunday embraces. She apologizes for not going with him. "How was the funeral?"

"The usual. You don't really want to know, do you?"

"No."

Georgeann plans for the retreat. She makes a doctor's appointment for Wednesday. She takes Shelby's suits to the cleaners. She visits some shut-ins she neglected to see on Sunday. She arranges with her mother to keep Tamara and Jason. Although her mother still believes Georgeann married unwisely, she now promotes the sanctity of the union. "Marriage is forever, but a preacher's marriage is longer than that," she says.

Today, Georgeann's mother sounds as though she is making excuses for Shelby. She knows very well that Georgeann is unhappy, but she says, "I never gave him much credit at first, but Lord knows he's ambitious. I'll say that for him. And practical. He knew he had to learn a trade so he could support himself in his dedication to the church."

"You make him sound like a junkie supporting a habit."

Georgeann's mother laughs uproariously. "It's the same thing! The same thing." She is a stout, good-looking woman who loves to drink at parties. She and Shelby have never had much to say to each other, and Georgeann gets very sad whenever she realizes how her mother treats her marriage like a joke. It isn't fair.

When Georgeann feeds the chickens, she notices the sick
hen is unable to get up on its feet. Its comb is turning black.
She picks it up and sets it in the henhouse. She puts some
mash in a Crisco can and sets it in front of the chicken. It
pecks indifferently at the mash. Georgeann goes to the house
and finds a margarine tub and fills it with water. There is nothing to do for a sick chicken, except to let it die. Or kill it to
keep disease from spreading to the others. She won't tell Shelby
the chicken is sick, because Shelby will get the ax and chop
its head off. Shelby isn't being cruel. He believes in the necessi-
ties of things.

Shelby will have a substitute in church next Sunday, while
he is at the retreat, but he has his sermon ready for the following
Sunday. On Tuesday evening, Georgeann types it for him. He
writes in longhand on yellow legal pads, the way Nixon wrote
his memoirs, and after ten years Georgeann has finally mastered his corkscrew handwriting. The sermon is on sex education in the schools. When Georgeann comes to a word she
doesn't know, she goes downstairs.

"There's no such word as pucelage," she says to Shelby,
who is at the kitchen table, trying to fix a gun-shaped hair
dryer. Parts are scattered all over the table.

"Sure there is," he says. "Pucelage means virginity."

"Why didn't you say so! Nobody will know what it means."

"But it's just the word I want."

"And what about this word in the next paragraph? Ma-
turescent? Are you kidding?"

"Now don't start in on how I'm making fun of you because
you haven't been to college," Shelby says.

Georgeann doesn't answer. She goes back to the study
and continues typing. Something pinches her on the stomach.
She raises her blouse and scratches a bite. She sees a tiny brown
speck scurrying across her flesh. Fascinated, she catches it by
moistening a fingertip. It drowns in her saliva. She puts it on
a scrap of yellow legal paper and folds it up. Something to
show the doctor. Maybe the doctor will let her look at it under
a microscope.

The next day, Georgeann goes to the doctor, taking the speck with her. "I started getting these bites after I cleaned out the henhouse," she tells the nurse. "And I've been handling a sick chicken."

The nurse scrapes the speck onto a slide and instructs Georgeann to get undressed and put on a paper robe so that it opens in the back. Georgeann piles her clothes in a corner behind a curtain and pulls on the paper robe. As she waits, she twists and stretches a corner of the robe, but the paper is tough, like the "quicker picker-upper" paper towel she has seen in TV ads. When the doctor bursts in, Georgeann gets a whiff of strong cologne.

The doctor says, "I'm afraid we can't continue with the examination until we treat you for that critter you brought in." He looks alarmed.

"I was cleaning out the henhouse," Georgeann explains. "I figured it was a chicken mite."

"What you have is a body louse. I don't know how you got it, but we'll have to treat it completely before we can look at you further."

"Do they carry diseases?"

"This *is* a disease," the doctor says. "What I want you to do is take off that paper gown and wad it up very tightly into a ball and put it in the wastebasket. Whatever you do, don't shake it! When you get dressed, I'll tell you what to do next."

Later, after prescribing a treatment, the doctor lets her look at the louse through the microscope. It looks like a bloated tick from a dog; it is lying on its back and its legs are flung around crazily.

"I just brought it in for fun," Georgeann says. "I had no idea."

At the library, she looks up lice in a medical book. There are three kinds, and to her relief she has the kind that won't get in the hair. The book says that body lice are common only in alcoholics and indigent elderly persons who rarely change their clothes. Georgeann cannot imagine how she got lice. When she goes to the drugstore to get her prescription filled, a woman brushes close to her, and Georgeann sends out a silent message: I have lice. She is enjoying this.

"I've got lice," she announces when Shelby gets home. "I have to take a fifteen-minute hot shower and put this cream on all over, and then I have to wash all the clothes and curtains and everything—and what's more, the same goes for you and Tamara and Jason. You're incubating them, the doctor said. They're in the bed covers and the mattresses and the rugs. Everywhere." Georgeann makes creepy crawling motions with her fingers.

The pain on Shelby's face registers with her after a moment. "What about the retreat?" he asks.

"I don't know if I'll have time to get all this done first."

"This sounds fishy to me. Where would you get lice?"

Georgeann shrugs. "He asked me if I'd been to a motel room lately. I probably got them from one of those shut-ins. Old Mrs. Speed maybe. That filthy old horsehair chair of hers."

Shelby looks really depressed, but Georgeann continues brightly, "I thought sure it was chicken mites because I'd been cleaning out the henhouse? But he let me look at it in the microscope and he said it was a body louse."

"Those doctors don't know everything," Shelby says. "Why don't you call a vet? I bet that doctor you went to wouldn't know a chicken mite if it crawled up his leg."

"He said it was lice."

"I've been itching ever since you brought this up."

"Don't worry. Why don't we just get you ready for the retreat—clean clothes and hot shower—and then I'll stay here and get the rest of us fumigated?"

"You don't really want to go to the retreat, do you?"

Georgeann doesn't answer. She gets busy in the kitchen. She makes a pork roast for supper, with fried apples and mashed potatoes. For dessert, she makes jello and peaches with Dream Whip. She is really hungry. While she peels potatoes, she sings a song to herself. She doesn't know the name of it, but it has a haunting melody. It is either a song her mother used to sing to her or a jingle from a TV ad.

They decide not to tell Tamara and Jason that the family

has lice. Tamara was inspected for head lice once at school, but there is no reason to make a show of this, Shelby tells Georgeann. He gets the children to take long baths by telling them it's a ritual cleansing, something like baptism. That night in bed, after long showers, Georgeann and Shelby don't touch each other. Shelby lies flat with his hands behind his head, looking at the ceiling. He talks about the value of spiritual renewal. He wants Georgeann to finish washing all the clothes so that she can go to the retreat. He says, "Every person needs to stop once in a while and take a look at what's around him. Even preaching wears thin."

"Your preaching's up-to-date," says Georgeann. "You're more up-to-date than a lot of those old-timey preachers who haven't even been to seminary." Georgeann is aware that she sounds too perky.

"You know what's going to happen, don't you? This little church is falling off so bad they're probably going to close it down and reassign me to Deep Springs."

"Well, you've been expecting that for a long time, haven't you?"

"It's awful," Shelby says. "These people depend on this church. They don't want to travel all the way to Deep Springs. Besides, everybody wants their own home church." He reaches across Georgeann and turns out the light.

The next day, after Shelby finishes wiring a house, he consults with a veterinarian about chicken mites. When he comes home, he tells Georgeann that in the veterinarian's opinion, the brown speck was a chicken mite. "The vet just laughed at that doctor," Shelby says. "He said the mites would leave of their own accord. They're looking for chickens, not people."

"Should I wash all these clothes or not? I'm half finished."

"I don't itch anymore, do you?"

Shelby has brought home a can of roost paint, a chemical to kill chicken mites. Georgeann takes the roost paint to the henhouse and applies it to the roosts. It smells like fumes from a paper mill and almost makes her gag. When she finishes, she gathers eggs, and then sees that the sick hen has flopped outside again and can't get up on her feet. Georgeann carries the chicken into the henhouse and sets her down by the food. She examines the chicken's feathers. Suddenly she notices that the chicken is covered with moving specks. Georgeann backs out of the henhouse and looks at her hands in the sunlight. The specks are swarming all over her hands. She watches them head up her arms, spinning crazily, disappearing on her.

The retreat is at a lodge at Kentucky Lake. In the mornings, a hundred people eat a country ham breakfast on picnic tables, out of doors by the lake. The dew is still on the grass. Now and then a speedboat races by, drowning out conversation. Georgeann wears a badge with her name on it and BACK TO BASICS, the theme of the gathering, in Gothic lettering. After the first day, Shelby's spirit seems renewed. He talks and laughs with old acquaintances, and during social hour, he seems cheerful and relaxed. At the workshops and lectures, he takes notes like mad on his yellow legal paper, which he carries on a clipboard. He already has fifty ideas for new sermons, he tells Georgeann happily. He looks handsome in his clean suit. She has begun to see him as someone remote, like a meter reader. Georgeann thinks: He is not the same person who once stole a ham.

On the second day, she skips silent prayers after breakfast and stays in the room watching Phil Donahue. Donahue is interviewing parents of murdered children; the parents have organized to support each other in their grief. There is an organization for everything, Georgeann realizes. When Shelby comes in before the noon meal, she is asleep and the farm market report is blaring from the TV. As she wakes up, he turns off the TV. Shelby is a kind and good man, she says to herself. He still thinks she has low blood. He wants to bring her food on a tray, but Georgeann refuses.

"I'm alive," she says. "There's a workshop this afternoon I want to go to. On marriage. Do you want to go to that one?"

"No, I can't make that one," says Shelby, consulting his schedule. "I have to attend The Changing Role of the Country Pastor."

"It will probably be just women," says Georgeann. "You wouldn't enjoy it." When he looks at her oddly, she says, "I mean the one on marriage."

Shelby winks at her. "Take notes for me."

The workshop concerns Christian marriage. A woman leading the workshop describes seven kinds of intimacy, and eleven women volunteer their opinions. Seven of the women present are ministers' wives. Georgeann isn't counting herself. The women talk about marriage enhancement, a term that is used five times.

A fat woman in a pink dress says, "God made man so that he can't resist a woman's adoration. She should treat him as a priceless treasure, for man is the highest form of creation. A man is born of God—and just think, *you* get to live with him."

"That's so exciting I can hardly stand it," says a young woman, giggling, then looking around innocently with an expansive smile.

"Christians are such beautiful people," says the fat woman. "And we have such nice-looking young people. We're not dowdy at all."

"People just get that idea," someone says.

A tall woman with curly hair stands up and says, "The world has become so filled with the false, the artificial—we have gotten so phony that we think the First Lady doesn't have smelly feet. Or the Pope doesn't go to the bathroom."

"Leave the Pope out of this," says the fat woman in pink. "He can't get married." Everyone laughs.

Georgeann stands up and asks a question. "What do you do if the man you're married to—this is just a hypothetical question—say he's the cream of creation and all, and he's sweet as can be, but he turns out to be the wrong one for you? What do you do if you're just simply mismatched?"

Everyone looks at her.

Shelby stays busy with the workshops and lectures, and Georgeann wanders in and out of them, as though she is visiting

someone else's dreams. She and Shelby pass each other casually
on the path, hurrying along between the lodge and the conference building. They wave hello like friendly acquaintances.
In bed she tells him, "Christella Simmons told me I looked
like Mindy on *Mork and Mindy*. Do you think I do?"

Shelby laughs."Don't be silly," he says. When he reaches
for her, she turns away.

Georgeann walks by the lake. She watches seagulls flying
over the water. It amazes her that seagulls have flown this
far inland, as though they were looking for something, the
source of all that water. They are above the water, flying away
from her. She expects them to return, like hurled boomerangs.
The sky changes as she watches, puffy clouds thinning out into
threads, a jet contrail intersecting them and spreading, like
something melting: an icicle. The sun pops out. Georgeann
walks past a family of picnickers. The family is having an
argument over who gets to use an inner tube first. The father
says threateningly, "I'm going to get me a switch!" Georgeann
feels a stiffening inside her. Instead of letting go, loosening
up, relaxing, she is tightening up. But this means she is growing
stronger.

Georgeann goes to the basement of the lodge to buy a
Coke from a machine, but she finds herself drawn to the electronic games along the wall. She puts a quarter in one of the
machines, the Galaxian. She is a Galaxian, with a rocket ship
something like the "Enterprise" on *Star Trek*, firing at a convoy
of fleeing, multicolored aliens. When her missiles hit them,
they make satisfying little bursts of color. Suddenly, as she is
firing away, three of them—two red ships and one yellow ship—
zoom down the screen and blow up her ship. She loses her
three ships one right after the other and the game is over.
Georgeann runs upstairs to the desk and gets change for a
dollar. She puts another quarter in the machine and begins
firing. She likes the sound of the firing and the siren wail of
the diving formation. She is beginning to get the hang of it.
The hardest thing is controlling the left and right movements
of her rocket ship with her left hand as she tries to aim or to

dodge the formation. The aliens keep returning and she keeps on firing and firing until she goes through all her quarters.

After supper, Georgeann removes her name badge and escapes to the basement again. Shelby has gone to the evening service, but she told him she had a headache. She has five dollars' worth of quarters, and she loses two of them before she can regain her control. Her game improves and she scores 3,660. The high score of the day, according to the machine, is 28,480. The situation is dangerous and thrilling, but Georgeann feels in control. She isn't running away; she is chasing the aliens. The basement is dim, and some men are playing at the other machines. One of them begins watching her game, making her nervous. When the game ends, he says, "You get eight hundred points when you get those three zonkers, but you have to get the yellow one last or it ain't worth as much."

"You must be an expert," says Georgeann, looking at him skeptically.

"You catch on after a while."

The man says he is a trucker. He wears a yellow billed cap and a denim jacket lined with fleece. He says, "You're good. Get a load of them fingers."

"I play the piano."

"Are you with them church people?"

"Unh-huh."

"You don't look like a church lady."

Georgeann plugs in another quarter. "This could be an expensive habit," she says idly. It has just occurred to her how good-looking the man is. He has curly sideburns that seem to match the fleece inside his jacket.

"I'm into Space Invaders myself," the trucker says. "See, in Galaxians you're attacking from behind. It's a kind of cowardly way to go at things."

"Well, they turn around and get you," says Georgeann. "And they never stop coming. There's always more of them."

The man takes off his cap and tugs at his hair, then puts his cap back on. "I'd ask you out for a beer, but I don't want to get in trouble with the church." He laughs. "Do you want a Coke? I'll buy you a Co-Cola."

Georgeann shakes her head no. She starts the new game. The aliens are flying in formation. She begins the chase. When the game ends—her best yet—she turns to look for the man, but he has left.

Georgeann spends most of the rest of the retreat in the basement, playing Galaxians. She doesn't see the trucker again. Eventually, Shelby finds her in the basement. She has lost track of time, and she has spent all their reserve cash. Shelby is treating her like a mental case. When she tries to explain to how how it feels to play the game, he looks at her indulgently, the way he looks at shut-ins when he takes them baskets of fruit. "You forget everything but who you are," Georgeann tells him. "Your mind leaves your body." Shelby looks depressed.

As they drive home, he says, "What can I do to make you happy?"

Georgeann doesn't answer at first. She's still blasting aliens off a screen in her mind. "I'll tell you when I can get it figured out," she says slowly. "Just let me work on it."

Shelby lets her alone. They drive home in silence. As they turn off the main highway toward the house, she says suddenly, "I was happy when I was playing that game."

"We're not children," says Shelby. "What do you want—toys?"

At home, the grass needs cutting. The brick house looks small and shabby, like something abandoned. In the mailbox, Shelby finds his reassignment letter. He has been switched to the Deep Springs church, sixty miles away. They will probably have to move. Shelby folds up the letter and puts it back in the envelope, then goes to his study. The children are not home yet, and Georgeann wanders around the house, pulling up the shades, looking for things that have changed in her absence. A short while later, she goes to Shelby's study, knocking first. One of his little rules. She says, "I can't go to Deep Springs. I'm not going with you."

Shelby stands up, blocking the light from the windows. "I don't want to move either," he says. "But it's too awful far to commute."

"You don't understand. I don't want to go at all. I want to stay here by myself so I can think straight."

"What's got into you lately, girl? Have you gone crazy?" Shelby draws the blind on the window so the sun doesn't glare in. He says, "You've got me so confused. Here I am in this big crisis and you're not standing by me."

"I don't know how."

Shelby snaps his fingers. "We can go to a counselor."

"I went to that marriage workshop and it was a lot of hooey."

Shelby's face has a pallor, Georgeann notices. He is distractedly thumbing through some papers, his notes from the conference. Georgeann realizes that Shelby is going to compose a sermon directed at her. "We're going to have to pray over this," he says quietly.

"Later," says Georgeann. "I have to go pick up the kids."

Before leaving, she goes to check on the chickens. A neighbor has been feeding them. The sick chicken is still alive, but it doesn't move from a corner under the roost. Its eyelids are half shut, and its comb is dark and crusty. The henhouse still smells of roost paint. Georgeann gathers eggs and takes them to the kitchen. Then, without stopping to reflect, she gets the ax from the shed and returns to the henhouse. She picks up the sick chicken and takes it outside to a stump behind the henhouse. She sets the chicken on the stump and examines its feathers. She doesn't see any mites on it now. Taking the hen by the feet, she lays it on its side, its head pointing away from her. She holds its body down, pressing its wings. The chicken doesn't struggle. When the ax crashes down blindly on its neck, Georgeann feels nothing, only that she has done her duty.

# The Ocean

The interstate highway was like the ocean. It seemed to go on forever and was a similar color. Mirages of heat were shining in the distance like whitecaps, and now and then Bill lost himself in his memories of the sea. He hummed happily. Driving the fancy camper made Bill feel like a big shot.

Finding the interstate had been a problem for Bill and Imogene Crittendon. Not trusting the toll roads, they had blazed a trail to Nashville. They figured it was a three-hour drive to Nashville, but it took five, including the time they spent getting lost in the city. After driving past the tall buildings downtown and through the poor areas on the outskirts, Bill finally pulled over to the curb and Imogene said, "Hey!" to a man in a straw hat who was walking along thoughtfully.

"Which way's 65!" she yelled.

The entrance to it turned out to be around the corner. The man's eyes roved over the big camper cruiser as if in disbelief.

"We're going to Florida," Bill said, more to himself than to the man.

The man told them I-65 wasn't the best way to go. It wasn't the most direct.

"He's not in any hurry," Imogene said.

"Yes, I am," said Bill. "Going through Alaska to get there wasn't my idea."

Imogene hit him with the map.

"I didn't recognize a thing in Nashville," Bill said a little later, as they sailed down the vast highway.

"It's been thirty-five years," said Imogene. "Hey, watch where you're going."

"You can't talk about all the wrecks there's been out here. You don't know the history."

Imogene had a habit of telling the history of the wrecks on any given stretch of road. There was one long hill east of town, and whenever they drove down it she would tell about the group of women who hit a bump there and scattered all over the highway. They were all killed except one woman, who insisted on going to work anyway, but she was in such a state later that they had to take her home.

"That happened twenty years ago," Bill would say when Imogene told the story. "I remember her. She was the one that prayed. How do you know the others didn't pray too?"

"Well, that's what they always said. Of course, she's dead now too," Imogene had said.

Bill was getting the hang of interstate driving. He hummed awhile, then burst loudly into an old song he remembered.

> Don't go walking down lovers' lane
> With anyone else but me
> Till I come marching home.

The song made him feel young and hopeful. He pictured himself with his hands in his pockets, whistling and walking along. He couldn't wait to be walking along the beach.

"He'll never do it," Imogene had always told all the kinfolks. "He won't set foot off this place for the rest of his born days. He's growed to it."

But he had. He had shown everybody. He had fifteen hundred dollars in his billfold right this minute and more in the bank. All the big money made him delirious. He spent hours adding figures, paying this, paying that. He had always carried a wad of bills with him, but not to spend. He just had them handy. Now he was spending right and left. The figures danced in his head.

Bill stopped at a roadside rest area, and they ate potato

salad and fried chicken Imogene had made that morning.

"This place ain't big enough to cuss a cat in," she said when they bumped into each other.

She opened a new jar of her squash pickles.

"Don't expect this grub to last," she said. "I can't can on the road."

"You won't have to," said Bill.

"You'll be wanting some field peas and country ham," said Imogene.

After eating, they lay down to rest, with the fan going and the traffic whizzing by. Bill studied the interior of the mobile home. He was not really familiar with it yet. He had bought the luxury model to please Imogene. He could live in a truckbed himself. He stretched out and shaded his eyes with his Worm-and-Germ cap from the feed mill.

A large family arrived at the rest area and noisily hauled out a picnic. They were laughing and talking and Bill couldn't get comfortably into his snooze. He got up and watched a boy and his dog play Frisbee. The boy was about eighteen, Bill guessed, and wore cut-off jeans. Bill was afraid the dog was going to run out in the road. It made him nervous to watch. Once the Frisbee sailed near the road and Bill had to fight to keep himself from racing after the dog. The dog did wild leaps trying to catch the Frisbee. Bill had seen dogs play Frisbee on television. Bill had never played Frisbee. He missed having a dog.

They drove on. The scenery changed back and forth from hills to flatlands, from fields to woods. Bill couldn't get over the fact that he was really going to see the ocean again. He just wanted to sit and look at it and memorize it. He drove along, singing. He liked the way they could sit up high in the camper, looking down on the other cars. He loved the way the camper handled, and the steady little noise of gasoline flowing through the carburetor.

Imogene sat with her hands in fists. When cars passed she grabbed the handle in front of her. Bill pointed out that with these wide highways she didn't have to worry about meeting traffic head-on, but Imogene said the cars sneaking around you were worse.

"I always heard when you retired you could start all over again at the beginning," said Imogene. "But my nerves is in too bad a shape."

She had said that over and over. She had cried at the sale and cried when she gave away her belongings to Judy and Bob and Sissy. She said it was her nerves.

"You're a lot of fun," said Bill in an exasperated tone. "I oughtn't to have brought you along."

"I've got this hurtin' in my side," she said.

Bill passed Volkswagens and Pintos and even trucks. He felt exhilarated when he passed another camper. He had a queer feeling inside, as though his whole body might jolt apart.

"You're going over fifty-five," Imogene said after a while.

Bill was an expert driver. He knew every road and cow path and Indian trail in the Jackson Purchase. If he was late coming home, Imogene always thought he had had a wreck. But he had never even been in a ditch, except on the tractor.

Imogene said, "Gladys had a hurtin' like this and come to find out she had kidney disease. She had to go to the bathroom every five minutes. At her husband's funeral she had to set by the door."

"Are you going to bellyache the whole way?"

Imogene laughed. "Listen to us! We'll kill each other before we get there. I'll be to bury. Or you'll have to put me in a asylum, one."

Bill laughed. A truck slowed him down, and he shifted gears. "You couldn't do this in China!" he exclaimed suddenly.

"Do what?"

"Go taking off like this. In China you can't go from one county to the next without a permit. And if you could, you'd have to go by bicycle."

"I think we might be in China before long, at the rate we're going. You're over fifty-five again."

"We'll be just like the Chinese if our goofy President has his way!" said Bill, ignoring Imogene's remark about the speed.

"What's this business about China again?" Imogene never read the papers, but Bill read the *Sun-Democrat* every night and watched NBC.

Bill tried to explain. "Well, see, after the war, the Chinese government was forced over to Taiwan, which was Formosa. And the rebels set up another country on the mainland, but China was on the island of Formosa. That was the true China. The ones that stayed back were Communists. The United States supported the true China." Bill looked at Imogene. "Are you listening?"

"Unh-huh. Go on." Imogene was clutching the sides of her seat. A Greyhound bus was passing them.

"And so the United States has a treaty with Taiwan, to protect them from the Communists."

"And so we broke the treaty," Imogene finished for him.

"That's right! And now our peanut President decides to be buddies with the Communists and he's going to have us in a war before you know it!"

Bill got upset when he thought of the President, with his phony grin. Bill couldn't stand him. He could see through every move he made. Bill had known too many like him.

"He gave Taiwan away, just like he did the Panama Canal," Bill said.

"I still want to see Plains," said Imogene.

"So you can see Billy Carter?" Bill laughed.

"I'd just like to say I went to the President's hometown."

"Well, O.K. We can probably get there tomorrow."

"Billy's always showing up somewhere—on a special or a talk show," said Imogene. "I bet he don't spend half his time in Plains anymore."

They looked for a campground. Imogene studied the guidebook and tried to watch the road at the same time. She located one that seemed reasonable, but Bill missed the turn.

"I think it was right back there," Imogene said. "Quick, turn around."

Bill made a U-turn, crossing the grassy strip. A car honked at him.

"Maybe you weren't supposed to do that," said Imogene, looking behind her.

The campground was pleasant. Music was playing and there were large shade trees and lots of dogs. Bill walked around the park while Imogene made supper. Being in a far-off place, wandering among strangers with license plates from everywhere, made Bill feel like a kid, off on his own. He nodded to a young man who hurried past him. The man, wearing rubber thong sandals and carrying a plastic shopping bag, had murmured a faint hello. For a moment Bill felt a desire to stop and have a conversation, a desire he felt only rarely.

Imogene made pork chops, butter beans, corn, slaw, and corn bread for supper, and they ate during the news. Bill made a face when the President came on.

"The days is getting longer," he said later, looking out the window.

"We're further south," said Imogene. She finished the dishes and sat down. "I don't hardly know what to do with myself. Without Mama to feed and watch over. Her complaining every ten minutes. I was thinking about her suppertime. I would go in there with her tray, her cornflakes and a little applesauce. And then get her ready for bed and bring her milk of magnesia and make sure she was covered up."

"Do you wish we had her along?" Bill asked, teasing. He knew Imogene would keep on if he let her. "We could have started out five years ago. I could have slept here, and you and her could have that bed."

"Oh, quit it! It hasn't been a month since we put her in the ground."

"I just thought you probably missed her snoring."

She shook her fist at him. "I tell you one thing. None of my younguns is going to have to put up with what I put up with." Imogene belched. "I've eat too much," she said.

Bill had a hard time sleeping. First the dogs barked half the night. Then a man kept hollering in the distance. And at one point during the night a motorcycle came roaring into camp, setting off the dogs again. Bill lay half awake, thinking of the ocean and remembering the rocking, cracking old ship

that he had feared would sink. The U.S.S. *Shaw* was a destroyer
that had been sunk at Pearl Harbor and then raised and re-
outfitted in an amazingly short time. He still heard the sounds
of the guns. They woke him sometimes at night. And he would
occasionally catch himself somewhere, standing as though in
a trance, still passing ammunition to the gunners, rhythmically
passing shell after shell. He had sailed the Pacific, but the Atlantic was connected—or it had been until Carter gave the canal
away, Bill thought in disgust as he rolled over on the narrow
bed.

"We might get there today!" Bill said when they got up
at four. No one else in the camp was up.

"You thought it was milking time," Imogene said. "I
couldn't sleep either. I was too wound up."

After a large breakfast of bacon, eggs, toast, and cereal,
they drove awhile, then stopped for a nap.

"We'll never get there," said Bill.

They drove south to Birmingham, then across several
smaller routes toward Plains. There was a lot of traffic on the
small roads. Georgia drivers were worse than Kentucky drivers,
Bill thought, as he tailed a woman who was straddling the
line in a battered old Buick with its rear end dragging.

"Look, there's a old mansion!" Imogene cried. "One of
those with the white columns!"

The mansion was so close to the road there was no yard,
and they could look through the front door and out the back.
Weeds had grown up around the place.

"See them old shacks out back," said Bill. "That's where
the slaves used to live."

"Looks like they're still living there," said Imogene, pointing to some ragged black children. "Law, I thought we had
poor people at home."

In Plains, Imogene bought postcards and sent them to the
kids, who were scattered all over. Imogene wrote the same
message on each card: "Your daddy and me's headed out to
see the world. Will let you know how it comes out. If I live
that long. (Oh!)" Bill and Imogene walked down the tiny main

street, which was crowded with buses and campers. People from everywhere were there. Imogene wanted to take the tourist bus, but Bill said they had a new twenty-thousand-dollar vehicle of their own and knew how to drive it, so they drove around awhile, doubling back on themselves. Then, at Imogene's insistence, Bill stopped at Billy Carter's filling station.

"I think that's him," Imogene said, peering toward the back of the station, where there was a crowd of people standing around. "No, that's not him. Looked like him, though."

A sweaty man in an undershirt with skinny straps filled up the tank.

"Reckon Billy ain't around," said Imogene, leaning over toward Bill's window.

"No, he's off. He's off over to Americus." The man pointed.

"We went through there," said Imogene.

"No, we didn't," said Bill.

"All these tourists just driving you folks crazy, I expect," said Imogene, ignoring Bill.

"Oh, you get used to it," the man said, leaning against the gas pump. "You never know what you're liable to see or who you'll meet. We get some characters in here, I tell you."

"I 'magine."

"Are you ready?" Bill asked Imogene.

"I guess."

"Y'all come back now, hear?" the man said.

"We will," said Imogene, waving.

"Seen enough?" Bill asked.

"I can say I've been here anyway."

Bill was getting tired, and he drove listlessly for a while. He could not make the connection between Plains and the White House. Plains looked like the old slave shacks outside the mansion they had passed. The mansion was the White House. Bill thought of Honest Abe splitting rails, but that was a long time ago. Things were more complicated now. Bill hated complications. If he were running the show, it would be pretty simple. He never had trusted those foot-washing, born-again Baptists anyway. And now the President had let a whole country in the Middle East be taken over by a religious maniac. It made him sick. What if Billy Graham decided to take over the United States? It would be the same thing.

Bill and Imogene, no longer talking, meandered throughout Georgia, through tiny towns that looked to Bill as though they hadn't changed since 1940. The grocery stores had front porches. Georgia still had Burma-Shave signs. Bill almost ran onto the shoulder trying to read one.

> YOUR HUSBAND
> MISBEHAVE
> GRUNT AND GRUMBLE
> RANT AND RAVE
> SHOOT THE BRUTE SOME
> BURMA-SHAVE

There was a word missing. The signs were faded and rotting.

Between Plains and the Florida border, Bill counted five dead animals—a possum, a groundhog, a cat, a dog, and one unidentifiable mass of hide and gristle. He tried to slow down.

They stopped at a camp on the border, and Bill filled up the water tank. The camper was dusty but still looked brand-new. Imogene checked to see if anything was broken.

"I don't see why this gas stove don't explode," she said. "All this shaking in this heat. They say not to take a gas can in your car."

"A camper is different," Bill said.

They walked around the campground. A lot of vehicles had motorcycles strapped onto them, and some people had already cranked up their motorcycles. The noise bothered Bill, but he liked to see the bikes take off, disappearing behind a swirl of dust.

Bill stopped to pet a friendly collie.

"That's Ishmael," said the girl who held the collie by a leash. "He's so friendly I never have any trouble meeting people. I meet lots of guys that way! People do that with dogs, you know?"

"You're a good boy," said Bill, patting the dog. "Nice boy."

Ishmael licked Bill's hand and then tried to sniff up Imogene's dress.

"Ishmael, don't be so obnoxious. He's always this friendly," the girl said apologetically. She had on a halter top and shorts. Her legs were smooth and brown, with golden hairs on her thighs.

"He loves dogs," said Imogene. "He can't stand to be without a dog. Or a cow or something! We sold all our cows and everything and here we are. Our whole farm's tied up in this." She waved at the camper.

"Wow, that's nice. That must have cost a fortune," the girl said, shading her eyes as she looked at the camper.

"Where are you headed?" Bill asked, with unusual politeness, which embarrassed him slightly.

"Oh, I was on the Coast, but it got to be a drag, so now I'm on my way to Atlanta, where I think I know this guy. I met him out in L.A. and he said if I was ever in Atlanta, to look him up. I hope he remembers me."

The girl said her name was Stephanie. Bill thought she might be college age. He wasn't sure. She looked very young to be traveling around alone. He thought of Sissy, his youngest daughter. Sissy had come home from San Francisco finally and had lived to tell the tale, though there was not much she would say about it.

"See, Ishmael is number one," Stephanie was saying. "If a guy can't take my dog, then I'm going to leave, right?" She looked up at Bill, as if for approval. Bill patted Ishmael, and the dog licked Bill's hand again.

"I got a ride with this guy who customizes rec-v's," Stephanie went on. She pointed to a beige van with designs of blue and red fish painted on the side. "See, people buy them stripped and he outfits them. He's supposed to be back any minute. He's checking out a deal." She looked around the campground. "See his license plate," she said. "KOOL-II. Isn't that cute? Here, look inside."

Bill and Imogene peered inside the van. It was lined with shag rug. In the back, crosswise, was a king-sized bed with a leopard-skin cover. The ceiling was shag carpeting too, white, with a red heart positioned above the bed.

"There's not a kitchen in it," said Imogene.

"Just a refrigerator, and a bar," said Stephanie. "Isn't it something? This interior just blows me away."

She let Ishmael inside the van and took his leash off. Ishmael hopped onto the bed and stretched his paws out. The bed seemed to ripple with the dog's movements.

"It's a water bed," Stephanie said with a laugh.

"We've been tied down on a farm all this time," said Imogene.

"We're going to travel around till we get it out of our system," said Bill, again feeling embarrassed to be telling the girl things about himself.

"That's really sweet," said Stephanie, pulling at her halter. "Wow, that's really sweet. Here I travel around and don't think anything about it, but I bet you've been waiting all these years!"

"You come and eat some supper with us," Imogene said. "You don't have a kitchen."

"Oh, no, thanks. I better wait for this guy. We were going to check out the McDonald's up on the highway. I'm sort of waiting around for him, see? Hey, thanks anyway."

Stephanie waved good-bye and wished them luck.

"We'll need it," said Imogene.

After supper Imogene and Bill sat in their folding chairs outside and watched the lights come on in the campers. It was still hot and they swatted at giant mosquitoes.

"I gave my antique preserve stand to Sissy," said Imogene. "She won't appreciate it."

Bill was quiet. He was listening to the sounds, the TV sets and radios all blending together. He watched a blond-headed boy enter the KOOL-II van.

"Can you just imagine the trouble that girl has been in?" said Imogene thoughtfully. "I believe she was one of those runaways they talk about."

"How do you know?"

"You never know, with people you meet, out."

Bill watched as the blond-headed boy emerged from the van and headed toward the shower building. Bill liked the way the boy walked, with his towel slung over his shoulder. He had hair like a girl's, and a short beard. The boy walked along so freely, as though he had nothing on his mind except that van with the red heart on the ceiling. Bill thought uncomfortably of how he had once promised Imogene that they would see the world, but they never had. He always knew it was a failure of courage. After the war he had rushed back home. He hated himself for the way he had stayed at home all that time.

Later, Imogene started crying. Bill was trying to watch *Charlie's Angels,* and he tried to pretend he didn't notice. In a few minutes she stopped. Then after a commercial she started again.

"Years ago," Imogene said, wiping her face, "when I took your mama to the doctor—when she had just moved in with us and I took her for a checkup?—I went in to talk to the doctor and he said to me, 'How are *you?*' and I said, 'I didn't come to see the doctor, I brought *her,*' and he said, 'I know, but how are *you?*' He said to me, 'She'll kill you! I've seen it before, and she'll kill you. You think they won't be much trouble and it's best, but mark my words, you may not see it now, but she'll take it out of you. She could destroy you. You could end up being a wreck.' He said, 'Now I'm not a psychiatrist'— or whatever they call them—'but I've seen it too many times. I'm just warning you.' I read about this woman that lived with her son and daughter-in-law and lived to be a hundred and three! Nobody ought to live that long!"

"Are you finished?" Imogene had interrupted a particularly exciting scene in *Charlie's Angels.* Bill didn't say anything and the program finished. Imogene made him nervous, bringing up the past. If she was going to do that, they might as well have stayed at home. Bill didn't know what to say. Imogene got a washrag and wiped her face. Her face was puffed up and red.

"I've been working up to say all that, what I just said,"

she went on later. "I get these headaches and I've got this hurtin'. And I can't taste."

"It's all in your mind," said Bill, teasing her gently. "You've been listening to too many old women talk."

"I get all sulled up," Imogene said. "Just some little something will bring it on. It wouldn't matter if we were here or in China or Kalamazoo."

"You just have to have something to bellyache about," Bill said. He would have to try to humor her.

"She was *your* mama," Imogene continued. "And I'm the one that took care of her all that time, keeping her house, putting up her canning, putting out her wash, and then waiting on her when she got down. And you never lifted a finger. You couldn't be around old people, you said; it give you the heebie-jeebies. Well, listen, buster, your time's a-coming and who's going to wait on you? You can stick me in a rest home, for all I care. And another thing, you don't see Miz Lillian living at the White House."

Bill felt sick. "You would go to a rest home and leave me by myself?" he asked, with a little whine.

"I've a good mind to," she said. She measured an inch off her index finger. "I like about this much from it," she said.

"You wouldn't do me that way, would you? Who would cook?"

"You can eat junk."

"I bought you this pretty playhouse. You don't want to leave me in it all by myself, do you?" He tousled her hair. "You're not any fun anymore. Always got to tune up and cry over some little something."

"I can't help it." She put her head in a pillow. "Don't tease me."

Awkwardly, Bill put his arms around her.

"You don't make over me anymore," she said.

"You just wait till we get to the ocean," Bill said, petting her. He felt like a fool. The muscles in his arms were so rigid he thought they were going to pop. His mouth was dry.

That night Bill slept fitfully. He could not get used to a

foam rubber mattress. He had a nightmare in which his mother
and Imogene sat in rocking chairs on either side of him, having
a contest to see who could rock the longest. Bill's job was to
keep score, but they kept on rocking. His kids gathered around,
mocking him, wanting to know the score. The steady, swinging,
endless rocking was making him feel seasick. He woke up almost crying out, but awake he could not understand why the
rocking chairs frightened him so. He told himself he was an
idiot and eventually he calmed himself down by thinking pleasant thoughts about Stephanie and the blond-headed boy. He
imagined what they were doing in the van with the red heart
on the ceiling. Later, he dreamed that he had a job driving
a van across the country. He wore a uniform, with a cowboy
hat that said KOOL-II on the front. He drove the van at top
speed and when he got to the ocean he boarded a ferry, which
turned out to be a destroyer. The destroyer zoomed across
the ocean. Imogene did not show up in the dream at all.

When he woke up he looked at her sleeping, with her
mouth open and a soft little snore coming out. He recalled
the time in the Andrew Jackson Hotel in Nashville when he
watched her sleep for a full hour, wanting to remember her
face while he was overseas. Then she had awakened, saying,
"I knew somebody was watching me. I dreamed it. You liked
to stared a hole through me." They had not been married
long, and they had stayed awake most of the night, holding
each other.

Now Imogene's face was fat and lined, but he could still
see her young face clearly. Her hair was gray and cut in short,
curly layers. Each curl was distinctly separate, like the coils
of a new pad of steel wool.

Bill bent down close to her and bellowed, "Rise and shine!"
Then he sang, "You're an angel, lighting up the morning."
Imogene woke up and glared at him.

"I can't wait to show you the ocean," said Bill. He pulled
on his clothes and slapped his cap on his head. He looked out
the window to see if KOOL-II had left. He had.

"KOOL-II's done gone," Bill said.

"She was a nice girl," said Imogene, getting up. "But taking up with that boy like that, I just don't know. There's so much meanness going on."

She put water and bacon strips on the stove and started dressing. Bill turned on the portable television. The *Today* show was in Minnesota. Jane Pauley was having breakfast with a farmer, who said that in fact it *was* possible to make a living as a dairy farmer these days.

"You have to like cows first," he said. He said he didn't name his cows anymore. He gave them numbers, "like social security numbers," the man said, laughing.

"How could you keep a cow without a name?" asked Bill. "How would you talk to it?"

"He's a big-dude farmer," said Imogene. "He couldn't remember all their names, he's got so many."

The farmer's wife claimed she was not a working wife, but Jane Pauley pointed out that the woman worked all the time making butter and cheese, dressing chickens, raising children, and so forth.

"That's fun work," she replied.

"If it don't kill you," said Imogene.

One of the farmer's seven children said he would be going to college. This day and age you had to be a businessman to be in agriculture. There was a lot his father couldn't teach him about the farm.

"Can you see us on TV, having breakfast and talking?" asked Imogene.

"Shoot," said Bill. "I'd be embarrassed to death. I'd go crawl in a hole."

The show switched to the original *Little House on the Prairie,* also in Minnesota. Tom Brokaw was interviewing Mike Landon. Mike Landon was telling how back then everybody lived mainly in one small room and they were forced to live together, to cooperate, to work together. You couldn't hide. Nowadays a kid could be off in his room and have a drug problem for six months and nobody would know. That couldn't have happened in the nineteenth century, Mike Landon said.

"Bet he lives in a mansion," said Bill, who was pacing the floor. "How does he explain that?"

Mike Landon said it didn't depend on the number of rooms, as long as you can communicate. His kids don't watch TV during the week, he said, except for *Little House on the Prairie.* "Or I give them a beating!" He laughed.

Bill grew more and more restless as they drove down into Florida. He kept an eye on the left side of the horizon so that he could catch that first glimpse of the ocean. He was afraid it might appear any second and he might miss it. He hardly noticed the changing terrain and the tourist signs.

"I thought I saw orange trees," Imogene said.

Imogene had stopped flinching every time a car passed, and she seemed to be in a better mood, Bill thought.

"I can't wait to show you the ocean," he said for the tenth time.

"Some folks is happy just to stay home," she said. "But that farmer on television—he had money. He could retire to Florida and still have something to show for all his years."

After bypassing Jacksonville, Bill headed for a campground. He still could not see the ocean.

"Whoa!" cried Imogene suddenly. "What's the matter with you? You scared the wadding out of me. You nearly run into that truck."

"That truck was half a mile down the road! Keep your britches on. We're almost there."

As they drove into the campground, which had a swimming pool but no trees, Imogene said, "You can tell this is Florida. Old folks everywhere."

Bill liked it better at the other places, with the dogs and the younger people. He didn't see any dogs here. They passed a man struggling along on a metal walker.

"I hope we don't get like that," said Imogene.

After selecting and paying for their parking place, they drove to the ocean, a couple of miles away. Bill's first sight of it was like something seen through a keyhole. Then it grew larger and larger.

"Is this what you brought me here to see?" said Imogene, as they examined the Atlantic from their high perches in the camper. "It all looks the same."

Bill was silent as they got out and locked the van. He dropped his keys in the sand, he was so nervous. They walked down a narrow pathway to the beach, and Bill kept wanting to break into a run, but Imogene was too slow. They walked down the beach together, now and then stopping while Bill faced the ocean. He kept his arm around Imogene's waist, in case she stumbled in the sand. She had on her straw wedgies.

Bill stopped her then and they stood still for a long while. Bill's eyes roved over the rolling sea. It was the same water, carried around by time, that he had sailed, but it was bluer than he remembered. He remembered the feeling of looking out over that expanse, fearing the sound of the Japanese planes, taking comfort at the sight of the big battleship and its family of destroyers. He had seen a kamikaze dive into a destroyer. The explosion was like a silent movie that played in his head endlessly, like reruns of *McHale's Navy*.

"How long will you be?" asked Imogene. "I need to find me some shade."

"I'll be along directly," said Bill, gazing out at battleships and destroyers riding on the horizon. He could not tell if they were coming or going, or whose they were.

# Graveyard Day

Waldeen's daughter Holly, swinging her legs from the kitchen stool, lectures her mother on natural foods. Holly is ten and too skinny.

Waldeen says, "I'll have to give your teacher a talking-to. She's put notions in your head. You've got to have meat to grow."

Waldeen is tenderizing liver, beating it with the edge of a saucer. Her daughter insists that she is a vegetarian. If Holly had said Rosicrucian, it would have sounded just as strange to Waldeen. Holly wants to eat peanuts, soyburgers, and yogurt. Waldeen is sure this new fixation has something to do with Holly's father, Joe Murdock, although Holly rarely mentions him. After Waldeen and Joe were divorced last September, Joe moved to Arizona and got a construction job. Joe sends Holly letters occasionally, but Holly won't let Waldeen see them. At Christmas he sent her a copper Indian bracelet with unusual marks on it. It is Indian language, Holly tells her. Waldeen sees Holly polishing the bracelet while she is watching TV.

Waldeen shudders when she thinks of Joe Murdock. If he weren't Holly's father, she might be able to forget him. Waldeen was too young when she married him, and he had a reputation for being wild. Now she could marry Joe McClain, who comes over for supper almost every night, always bringing something special, such as a roast or dessert. He seems to be oblivious to what things cost, and he frequently brings Holly presents. If Waldeen married Joe, then Holly would have a stepfather—something like a sugar substitute, Waldeen imagines. Shifting relationships confuse her. She tells Joe they must wait. Her ex-husband is still on her mind, like the lingering aftereffects of an illness.

Joe McClain is punctual, considerate. Tonight he brings fudge ripple ice cream and a half gallon of Coke in a plastic jug. He kisses Waldeen and hugs Holly.

Waldeen says, "We're having liver and onions, but Holly's mad 'cause I won't make Soybean Supreme."

"Soybean *Delight,*" says Holly.

"Oh, excuse me!"

"Liver is full of poison. The poisons in the feed settle in the liver."

"Do you want to stunt your growth?" Joe asks, patting Holly on the head. He winks at Waldeen and waves his walking stick at her playfully, like a conductor. Joe collects walking sticks, and he has an antique one that belonged to Jefferson Davis. On a gold band, in italics, it says *Jefferson Davis.* Joe doesn't go anywhere without a walking stick, although he is only thirty. It embarrasses Waldeen to be seen with him.

"Sometimes a cow's liver just explodes from the poison," says Holly. "Poisons are *oozing* out."

"Oh, Holly, hush, that's disgusting." Waldeen plops the pieces of liver onto a plate of flour.

"There's this restaurant at the lake that has Liver Lovers' Night," Joe says to Holly. "Every Tuesday is Liver Lovers' Night."

"Really?" Holly is wide-eyed, as if Joe is about to tell a long story, but Waldeen suspects Joe is bringing up the restaurant—Bob's Cove at Kentucky Lake—to remind her that it was the scene of his proposal. Waldeen, not accustomed to eating out, studied the menu carefully, wavering between pork chops and T-bone steak, and then suddenly, without thinking, ordering catfish. She was disappointed to learn that the catfish was not even local, but frozen ocean cat. "Why would they do that," she kept saying, interrupting Joe, "when they've got all the fresh channel cat in the world right here at Kentucky Lake?"

During supper, Waldeen snaps at Holly for sneaking liver to the cat, but with Joe gently persuading her, Holly manages to eat three bites of liver without gagging. Holly is trying to please him, as though he were some TV game-show host who happened to live in the neighborhood. In Waldeen's opinion, families shouldn't shift membership, like clubs. But here they are, trying to be a family. Holly, Waldeen, Joe McClain. Sometimes Joe spends the weekends, but Holly prefers weekends at Joe's house because of his shiny wood floors and his parrot that tries to sing "Inka-Dinka-Doo." Holly likes the idea of packing an overnight bag.

Waldeen dishes out the ice cream. Suddenly inspired, she suggests a picnic Saturday. "The weather's fairing up," she says.

"I can't," says Joe. "Saturday's graveyard day."

"Graveyard day?" Holly and Waldeen say together.

"It's my turn to clean off the graveyard. Every spring and fall somebody has to rake it off." Joe explains that he is responsible for taking geraniums to his grandparents' graves. His grandmother always kept them in her basement during the winter, and in the spring she took them to her husband's grave, but she had died in November.

"Couldn't we have a picnic at the graveyard?" asks Waldeen.

"That's gruesome."

"We never get to go on picnics," says Holly. "Or anywhere." She gives Waldeen a look.

"Well, O.K.," Joe says. "But remember, it's serious. No fooling around."

"We'll be real quiet," says Holly.

"Far be it from me to disturb the dead," Waldeen says, wondering why she is speaking in a mocking tone.

After supper, Joe plays rummy with Holly while Waldeen cracks pecans for a cake. Pecan shells fly across the floor, and the cat pounces on them. Holly and Joe are laughing together, whooping loudly over the cards. They sound like contestants on *Let's Make a Deal*. Joe Murdock had wanted desperately to be on a game show and strike it rich. He wanted to go to California so he would have a chance to be on TV and so he could travel the freeways. He drove in the stock car races, and he had been drag racing since he learned to drive. Evel Knievel was his hero. Waldeen couldn't look when the TV showed Evel Knievel leaping over canyons. She told Joe many times, "He's nothing but a show-off. But if you want to break your fool neck, then go right ahead. Nobody's stopping you." She is better off without Joe Murdock. If he were still in town, he would do something to make her look foolish, such as paint her name on his car door. He once had WALDEEN painted in large red letters on the door of his LTD. It was like a tattoo. It is probably a good thing he is in Arizona. Still, she cannot really understand why he had to move so far away from home.

After Holly goes upstairs, carrying the cat, whose name is Mr. Spock, Waldeen says to Joe, "In China they have a law that the men have to help keep house." She is washing the dishes.

Joe grins. "That's in China. This is *here*."

Waldeen slaps at him with the dish towel, and Joe jumps up and grabs her. "I'll do all the housework if you marry me," he says. "You can get the Chinese to arrest me if I don't."

"You sound just like my ex-husband. Full of promises."

"Guys named Joe are good at making promises." Joe laughs and hugs her.

"All the important men in my life were named Joe," says Waldeen, with pretended seriousness. "My first real boyfriend was named Joe. I was fourteen."

"You always bring that up," says Joe. "I wish you'd forget about them. You love *me*, don't you?"

"Of course, you idiot."

"Then why don't you marry me?"

"I just said I was going to think twice is all."

"But if you love me, what are you waiting for?"
"That's the easy part. Love is easy."

In the middle of *The Waltons,* C. W. Redmon and Betty
Mathis drop by. Betty, Waldeen's best friend, lives with
C. W., who works with Joe on a construction crew. Waldeen
turns off the TV and clears magazines from the couch. C. W.
and Betty have just returned from Florida and they are full
of news about Sea World. Betty shows Waldeen her new tote
bag with a killer whale pictured on it.
    "Guess who we saw at the Louisville airport," Betty says.
    "I give up," says Waldeen.
    "Colonel Sanders!"
    "He's eighty-four if he's a day," C. W. adds.
    "You couldn't miss him in that white suit," Betty says.
"I'm sure it was him. Oh, Joe! He had a walking stick. He
went strutting along—"
    "No kidding!"
    "He probably beats chickens to death with it," says Holly,
who is standing around.
    "That would be something to have," says Joe. "Wow, one
of the Colonel's walking sticks."
    "Do you know what I read in a magazine?" says Betty.
"That the Colonel Sanders outfit is trying to grow a three-
legged chicken."
    "No, a four-legged chicken," says C. W.
    "Well, whatever."
    Waldeen is startled by the conversation. She is rattling
ice cubes, looking for glasses. She finds an opened Coke in
the refrigerator, but it may have lost its fizz. Before she can
decide whether to open the new one Joe brought, C. W. and
Betty grab glasses of ice from her and hold them out. Waldeen
pours the Coke. There is a little fizz.
    "We went first class the whole way," says C. W. "I always
say, what's a vacation for if you don't splurge?"
    "We spent a fortune," says Betty. "Plus, I gained a ton."

"Man, those big jets are really nice," says C. W.

C. W. and Betty seem changed, exactly like all the people Waldeen has known who come back from Florida with tales of adventure and glowing tans, except that C. W. and Betty did not get tans. It rained. Waldeen cannot imagine flying, or spending that much money. Her ex-husband tried to get her to go up in an airplane with him once—a seven-fifty ride in a Cessna—but she refused. If Holly goes to Arizona to visit him, she will have to fly. Arizona is probably as far away as Florida.

When C. W. says he is going fishing on Saturday, Holly demands to go along. Waldeen reminds her about the picnic. "You're full of wants," she says.

"I just wanted to go somewhere."

"I'll take you fishing one of these days soon," says Joe.

"Joe's got to clean off his graveyard," says Waldeen. Before she realizes what she is saying, she has invited C. W. and Betty to come along on the picnic. She turns to Joe. "Is that O.K.?"

"I'll bring some beer," says C. W. "To hell with fishing."

"I never heard of a picnic at a graveyard," says Betty. "But it sounds neat."

Joe seems embarrassed. "I'll put you to work," he warns.

Later, in the kitchen, Waldeen pours more Coke for Betty. Holly is playing solitaire on the kitchen table. As Betty takes the Coke, she says, "Let C. W. take Holly fishing if he wants a kid so bad." She has told Waldeen that she wants to marry C. W., but she does not want to ruin her figure by getting pregnant. Betty pets the cat. "Is this cat going to have kittens?"

Mr. Spock, sitting with his legs tucked under his stomach, is shaped somewhat like a turtle.

"Heavens, no," says Waldeen. "He's just fat because I had him nurtured."

"The word is *neutered*!" cries Holly, jumping up. She grabs Mr. Spock and marches up the stairs.

"That youngun," Waldeen says. She feels suddenly afraid. Once, Holly's father, unemployed and drunk on tequila, snatched Holly from the school playground and took her on a wild ride around town, buying her ice cream at the Tastee-Freez, and stopping at Newberry's to buy her an *All in the Family* Joey doll, with correct private parts. Holly was eight. When Joe brought her home, both were tearful and quiet. The excitement had worn off, but Waldeen had vividly imagined how it was. She wouldn't be surprised if Joe tried the same trick again, this time carrying Holly off to Arizona. She has heard of divorced parents who kidnap their own children.

The next day Joe McClain brings a pizza at noon. He is working nearby and has a chance to eat lunch with Waldeen. The pizza is large enough for four people. Waldeen is not hungry.

"I'm afraid we'll end up horsing around and won't get the graveyard cleaned off," Joe says. "It's really a lot of work."

"Why's it so important, anyway?"

"It's a family thing."

"Family. Ha!"

"What do you mean?"

"I don't know what's what anymore," Waldeen wails. "I've got this kid that wants to live on peanuts and sleeps with a cat—and didn't even see her daddy at Christmas. And here *you* are, talking about family. What do you know about family? You don't know the half of it."

"What's got into you lately?"

Waldeen tries to explain. "Take Colonel Sanders, for instance. He was on *I've Got a Secret* once, years ago, when nobody knew who he was? His secret was that he had a million-dollar check in his pocket for selling Kentucky Fried Chicken to John Y. Brown. *Now* look what's happened. Colonel Sanders sold it but didn't get rid of it. He couldn't escape from being Colonel Sanders. John Y. sold it too, and he can't get rid of it either. Everybody calls him the Chicken King, even though he's governor. That's not very dignified, if you ask me."

"What in Sam Hill are you talking about? What's that got to do with families?"

"Oh, Colonel Sanders just came to mind because C. W.

and Betty saw him. What I mean is, you can't just do something by itself. Everything else drags along. It's all *involved*. I can't get rid of my ex-husband just by signing a paper. Even if he *is* in Arizona and I never lay eyes on him again."

Joe stands up, takes Waldeen by the hand, and leads her to the couch. They sit down and he holds her tightly for a moment. Waldeen has the strange impression that Joe is an old friend who moved away and returned, years later, radically changed. She doesn't understand the walking sticks, or why he would buy such an enormous pizza.

"One of these days you'll see," says Joe, kissing her.

"See what?" Waldeen mumbles.

"One of these days you'll see. I'm not such a bad catch."

Waldeen stares at a split in the wallpaper.

"Who would cut your hair if it wasn't for me?" he asks, rumpling her curls. "I should have gone to beauty school."

"I don't know."

"Nobody else can do Jimmy Durante imitations like I can."

"I wouldn't brag about it."

On Saturday, Waldeen is still in bed when Joe arrives. He appears in the doorway of her bedroom, brandishing a shiny black walking stick. It looks like a stiffened black racer snake.

"I overslept," Waldeen says, rubbing her eyes. "First I had insomnia. Then I had bad dreams. Then—"

"You said you'd make a picnic."

"Just a minute. I'll go make it."

"There's not time now. We've got to pick up C. W. and Betty."

Waldeen pulls on her jeans and a shirt, then runs a brush through her hair. In the mirror she sees blue pouches under her eyes. She catches sight of Joe in the mirror. He looks like an actor in a vaudeville show.

They go into the kitchen, where Holly is eating granola. "She promised me she'd make carrot cake," Holly tells Joe.

"I get blamed for everything," says Waldeen. She is rushing around, not sure why. She is hardly awake.

"How could you forget?" asks Joe. "It was your idea in the first place."

"I didn't forget. I just overslept." Waldeen opens the refrigerator. She is looking for something. She stares at a ham.

When Holly leaves the kitchen, Waldeen asks Joe, "Are you mad at me?" Joe is thumping his stick on the floor.

"No. I just want to get this show on the road."

"My ex-husband always said I was never dependable, and he was right. But *he* was one to talk! He had his head in the clouds."

"Forget your ex-husband."

"His name is Joe. Do you want some fruit juice?" Waldeen is looking for orange juice, but she cannot find it.

"No." Joe leans on his stick. "He's over and done with. Why don't you just cross him off your list?"

"Why do you think I had bad dreams? Answer me that. I must be afraid of something."

There is no orange juice. Waldeen closes the refrigerator door. Joe is smiling at her enigmatically. What she is really afraid of, she realizes, is that he will turn out to be just like Joe Murdock. But it must be only the names, she reminds herself. She hates the thought of a string of husbands, and the idea of a stepfather is like a substitute host on a talk show. It makes her think of Johnny Carson's many substitute hosts.

"You're just afraid to do anything new, Waldeen," Joe says. "You're afraid to cross the street. Why don't you get your ears pierced? Why don't you adopt a refugee? Why don't you get a dog?"

"You're crazy. You say the weirdest things." Waldeen searches the refrigerator again. She pours a glass of Coke and watches it foam.

It is afternoon before they reach the graveyard. They had to wait for C. W. to finish painting his garage door, and Betty was in the shower. On the way, they bought a bucket of fried chicken. Joe said little on the drive into the country. When he gets quiet, Waldeen can never figure out if he is angry or calm. When he put the beer cooler in the trunk, she caught a glimpse of the geraniums in an ornate concrete pot with a handle. It looked like a petrified Easter basket. On the drive, she closed her eyes and imagined that they were in a funeral procession.

The graveyard is next to the woods on a small rise fenced in with barbed wire. A herd of Holsteins grazes in the pasture nearby, and in the distance the smokestacks of the new industrial park send up lazy swirls of smoke. Waldeen spreads out a blanket, and Betty opens beers and hands them around. Holly sits under a tree, her back to the gravestones, and opens a Vicki Barr flight stewardess novel.

Joe won't sit down to eat until he has unloaded the geraniums. He fusses over the heavy basket, trying to find a level spot. The flowers are not yet blooming.

"Wouldn't plastic flowers keep better?" asks Waldeen. "Then you wouldn't have to lug that thing back and forth." There are several bunches of plastic flowers on the graves. Most of them have fallen out of their containers.

"Plastic, yuck!" cries Holly.

"I should have known I'd say the wrong thing," says Waldeen.

"My grandmother liked geraniums," Joe says.

At the picnic, Holly eats only slaw and the crust from a drumstick. Waldeen remarks, "Mr. Spock is going to have a feast."

"You've got a treasure, Waldeen," says C. W. "Most kids just want to load up on junk."

"Wonder how long a person can survive without meat," says Waldeen, somewhat breezily. But she suddenly feels miserable about the way she treats Holly. Everything Waldeen does is so roundabout, so devious. Disgusted, Waldeen flings a chicken bone out among the graves. Once, her ex-husband wouldn't bury the dog that was hit by a car. It lay in a ditch for over a week. She remembers Joe saying several times, "Wonder if the dog is still there." He wouldn't admit that he didn't want to bury it. Waldeen wouldn't do it because he had said he would do it. It was a war of nerves. She finally called the Highway Department to pick it up. Joe McClain, she thought now, would never be that barbaric.

Joe pats Holly on the head and says, "My girl's stubborn, but she knows what she likes." He makes a Jimmy Durante face, which causes Holly to smile. Then he brings out a surprise for her, a bag of trail mix, which includes pecans and raisins. When Holly pounces on it, Waldeen notices that Holly is not wearing the Indian bracelet her father gave her. Waldeen wonders if there are vegetarians in Arizona.

Blue sky burns through the intricate spring leaves of the maples on the fence line. The light glances off the gravestones—a few thin slabs that date back to the last century and eleven sturdy blocks of marble and granite. Joe's grandmother's grave is a brown heap.

Waldeen opens another beer. She and Betty are stretched out under a maple tree and Holly is reading. Betty is talking idly about the diet she intends to go on. Waldeen feels too lazy to move. She watches the men work. While C. W. rakes leaves, Joe washes off the gravestones with water he brought in a plastic jug. He scrubs out the carvings with a brush. He seems as devoted as a man washing and polishing his car on a Saturday afternoon. Betty plays he-loves-me-he-loves-me-not with the fingers of a maple leaf. The fragments fly away in a soft breeze.

From her Sea World tote bag, Betty pulls out playing cards with Holly Hobbie pictures on them. The old-fashioned child with the bonnet hiding her face is just the opposite of Waldeen's own strange daughter. Waldeen sees Holly watching the men. They pick up their beer cans from a pink, shiny tombstone and drink a toast to Joe's great-great-grandfather, Joseph McClain, who was killed in the Civil War. His stone, almost hidden in dead grasses, says 1841–1862.

"When I die, they can burn me and dump the ashes in the lake," says C. W.

"Not me," says Joe. "I want to be buried right here."

"*Want* to be? You planning to die soon?"

Joe laughs. "No, but if it's my time, then it's my time. I wouldn't be afraid to go."

"I guess that's the right way to look at it."

Betty says to Waldeen, "He'd marry me if I'd have his kid."

"What made you decide you don't want a kid, anyhow?" Waldeen is shuffling the cards, fifty-two identical children in bonnets.

"Who says I decided? You just do whatever comes natural. Whatever's right for you." Betty drinks from her can of beer.

"Most people do just the opposite," Waldeen says. "They have kids without thinking."

"Talk about decisions," Betty goes on, "did you see *Sixty Minutes* when they were telling about Palm Springs? And how all those rich people live? One woman had hundreds of dresses, and Morley Safer was asking her how she ever decided what on earth to wear. He was *strolling* through her closet. He could have played *golf* in her closet."

"Rich people don't know beans," says Waldeen. She drinks some beer, then deals out the cards for a game of hearts. Betty snatches each card eagerly. Waldeen does not look at her own cards right away. In the pasture, the cows are beginning to move. The sky is losing its blue. Holly seems lost in her book, and the men are laughing. C. W. stumbles over a footstone hidden in the grass and falls onto a grave. He rolls over, curled up with laughter.

"Y'all are going to kill yourselves," Waldeen says, calling across the graveyard.

Joe tells C. W. to shape up. "We've got work to do," he says.

Joe looks over at Waldeen and mouths something. "I love you"? She suddenly remembers a Ku Klux Klansman she saw on TV. He was being arrested at a demonstration, and as he was led away in handcuffs, he spoke to someone off-camera, ending with a solemn message, "I love you." He was acting for the camera, as if to say, "Look what a nice guy I am." He gave Waldeen the creeps. That could have been Joe Murdock, Waldeen thinks. Not Joe McClain. Maybe she is beginning to get them straight in her mind. They have different ways of trying to get through to her.

Waldeen and Betty play several hands of hearts and drink more beer. Betty is clumsy with the cards and loses three hands in a row. Waldeen cannot keep her mind on the cards either. She wins accidentally. She can't concentrate because of the graves, and Joe standing there saying "I love you." If she marries Joe, and doesn't get divorced again, they will be buried here together. She picks out a likely spot and imagines the headstone and the green carpet and the brown leaves that will someday cover the twin mounds. Joe and C. W. are bringing leaves to the center of the graveyard and piling them on the place she has chosen. Waldeen feels peculiar, as if the burial plot, not a diamond ring, symbolizes the promise of marriage. But there is something comforting about the thought, which she tries to explain to Betty.

"Ooh, that's gross," says Betty. She slaps down a heart and takes the trick.

Waldeen shuffles the cards for a long time. The pile of leaves is growing dramatically. Joe and C. W. have each claimed a side of the graveyard, and they are racing. It occurs to Waldeen that she has spent half her life watching guys named Joe show off for her. Once, when Waldeen was fourteen, she went out onto the lake with Joe Suiter in a rented pedal boat. When Waldeen sees him at the bank, where he works, she always remembers the pedal boat and how they stayed out in the silver-blue lake all afternoon, ignoring the people waving them in from the shore. When they finally returned, Joe owed ten dollars in overtime on the boat, so he worked Saturdays, mowing yards, to pay for their spree. Only recently in the bank, when they laughed together over the memory, he told her that it was worth it, for it was one of the great adventures of his life, going out in a pedal boat with Waldeen, with nothing but the lake and time.

Betty is saying, "We could have a nice bonfire and a wienie roast—what *are* you doing?"

Waldeen has pulled her shoes off. Then she is taking a long, running start, like a pole vaulter, and then with a flying leap she lands in the immense pile of leaves, up to her elbows. Leaves are flying and everyone is standing around her, forming a stern circle, and Holly, with her book closed on her fist, is saying, "Don't you know *any*thing?"

# Nancy Culpepper

When Nancy received her parents' letter saying they were moving her grandmother to a nursing home, she said to her husband, "I really should go help them out. And I've got to save Granny's photographs. They might get lost." Jack did not try to discourage her, and she left for Kentucky soon after the letter came.

Nancy has been vaguely wanting to move to Kentucky, and she has persuaded Jack to think about relocating his photography business. They live in the country, near a small town an hour's drive from Philadelphia. Their son, Robert, who is eight, has fits when they talk about moving. He does not want to leave his room or his playmates. Once, he asked, "What about our chickens?"

"They have chickens in Kentucky," Nancy explained. "Don't worry. We're not going yet."

Later he asked, "But what about the fish in the pond?"

"I don't know," said Nancy. "I guess we'll have to rent a U-Haul."

When Nancy arrives at her parents' farm in western Kentucky, her mother says, "Your daddy and me's both got inner ear and nerves. And we couldn't lift Granny, or anything, if we had to all of a sudden."

"The flu settled in my ears," Daddy says, cocking his head at an angle.

"Mine's still popping," says Mother.

In a few days they plan to move Granny, and they will return to their own house, which they have been renting out.

For nine years, they have lived next door, in Granny's house, in order to care for her. There Mother has had to cook on an ancient gas range, with her mother-in-law hovering over her, supervising. Granny used only lye soap on dishes, and it was five years before Nancy's mother defied her and bought some Joy. By then, Granny was confined to her bed, crippled with arthritis. Now she is ninety-three.

"You didn't have to come back," Daddy says to Nancy at the dinner table. "We could manage."

"I want to help you move," Nancy says. "And I want to make sure Granny's pictures don't get lost. Nobody cares about them but me, and I'm afraid somebody will throw them away."

Nancy wants to find out if Granny has a picture of a great-great-aunt named Nancy Culpepper. No one in the family seems to know anything about her, but Nancy is excited by the thought of an ancestor with the same name as hers. Since she found out about her, Nancy has been going by her maiden name, but she has given up trying to explain this to her mother, who persists in addressing letters to "Mr. and Mrs. Jack Cleveland."

"There's some pictures hid behind Granny's closet wall," Daddy tells Nancy. "When we hooked up the coal-oil stove through the fireplace a few years ago, they got walled in."

"That's ridiculous! Why would you do that?"

"They were in the way." He stands up and puts on his cap, preparing to go out to feed his calves.

"Will Granny care if I tear the wall down?" Nancy asks, joking.

Daddy laughs, acting as though he understood, but Nancy knows he is pretending. He seems tired, and his billed cap looks absurdly small perched on his head.

When Nancy and Jack were married, years ago, in Massachusetts, Nancy did not want her parents to come to the wedding. She urged them not to make the long trip. "It's no big deal," she told them on the telephone. "It'll last ten minutes.

We're not even going on a honeymoon right away, because we both have exams Monday."

Nancy was in graduate school, and Jack was finishing his B.A. For almost a year they had been renting a large old house on a lake. The house had a field-rock fireplace with a heart-shaped stone centered above the mantel. Jack, who was studying design, thought the heart was tasteless, and he covered it with a Peter Max poster.

At the ceremony, Jack's dog, Grover, was present, and instead of organ music, a stereo played *Sgt. Pepper's Lonely Hearts Club Band.* It was 1967. Nancy was astonished by the minister's white robe and his beard and by the fact that he chain-smoked. The preachers she remembered from childhood would have called him a heathen, she thought. Most of the wedding pictures, taken by a friend of Jack's, turned out to be trick photography—blurred faces and double exposures.

The party afterward lasted all night. Jack blew up two hundred balloons and kept the fire going. They drank too much wine-and-7Up punch. Guests went in and out, popping balloons with cigarettes, taking walks by the lake. Everyone was looking for the northern lights, which were supposed to be visible that evening. Holding on to Jack, Nancy searched the murky sky, feeling that the two of them were lone travelers on the edge of some outer-space adventure. At the same time, she kept thinking of her parents at home, probably watching *Gunsmoke.*

"I saw them once," Jack said. "They were fantastic."

"What was it like?"

"Shower curtains."

"Really? That's amazing."

"Luminescent shower curtains."

"I'm shivering," Nancy said. The sky was blank.

"Let's go in. It's too cloudy anyway. Someday we'll see them. I promise."

Someone had taken down the poster above the fireplace and put up the picture of Sgt. Pepper—the cutout that came

with the album. Sgt. Pepper overlooked the room like a stern
father.

"What's the matter?" a man asked Nancy. He was Dr.
Doyle, her American History 1861–1865 professor. "This is your
wedding. Loosen up." He burst a balloon and Nancy jumped.

When someone offered her a joint, she refused, then wondered why. The house was filled with strangers, and the Beatles
album played over and over. Jack and Nancy danced, hugging
each other in a slow two-step that was all wrong for the music.
They drifted past the wedding presents, lined up on a table
Jack had fashioned from a door—hand-dipped candles, a silver
roach clip, *Joy of Cooking,* signed pottery in nonfunctional
shapes. Nancy wondered what her parents had eaten for supper. Possibly fried steak, two kinds of peas, biscuits, blackberry
pie. The music shifted and the songs merged together; Jack
and Nancy kept dancing.

"There aren't any stopping places," Nancy said. She was
crying. "Songs used to have stopping places in between."

"Let's just keep on dancing," Jack said.

Nancy was thinking of the blackberry bushes at the farm
in Kentucky, which spread so wildly they had to be burned
down every few years. They grew on the banks of the creek,
which in summer shrank to still, small occasional pools. After
a while Nancy realized that Jack was talking to her. He was
explaining how he could predict exactly when the last, dying
chord on the album was about to end.

"Listen," he said. *"There.* Right there."

Nancy's parents had met Jack a few months before the
wedding, during spring break, when Jack and Nancy stopped
in Kentucky on their way to Denver to see an old friend of
Jack's. The visit involved some elaborate lies about their sleeping arrangements on the trip.

At the supper table, Mother and Daddy passed bowls of
food self-consciously. The table was set with some napkins left
over from Christmas. The vegetables were soaked in bacon
grease, and Jack took small helpings. Nancy sat rigidly, watch-

ing every movement, like a cat stationed near a bird feeder. Mother had gathered poke, because it was spring, and she said to Jack, "I bet you don't eat poke salet up there."

"It's weeds," said Nancy.

"I've never heard of it," Jack said. He hesitated, then took a small serving.

"It's poison if it gets too big," Daddy said. He turned to Nancy's mother. "I think you picked this too big. You're going to poison us all."

"He's teasing," Nancy said.

"The berries is what's poison," said Mother, laughing. "Wouldn't that be something? They'll say up there I tried to poison your boyfriend the minute I met him!"

Everyone laughed. Jack's face was red. He was wearing an embroidered shirt. Nancy watched him trim the fat from his ham as precisely as if he were using an X-Acto knife on mat board.

"How's Granny?" asked Nancy. Her grandmother was then living alone in her own house.

"Tolerable well," said Daddy.

"We'll go see her," Jack said. "Nancy told me all about her."

"She cooks her egg in her oats to keep from washing a extry dish," Mother said.

Nancy played with her food. She was looking at the pink dining room wall and the plastic flowers in the window. On the afternoon Jack and Nancy first met, he took her to a junk shop, where he bought a stained-glass window for his bathroom. Nancy would never have thought of going to a junk shop. It would not have occurred to her to put a stained-glass window in a bathroom.

"What do you aim to be when you graduate?" Daddy asked Jack abruptly, staring at him. Jack's hair looked oddly like an Irish setter's ears, Nancy thought suddenly.

"Won't you have to go in the army?" Mother asked.

"I'll apply for an assistantship if my grades are good enough," Jack said. "Anything to avoid the draft."

Nancy's father was leaning into his plate, as though he were concentrating deeply on each bite.

"He makes good grades," Nancy said.

"Nancy always made all A's," Daddy said to Jack.

"We gave her a dollar for ever' one," said Mother. "She kept us broke."

"In graduate school they don't give A's," said Nancy. "They just give S's and U's."

Jack wadded up his napkin. Then Mother served fried pies with white sauce. "Nancy always loved these better than anything," she said.

After supper, Nancy showed Jack the farm. As they walked through the fields, Nancy felt that he was seeing peaceful landscapes—arrangements of picturesque cows, an old red barn. She had never thought of the place this way before; it reminded her of prints in a dime store.

While her mother washes the dishes, Nancy takes Granny's dinner to her, and sits in a rocking chair while Granny eats in bed. The food is on an old TV-dinner tray. The compartments hold chicken and dressing, mashed potatoes, field peas, green beans, and vinegar slaw. The servings are tiny—six green beans, a spoonful of peas.

Granny's teeth no longer fit, and she has to bite sideways, like a cat. She wears the lower teeth only during meals, but she will not get new ones. She says it would be wasteful to be buried with a new three-hundred-dollar set of teeth. In between bites, Granny guzzles iced tea from a Kentucky Lakes mug. "That slaw don't have enough sugar in it," she says. "It makes my mouth draw up." She smacks her lips.

Nancy says, "I've heard the food is really good at the Orchard Acres Rest Home."

Granny does not reply for a moment. She is working on a chicken gristle, which causes her teeth to clatter. Then she says, "I ain't going nowhere."

"Mother and Daddy are moving back into their house. You don't want to stay here by yourself, do you?" Nancy's voice sounds hollow to her.

"I'll be all right. I can do for myself."

When Granny swallows, it sounds like water spilling from a bucket into a cistern. After Nancy's parents moved in, they covered Granny's old cistern, but Nancy still remembers drawing the bucket up from below. The chains made a sound like crying.

Granny pushes her food with a piece of bread, cleaning her tray. "I can do a little cooking," she says. "I can sweep."

"Try this boiled custard, Granny. I made it just for you. Just the way you used to make it."

"It ain't yaller enough," says Granny, tasting the custard. "Store-bought eggs."

When she finishes, she removes her lower teeth and sloshes them in a plastic tumbler on the bedside table. Nancy looks away. On the wall are Nancy's high school graduation photograph and a picture of Jesus. Nancy looks sassy; her graduation hat resembles a tilted lid. Jesus has a halo, set at about the same angle.

Now Nancy ventures a question about the pictures hidden behind the closet wall. At first Granny is puzzled. Then she seems to remember.

"They're behind the stovepipe," she says. Grimacing with pain, she stretches her legs out slowly, and then, holding her head, she sinks back into her pillows and draws the quilt over her shoulders. "I'll look for them one of these days—when I'm able."

Jack photographs weeds, twigs, pond reflections, silhouettes of Robert against the sun with his arms flung out like a scarecrow's. Sometimes he works in the evenings in his studio at home, drinking tequila sunrises and composing bizarre still lifes with light bulbs, wine bottles, Tinker Toys, Lucite cubes. He makes arrangements of gourds look like breasts.

On the day Nancy tried to explain to Jack about her need to save Granny's pictures, a hailstorm interrupted her. It was the only hailstorm she had ever seen in the North, and she had forgotten all about them. Granny always said a hailstorm meant that God was cleaning out his icebox. Nancy stood against a white Masonite wall mounted with a new series of photographs and looked out the window at tulips being smashed. The ice pellets littered the ground like shattered glass. Then, as suddenly as it had arrived, the hailstorm was over.

"Pictures didn't use to be so common," Nancy said. Jack's trash can was stuffed with rejected prints, and Robert's face was crumpled on top. "I want to keep Granny's pictures as reminders."

"If you think that will solve anything," said Jack, squinting at a negative he was holding against the light.

"I want to see if she has one of Nancy Culpepper."

"That's *you*."

"There was another one. She was a great-great-aunt or something, on my daddy's side. She had the same name as mine."

"There's another one of you?" Jack said with mock disbelief.

"I'm a reincarnation," she said, playing along.

"There's nobody else like you. You're one of a kind."

Nancy turned away and stared deliberately at Jack's pictures, which were held up by clear-headed pushpins, like translucent eyes dotting the wall. She examined them one by one, moving methodically down the row—stumps, puffballs, tree roots, close-ups of cat feet.

Nancy first learned about her ancestor on a summer Sunday a few years before, when she took her grandmother to visit the Culpepper graveyard, beside an oak grove off the Paducah highway. The old oaks had spread their limbs until they shaded the entire cemetery, and the tombstones poked through weeds like freak mushrooms. Nancy wandered among the graves, while Granny stayed beside her husband's gravestone. It had her own name on it too, with a blank space for the date.

Nancy told Jack afterward that when she saw the stone marked "NANCY CULPEPPER, 1833–1905," she did a double take. "It was like time-lapse photography," she said. "I mean,

I was standing there looking into the past and the future at the same time. It was weird."

"She wasn't kin to me, but she lived down the road," Granny explained to Nancy. "She was your granddaddy's aunt."

"Did she look like me?" Nancy asked.

"I don't know. She was real old." Granny touched the stone, puzzled. "I can't figure why she wasn't buried with her husband's people," she said.

On Saturday, Nancy helps her parents move some of their furniture to the house next door. It is only a short walk, but when the truck is loaded they all ride in it, Nancy sitting between her parents. The truck's muffler sounds like thunder, and they drive without speaking. Daddy backs up to the porch.

The paint on the house is peeling, and the latch of the storm door is broken. Daddy pulls at the door impatiently, saying, "I sure wish I could burn down these old houses and retire to Arizona." For as long as Nancy can remember, her father has been sending away for literature on Arizona.

Her mother says, "We'll never go anywhere. We've got our dress tail on a bedpost."

"What does that mean?" asks Nancy, in surprise.

"Use to, if a storm was coming, people would put a bedpost on a child's dress tail, to keep him from blowing away. In other words, we're tied down."

"That's funny. I never heard of that."

"I guess you think we're just ignorant," Mother says. "The way we talk."

"No, I don't."

Daddy props the door open, and Nancy helps him ease a mattress over the threshold. Mother apologizes for not being able to lift anything.

"I'm in your way," she says, stepping off the porch into a dead canna bed.

Nancy stacks boxes in her old room. It seems smaller than she remembered, and the tenants have scarred the woodwork. Mentally, she refurnishes the room—the bed by the window, the desk opposite. The first time Jack came to Kentucky he slept here, while Nancy slept on the couch in the living room. Now Nancy recalls the next day, as they headed west, with Jack accusing her of being dishonest, foolishly trying to protect her parents. "You let them think you're such a goody-goody, the ideal daughter," he said. "I bet you wouldn't tell them if you made less than an A."

Nancy's father comes in and runs his hand across the ceiling, gathering up strings of dust. Tugging at a loose piece of door facing, he says to Nancy, "Never trust renters. They won't take care of a place."

"What will you do with Granny's house?"

"Nothing. Not as long as she's living."

"Will you rent it out then?"

"No. I won't go through that again." He removes his cap and smooths his hair, then puts the cap back on. Leaning against the wall, he talks about the high cost of the nursing home. "I never thought it would come to this," he says. "I wouldn't do it if there was any other way."

"You don't have any choice," says Nancy.

"The government will pay you to break up your family," he says. "If I get like your granny, I want you to just take me out in the woods and shoot me."

"She told me she wasn't going," Nancy says.

"They've got a big recreation room for the ones that can get around," Daddy says. "They've even got disco dancing."

When Daddy laughs, his voice catches, and he has to clear his throat. Nancy laughs with him. "I can just see Granny disco dancing. Are you sure you want me to shoot you? That place sounds like fun."

They go outside, where Nancy's mother is cleaning out a patch of weed-choked perennials. "I planted these iris the year we moved," she says.

"They're pretty," says Nancy. "I haven't seen that color up North."

Mother stands up and shakes her foot awake. "I sure hope y'all can move down here," she says. "It's a shame you have to be so far away. Robert grows so fast I don't know him."

"We might someday. I don't know if we can."

"Looks like Jack could make good money if he set up a studio in town. Nowadays people want fancy pictures."

"Even the school pictures cost a fortune," Daddy says.

"Jack wants to free-lance for publications," says Nancy. "And there aren't any here. There's not even a camera shop within fifty miles."

"But people want pictures," Mother says. "They've gone back to decorating living rooms with family pictures. In antique frames."

Daddy smokes a cigarette on the porch, while Nancy circles the house. A beetle has infested the oak trees, causing clusters of leaves to turn brown. Nancy stands on the concrete lid of an old cistern and watches crows fly across a cornfield. In the distance a series of towers slings power lines across a flat sea of soybeans. Her mother is talking about Granny. Nancy thinks of Granny on the telephone, the day of her wedding, innocently asking, "What are you going to cook for your wedding breakfast?" Later, seized with laughter, Nancy told Jack what Granny had said.

"I almost said to her, 'We usually don't eat breakfast, we sleep so late!' "

Jack was busy blowing up balloons. When he didn't laugh, Nancy said, "Isn't that hilarious? She's really out of the nineteenth century."

"You don't have to make me breakfast," said Jack.

"In her time, it meant something really big," Nancy said helplessly. "Don't you see?"

Now Nancy's mother is saying, "The way she has to have that milk of magnesia every night, when I know good and well she don't need it. She thinks she can't live without it."

"What's wrong with her?" asks Nancy.

"She thinks she's got a knot in her bowels. But ain't nothing wrong with her but that head-swimming and arthritis." Mother jerks a long morning glory vine out of the marigolds. "Hardening of the arteries is what makes her head swim," she says.

"We better get back and see about her," Daddy says, but he does not get up immediately. The crows are racing above the power lines.

Later, Nancy spreads a Texaco map of the United States out on Granny's quilt. "I want to show you where I live," she says. "Philadelphia's nearly a thousand miles from here."

"Reach me my specs," says Granny, as she struggles to sit up. "How did you get here?"

"Flew. Daddy picked me up at the airport in Paducah."

"Did you come by the bypass or through town?"

"The bypass," says Nancy. Nancy shows her where Pennsylvania is on the map. "I flew from Philadelphia to Louisville to Paducah. There's California. That's where Robert was born."

"I haven't seen a geography since I was twenty years old," Granny says. She studies the map, running her fingers over it as though she were caressing fine material. "Law, I didn't know *where* Floridy was. It's way down there."

"I've been to Florida," Nancy says.

Granny lies back, holding her head as if it were a delicate china bowl. In a moment she says, "Tell your mama to thaw me up some of them strawberries I picked."

"When were you out picking strawberries, Granny?"

"They're in the freezer of my refrigerator. Back in the back. In a little milk carton." Granny removes her glasses and waves them in the air.


"Larry was going to come and play with me, but he couldn't come," Robert says to Nancy on the telephone that evening. "He had a stomachache."

"That's too bad. What did you do today?"

"We went to the Taco Bell and then we went to the woods so Daddy could take pictures of Indian pipes."

"What are those?"

"I don't know. Daddy knows."

"We didn't find any," Jack says on the extension. "I think it's the wrong time of year. How's Kentucky?"

Nancy tells Jack about helping her parents move. "My

bed is gone, so tonight I'll have to sleep on a couch in the hallway," she says. "It's really dreary here in this old house. Everything looks so bare."

"How's your grandmother?"

"The same. She's dead set against that rest home, but what can they do?"

"Do you still want to move down there?" Jack asks.

"I don't know."

"I know how we could take the chickens to Kentucky," says Robert in an excited burst.

"How?"

"We could give them sleeping pills and then put them in the trunk so they'd be quiet."

"That sounds gruesome," Jack says.

Nancy tells Robert not to think about moving. There is static on the line. Nancy has trouble hearing Jack. "We're your family too," he is saying.

"I didn't mean to abandon you," she says.

"Have you seen the pictures yet?"

"No. I'm working up to that."

"Nancy Culpepper, the original?"

"You bet," says Nancy, a little too quickly. She hears Robert hang up. "Is Robert O.K.?" she asks through the static.

"Oh, sure."

"He doesn't think I moved without him?"

"He'll be all right."

"He didn't tell me good-bye."

"Don't worry," says Jack.

"She's been after me about those strawberries till I could wring her neck," says Mother as she and Nancy are getting ready for bed. "She's talking about some strawberries she put up in nineteen seventy-*one*. I've told her and told her that she eat them strawberries back then, but won't nothing do but for her to have them strawberries."

"Give her some others," Nancy says.

"She'd know the difference. She don't miss a thing when

it comes to what's *hers*. But sometimes she's just as liable to forget her name."

Mother is trembling, and then she is crying. Nancy pats her mother's hair, which is gray and wiry and sticks out in sprigs. Wiping her eyes, Mother says, "All the kinfolks will talk. 'Look what they done to her, poor helpless thing.' It'll probably kill her, to move her to that place."

"When you move back home you can get all your antiques out of the barn," Nancy says. "You'll be in your own house again. Won't that be nice?"

Mother does not answer. She takes some sheets and quilts from a closet and hands them to Nancy. "That couch lays good," she says.

When Nancy wakes up, the covers are on the floor, and for a moment she does not remember where she is. Her digital watch says 2:43. Then it tells the date. In the darkness she has no sense of distance, and it seems to her that the red numerals could be the size of a billboard, only seen from far away.

Jack has told her that this kind of insomnia is a sign of depression, while the other kind—inability to fall asleep at bedtime—is a sign of anxiety. Nancy always thought he had it backward, but now she thinks he may be right. A flicker of distant sheet lightning exposes the bleak walls with the suddenness of a flashbulb. The angles of the hall seem unfamiliar, and the narrow couch makes Nancy feel small and alone. When Jack and Robert come to Kentucky with her, they all sleep in the living room, and in the early morning Nancy's parents pass through to get to the bathroom. "We're just one big happy family," Daddy announces, to disguise his embarrassment when he awakens them. Now, for some reason, Nancy recalls Jack's strange still lifes, and she thinks of the black irises and the polished skulls of cattle suspended in the skies of O'Keeffe paintings. The irises are like thunderheads. The night they were married, Nancy and Jack collapsed into bed, falling asleep immediately, their heads swirling. The party was still going on, and friends from New York were staying over. Nancy woke up the next day saying her new name, and feeling that once again, in another way, she had betrayed her parents. "The one time they really thought they knew what I was doing, they didn't at all," she told Jack, who was barely awake. The visitors had gone out for the Sunday newspapers, and they brought back doughnuts. They had doughnuts and wine for breakfast. Someone made coffee later.

In the morning, a slow rain blackens the fallen oak branches in the yard. In Granny's room the curtains are gray with shadows. Nancy places an old photograph album in Granny's lap. Silently, Granny turns pages of blank-faced babies in long white dresses like wedding gowns. Nancy's father is a boy in a sailor suit. Men and women in pictures the color of café au lait stand around picnic tables. The immense trees in these settings are shaggy and dark. Granny cannot find Nancy Culpepper in the album. Quickly, she flips past a picture of her husband. Then she almost giggles as she points to a girl. "That's me."

"I wouldn't have recognized you, Granny."

"Why, it looks just *like* me." Granny strokes the picture, as though she were trying to feel the dress. "That was my favorite dress," she says. "It was brown poplin, with grosgrain ribbon and self-covered buttons. Thirty-two of them. And all those tucks. It took me three weeks to work up that dress."

Nancy points to the pictures one by one, asking Granny to identify them. Granny does not notice Nancy writing the names in a notebook. Aunt Sass, Uncle Joe, Dove and Pear Culpepper, Hortense Culpepper.

"Hort Culpepper went to Texas," says Granny. "She had TB."

"Tell me about that," Nancy urges her.

"There wasn't anything to tell. She got homesick for her mammy's cooking." Granny closes the album and falls back against her pillows, saying, "All those people are gone."

While Granny sleeps, Nancy gets a flashlight and opens the closet. The inside is crammed with the accumulation of decades—yellowed newspapers, boxes of greeting cards, bags of string, and worn-out stockings. Granny's best dress, a blue bonded knit she has hardly worn, is in plastic wrapping. Nancy pushes the clothing aside and examines the wall. To her right, a metal pipe runs vertically through the closet. Backing up against the dresses, Nancy shines the light on the corner and discovers a large framed picture wedged behind the pipe. By tugging at the frame, she is able to work it gradually through the narrow space between the wall and the pipe. In the picture a man and woman, whose features are sharp and clear, are sitting expectantly on a brocaded love seat. Nancy imagines that this is a wedding portrait.

In the living room, a TV evangelist is urging viewers to call him, toll free. Mother turns the TV off when Nancy appears with the picture, and Daddy stands up and helps her hold it near a window.

"I think that's Uncle John!" he says excitedly. "He was my favorite uncle."

"They're none of my people," says Mother, studying the picture through her bifocals.

"He died when I was little, but I think that's him," says Daddy. "Him and Aunt Lucy Culpepper."

"Who was she?" Nancy asks.

"Uncle John's wife."

"I figured that," says Nancy impatiently. "But who *was* she?"

"I don't know." He is still looking at the picture, running his fingers over the man's face.

Back in Granny's room, Nancy pulls the string that turns on the ceiling light, so that Granny can examine the picture. Granny shakes her head slowly. "I never saw them folks before in all my life."

Mother comes in with a dish of strawberries.

"Did I pick these?" Granny asks.

"No. You eat yours about ten years ago," Mother says.

Granny puts in her teeth and eats the strawberries in slurps, missing her mouth twice. "Let me see them people again," she says, waving her spoon. Her teeth make the sound of a baby rattle.

"Nancy Hollins," says Granny. "She was a Culpepper."

"That's Nancy Culpepper?" cries Nancy.

"*That*'s not Nancy Culpepper," Mother says. "That woman's got a rat in her hair. They wasn't in style back when Nancy Culpepper was alive."

Granny's face is flushed and she is breathing heavily. "She was a real little-bitty old thing," she says in a high, squeaky voice. "She never would talk. Everybody thought she was curious. Plumb curious."

"Are you sure it's her?" Nancy says.

"If I'm not mistaken."

"She don't remember," Mother says to Nancy. "Her mind gets confused."

Granny removes her teeth and lies back, her bones grinding. Her chest heaves with exhaustion. Nancy sits down in the rocking chair, and as she rocks back and forth she searches the photograph, exploring the features of the young woman, who is wearing an embroidered white dress, and the young man, in a curly beard that starts below his chin, framing his face like a ruffle. The woman looks frightened—of the camera perhaps—but nevertheless her deep-set eyes sparkle like shards of glass. This young woman would be glad to dance to "Lucy in the Sky with Diamonds" on her wedding day, Nancy thinks. The man seems bewildered, as if he did not know what to expect, marrying a woman who has her eyes fixed on something so far away.

# Lying Doggo

Grover Cleveland is growing feeble. His eyes are cloudy, and his muzzle is specked with white hairs. When he scoots along on the hardwood floors, he makes a sound like brushes on drums. He sleeps in front of the woodstove, and when he gets too hot he creeps across the floor.

When Nancy Culpepper married Jack Cleveland, she felt, in a way, that she was marrying a divorced man with a child. Grover was a young dog then. Jack had gotten him at the humane society shelter. He had picked the shyest, most endearing puppy in a boisterous litter. Later, he told Nancy that someone said he should have chosen an energetic one, because quiet puppies often have something wrong with them. That chance remark bothered Nancy; it could have applied to her as well. But that was years ago. Nancy and Jack are still married, and Grover has lived to be old. Now his arthritis stiffens his legs so that on some days he cannot get up. Jack has been talking of having Grover put to sleep.

"Why do you say 'put to sleep'?" their son, Robert, asks. "I know what you mean." Robert is nine. He is a serious boy, quiet, like Nancy.

"No reason. It's just the way people say it."

"They don't say they put *people* to sleep."

"It doesn't usually happen to people," Jack says.

"Don't you dare take him to the vet unless you let me go along. I don't want any funny stuff behind my back."

"Don't worry, Robert," Nancy says.

Later, in Jack's studio, while developing photographs of

broken snow fences on hillsides, Jack says to Nancy, "There's a first time for everything, I guess."

"What?"

"Death. I never really knew anybody who died."

"You're forgetting my grandmother."

"I didn't really know your grandmother." Jack looks down at Grover's face in the developing fluid. Grover looks like a wolf in the snow on the hill. Jack says, "The only people I ever cared about who died were rock heroes."

Jack has been buying special foods for the dog—pork chops and liver, vitamin supplements. All the arthritis literature he has been able to find concerns people, but he says the same rules must apply to all mammals. Until Grover's hind legs gave way, Jack and Robert took Grover out for long, slow walks through the woods. Recently, a neighbor who keeps Alaskan malamutes stopped Nancy in the Super Duper and inquired about Grover. The neighbor wanted to know which kind of arthritis Grover had—osteo- or rheumatoid? The neighbor said he had rheumatoid and held out knobbed fingers. The doctor told him to avoid zucchini and to drink lots of water. Grover doesn't like zucchini, Nancy said.

Jack and Nancy and Robert all deal with Grover outside. It doesn't help that the temperature is dropping below twenty degrees. It feels even colder because they are conscious of the dog's difficulty. Nancy holds his head and shoulders while Jack supports his hind legs. Robert holds up Grover's tail.

Robert says, "I have an idea."

"What, sweetheart?" asks Nancy. In her arms, Grover lurches. Nancy squeezes against him and he whimpers.

"We could put a diaper on him."

"How would we clean him up?"

"They do that with chimpanzees," says Jack, "but it must be messy."

"You mean I didn't have an original idea?" Robert cries. "Curses, foiled again!" Robert has been reading comic books about masked villains.

"There aren't many original ideas," Jack says, letting go of Grover. "They just look original when you're young." Jack lifts Grover's hind legs again and grasps him under the stomach. "Let's try one more time, boy."

Grover looks at Nancy, pleading.

Nancy has been feeling that the dying of Grover marks a milestone in her marriage to Jack, a marriage that has somehow lasted almost fifteen years. She is seized with an irrational dread—that when the dog is gone, Jack will be gone too. Whenever Nancy and Jack are apart—during Nancy's frequent trips to see her family in Kentucky, or when Jack has gone away "to think"—Grover remains with Jack. Actually, Nancy knew Grover before she knew Jack. When Jack and Nancy were students, in Massachusetts, the dog was a familiar figure around campus. Nancy was drawn to the dog long before she noticed the shaggy-haired student in the sheepskin-lined corduroy jacket who was usually with him. Once, in a seminar on the Federalist period that Nancy was auditing, Grover had walked in, circled the room, and then walked out, as if performing some routine investigation, like the man who sprayed Nancy's apartment building for silverfish. Grover was a beautiful dog, a German shepherd, gray, dusted with a sooty topcoat. After the seminar, Nancy followed the dog out of the building, and she met Jack then. Eventually, when Nancy and Jack made love in his apartment in Amherst, Grover lay sprawled by the bed, both protective and quietly participatory. Later, they moved into a house in the country, and Nancy felt that she had an instant family. Once, for almost three months, Jack and Grover were gone. Jack left Nancy in California, pregnant and terrified, and went to stay at an Indian reservation in New Mexico. Nancy lived in a room on a street with palm trees. It was winter. It felt like a Kentucky October. She went to a park every day and watched people with their dogs, their children, and tried to comprehend that she was there, alone, a mile from the San Andreas fault, reluctant to return to Kentucky. "We need to decide where we stand with each other," Jack had said when he left. "Just when I start to think I know where you're at, you seem to disappear." Jack always seemed to stand back and watch her, as though he expected her to do something excitingly original. He expected her to be herself, not someone she thought people wanted her to be. That was a twist: he expected the unexpected. While Jack was away, Nancy indulged in crafts projects. At the Free University, she learned batik and macramé. On her own, she learned to crochet. She had never done anything like that before. She threw away her file folders of history notes for the article she had wanted to write. Suddenly, making things with her hands was the only endeavor that made sense. She crocheted a bulky, shapeless sweater in a shell stitch for Jack. She made baby things, using large hooks. She did not realize that such heavy blankets were unsuitable for a baby until she saw Robert—a tiny, warped-looking creature, like one of her clumsily made crafts. When Jack returned, she was in a sprawling adobe hospital, nursing a baby the color of scalded skin. The old song "In My Adobe Hacienda" was going through her head. Jack stood over her behind an unfamiliar beard, grinning in disbelief, stroking the baby as though he were a new pet. Nancy felt she had fooled Jack into thinking she had done something original at last.

"Grover's dying to see you," he said to her. "They wouldn't let him in here."

"I'll be glad to see Grover," said Nancy. "I missed him."

She had missed, she realized then, his various expressions: the staccato barks of joy, the forceful, menacing barks at strangers, the eerie howls when he heard cat fights at night.

Those early years together were confused and dislocated. After leaving graduate school, at the beginning of the seventies, they lived in a number of places—sometimes on the road, with Grover, in a van—but after Robert was born they settled in Pennsylvania. Their life is orderly. Jack is a free-lance photographer, with his own studio at home. Nancy, unable to find a use for her degree in history, returned to school, taking education and administration courses. Now she is assistant principal

of a small private elementary school, which Robert attends.
Now and then Jack frets about becoming too middle-class. He
has become semipolitical about energy, sometimes attending
anti-nuclear power rallies. He has been building a sun space
for his studio and has been insulating the house. "Retrofitting"
is the term he uses for making the house energy-efficient.

"Insulation is his hobby," Nancy told an old friend from
graduate school, Tom Green, who telephoned unexpectedly
one day recently. "He insulates on weekends."

"Maybe he'll turn into a butterfly—he could insulate himself into a cocoon," said Tom, who Nancy always thought was
funny. She had not seen him in ten years. He called to say
he was sending a novel he had written—"about all the crazy
stuff we did back then."

The dog is forcing Nancy to think of how Jack has changed
in the years since then. He is losing his hair, but he doesn't
seem concerned. Jack was always fanatical about being honest.
He used to be insensitive about his directness. "I'm just being
honest," he would say pleasantly, boyishly, when he hurt people's feelings. He told Nancy she was uptight, that no one ever
knew what she thought, that she should be more expressive.
He said she "played games" with people, hiding her feelings
behind her coy Southern smile. He is more tolerant now, less
judgmental. He used to criticize her for drinking Cokes and
eating pastries. He didn't like her lipstick, and she stopped
wearing it. But Nancy has changed too. She is too sophisticated
now to eat fried foods and rich pies and cakes, indulging in
them only when she goes to Kentucky. She uses makeup now—
so sparingly that Jack does not notice. Her cool reserve, her
shyness, has changed to cool assurance, with only the slightest
shift. Inwardly, she has reorganized. "It's like retrofitting," she
said to Jack once, but he didn't notice any irony.

It wasn't until two years ago that Nancy learned that he
had lied to her when he told her he had been at the Beatles'
Shea Stadium concert in 1966, just as she had, only two months
before they met. When he confessed his lie, he claimed he
had wanted to identify with her and impress her because he

thought of her as someone so mysterious and aloof that he could not hold her attention. Nancy, who had in fact been intimidated by Jack's directness, was troubled to learn about his peculiar deception. It was out of character. She felt a part of her past had been ripped away. More recently, when John Lennon died, Nancy and Jack watched the silent vigil from Central Park on TV and cried in each other's arms. Everybody that week was saying that they had lost their youth.

Jack was right. That was the only sort of death they had known.

Grover lies on his side, stretched out near the fire, his head flat on one ear. His eyes are open, expressionless, and when Nancy speaks to him he doesn't respond.

"Come on, Grover!" cries Robert, tugging the dog's leg. "Are you dead?"

"Don't pull at him," Nancy says.

"He's lying doggo," says Jack.

"That's funny," says Robert. "What does that mean?"

"Dogs do that in the heat," Jack explains. "They save energy that way."

"But it's winter," says Robert. "I'm freezing." He is wearing a wool pullover and a goose-down vest. Jack has the thermostat set on fifty-five, relying mainly on the woodstove to warm the house.

"I'm cold too," says Nancy. "I've been freezing since 1965, when I came North."

Jack crouches down beside the dog. "Grover, old boy. Please. Just give a little sign."

"If you don't get up, I won't give you your treat tonight," says Robert, wagging his finger at Grover.

"Let him rest," says Jack, who is twiddling some of Grover's fur between his fingers.

"Are you sure he's not dead?" Robert asks. He runs the zipper of his vest up and down.

"He's just pretending," says Nancy.

The tip of Grover's tail twitches, and Jack catches it, the

way he might grab at a fluff of milkweed in the air.

Later, in the kitchen, Jack and Nancy are preparing for a dinner party. Jack is sipping whiskey. The woodstove has been burning all day, and the house is comfortably warm now. In the next room, Robert is lying on the rug in front of the stove with Grover. He is playing with a computer football game and watching *Mork and Mindy* at the same time. Robert likes to do several things at once, and lately he has included Grover in his multiple activities.

Jack says, "I think the only thing to do is just feed Grover pork chops and steaks and pet him a lot, and then when we can stand it, take him to the vet and get it over with."

"When can we stand it?"

"If I were in Grover's shape, I'd just want to be put out of my misery."

"Even if you were still conscious and could use your mind?"

"I guess so."

"I couldn't pull the plug on you," says Nancy, pointing a carrot at Jack. "You'd have to be screaming in agony."

"Would you want me to do it to you?"

"No. I can see right now that I'd be the type to hang on. I'd be just like my Granny. I think she just clung to life, long after her body was ready to die."

"Would you really be like that?"

"You said once I was just like her—repressed, uptight."

"I didn't mean that."

"You've been right about me before," Nancy says, reaching across Jack for a paring knife. "Look, all I mean is that it shouldn't be a matter of *our* convenience. If Grover needs assistance, then it's our problem. We're responsible."

"I'd want to be put out of my misery," Jack says.

During that evening, Nancy has the impression that Jack is talking more than usual. He does not notice the food. She has made chicken Marengo and is startled to realize how much it resembles chicken cacciatore, which she served the last time she had the same people over. The recipes are side by side in the cookbook, gradations on a theme. The dinner is for Stewart and Jan, who are going to Italy on a teaching exchange.

"Maybe I shouldn't even have made Italian," Nancy tells them apologetically. "You'll get enough of that in Italy. And it will be real."

Both Stewart and Jan say the chicken Marengo is wonderful. The olives are the right touch, Jan says. Ted and Laurie nod agreement. Jack pours more wine. The sound of a log falling in the woodstove reminds Nancy of the dog in the other room by the stove, and in her mind she stages a scene: finding the dog dead in the middle of the dinner party.

Afterward, they sit in the living room, with Grover lying there like a log too large for the stove. The guests talk idly. Ted has been sandblasting old paint off a brick fireplace, and Laurie complains about the gritty dust. Jack stokes the fire. The stove, hooked up through the fireplace, looks like a robot from an old science fiction movie. Nancy and Jack used to sit by the fireplace in Massachusetts, stoned, watching the blue frills of the flames, imagining that they were musical notes, visual textures of sounds on the stereo. Nobody they know smokes grass anymore. Now people sit around and talk about investments and proper flue linings. When Jack passes around the Grand Marnier, Nancy says, "In my grandparents' house years ago, we used to sit by their fireplace. They burned coal. They didn't call it a fireplace, though. They called it a grate."

"Coal burns more efficiently than wood," Jack says.

"Coal's a lot cheaper in this area," says Ted. "I wish I could switch."

"My grandparents had big stone fireplaces in their country house," says Jan, who comes from Connecticut. "They were so pleasant. I always looked forward to going there. Sometimes in the summer the evenings were cool and we'd have a fire. It was lovely."

"I remember being cold," says Nancy. "It was always very cold, even in the South."

"The heat just goes up the chimney in a fireplace," says Jack.

Nancy stares at Jack. She says, "I would stand in front of

the fire until I was roasted. Then I would turn and roast the other side. In the evenings, my grandparents sat on the hearth and read the Bible. There wasn't anything *lovely* about it. They were trying to keep warm. Of course, nobody had heard of insulation."

"There goes Nancy, talking about her deprived childhood," Jack says with a laugh.

Nancy says, "Jack is so concerned about wasting energy. But when he goes out he never wears a hat." She looks at Jack. "Don't you know your body heat just flies out the top of your head? It's a chimney."

Surprised by her tone, she almost breaks into tears.

It is the following evening, and Jack is flipping through some contact sheets of a series on solar hot-water heaters he is doing for a magazine. Robert sheds his goose-down vest, and he and Grover, on the floor, simultaneously inch away from the fire. Nancy is trying to read the novel written by the friend from Amherst, but the book is boring. She would not have recognized her witty friend from the past in the turgid prose she is reading.

"It's a dump on the sixties," she tells Jack when he asks. "A really cynical look. All the characters are types."

"Are we in it?"

"No. I hope not. I think it's based on that Phil Baxter who cracked up at that party."

Grover raises his head, his eyes alert, and Robert jumps up, saying, "It's time for Grover's treat."

He shakes a Pet-Tab from a plastic bottle and holds it before Grover's nose. Grover bangs his tail against the rug as he crunches the pill.

Jack turns on the porch light and steps outside for a moment, returning with a shroud of cold air. "It's starting to snow," he says. "Come on out, Grover."

Grover struggles to stand, and Jack heaves the dog's hind legs over the threshold.

Later, in bed, Jack turns on his side and watches Nancy,

reading her book, until she looks up at him.

"You read so much," he says. "You're always reading."

"Hmm."

"We used to have more fun. We used to be silly together."

"What do you want to do?"

"Just something silly."

"I can't think of anything silly." Nancy flips the page back, rereading. "God, this guy can't write. I used to think he was so clever."

In the dark, touching Jack tentatively, she says, "We've changed. We used to lie awake all night, thrilled just to touch each other."

"We've been busy. That's what happens. People get busy."

"That scares me," says Nancy. "Do you want to have another baby?"

"No. I want a dog." Jack rolls away from her, and Nancy can hear him breathing into his pillow. She waits to hear if he will cry. She recalls Jack returning to her in California after Robert was born. He brought a God's-eye, which he hung from the ceiling above Robert's crib, to protect him. Jack never wore the sweater Nancy made for him. Instead, Grover slept on it. Nancy gave the dog her granny-square afghan too, and eventually, when they moved back East, she got rid of the pathetic evidence of her creative period—the crochet hooks, the piles of yarn, some splotchy batik tapestries. Now most of the objects in the house are Jack's. He made the oak counters and the dining room table; he remodeled the studio; he chose the draperies; he photographed the pictures on the wall. If Jack were to leave again, there would be no way to remove his presence, the way the dog can disappear completely, with his sounds. Nancy revises the scene in her mind. The house is still there, but Nancy is not in it.

In the morning, there is a four-inch snow, with a drift blowing up the back-porch steps. From the kitchen window, Nancy watches her son float silently down the hill behind the house. At the end, he tumbles off his sled deliberately, wallowing in the snow, before standing up to wave, trying to catch her attention.

On the back porch, Nancy and Jack hold Grover over newspapers. Grover performs unselfconsciously now. Nancy says, "Maybe he can hang on, as long as we can do this."

"But look at him, Nancy," Jack says. "He's in misery."

Jack holds Grover's collar and helps him slide over the threshold. Grover aims for his place by the fire.

After the snowplow passes, late in the morning, Nancy drives Robert to the school on slushy roads, all the while lecturing him on the absurdity of raising money to buy official Boy Scout equipment, especially on a snowy Saturday. The Boy Scouts are selling water-savers for toilet tanks in order to earn money for camping gear.

"I thought Boy Scouts spent their time earning badges," says Nancy. "I thought you were supposed to learn about nature, instead of spending money on official Boy Scout pots and pans."

"This is nature," Robert says solemnly. "It's ecology. Saving water when you flush is ecology."

Later, Nancy and Jack walk in the woods together. Nancy walks behind Jack, stepping in his boot tracks. He shields her from the wind. Her hair is blowing. They walk briskly up a hill and emerge on a ridge that overlooks a valley. In the distance they can see a housing development, a radio tower, a winding road. House trailers dot the hillsides. A snowplow is going up a road, like a zipper in the landscape.

Jack says, "I'm going to call the vet Monday."

Nancy gasps in cold air. She says, "Robert made us promise you won't do anything without letting him in on it. That goes for me too." When Jack doesn't respond, she says, "I'd want to hang on, even if I was in a coma. There must be some spark, in the deep recesses of the mind, some twitch, a flicker of a dream—"

"A twitch that could make life worth living?" Jack laughs bitterly.

"Yes." She points to the brilliantly colored sparkles the

sun is making on the snow. "Those are the sparks I mean," she says. "In the brain somewhere, something like that. That would be beautiful."

"You're weird, Nancy."

"I learned it from you. I never would have noticed anything like that if I hadn't known you, if you hadn't got me stoned and made me look at your photographs." She stomps her feet in the snow. Her toes are cold. "You educated me. I was so out of it when I met you. One day I was listening to Hank Williams and shelling corn for the chickens and the next day I was expected to know what wines went with what. Talk about weird."

"You're exaggerating. That was years ago. You always exaggerate your background." He adds in a teasing tone, "Your humble origins."

"We've been together fifteen years," says Nancy. She stops him, holding his arm. Jack is squinting, looking at something in the distance. She goes on, "You said we didn't do anything silly anymore. What should we do, Jack? Should we make angels in the snow?"

Jack touches his rough glove to her face. "We shouldn't unless we really feel like it."

It was the same as Jack chiding her to be honest, to be expressive. The same old Jack, she thought, relieved.

"Come and look," Robert cries, bursting in the back door. He and Jack have been outside making a snowman. Nancy is rolling dough for a quiche. Jack will eat a quiche but not a custard pie, although they are virtually the same. She wipes her hands and goes to the door of the porch. She sees Grover swinging from the lower branch of the maple tree. Jack has rigged up a sling, so that the dog is supported in a harness, with the canvas from the back of a deck chair holding his stomach. His legs dangle free.

"Oh, Jack," Nancy calls. "The poor thing."

"I thought this might work," Jack explains. "A support for his hind legs." His arms cradle the dog's head. "I did it

for you," he adds, looking at Nancy. "Don't push him, Robert.
I don't think he wants to swing."

Grover looks amazingly patient, like a cat in a doll bonnet.

"He hates it," says Jack, unbuckling the harness.

"He can learn to like it," Robert says, his voice rising shrilly.

On the day that Jack has planned to take Grover to the
veterinarian, Nancy runs into a crisis at work. One of the children has been exposed to hepatitis, and it is necessary to vacci-
nate all of them. Nancy has to arrange the details, which means
staying late. She telephones Jack to ask him to pick up Robert
after school.

"I don't know when I'll be home," she says. "This is an
administrative nightmare. I have to call all the parents, get
permissions, make arrangements with family doctors."

"What will we do about Grover?"

"Please postpone it. I want to be with you then."

"I want to get it over with," says Jack impatiently. "I hate
to put Robert through another day of this."

"Robert will be glad of the extra time," Nancy insists. "So
will I."

"I just want to face things," Jack says. "Don't you understand? I don't want to cling to the past like you're doing."

"Please wait for us," Nancy says, her voice calm and controlled.

On the telephone, Nancy is authoritative, a quick decision-
maker. The problem at work is a reprieve. She feels free, on
her own. During the afternoon, she works rapidly and efficiently, filing reports, consulting health authorities, notifying
parents. She talks with the disease-control center in Atlanta,
inquiring about guidelines. She checks on supplies of gamma
globulin. She is so preoccupied that in the middle of the afternoon, when Robert suddenly appears in her office, she is startled, for a fleeting instant not recognizing him.

He says, "Kevin has a sore throat. Is that hepatitis?"

"It's probably just a cold. I'll talk to his mother." Nancy

is holding Robert's arm, partly to keep him still, partly to steady herself.

"When do I have to get a shot?" Robert asks.

"Tomorrow."

"Do I have to?"

"Yes. It won't hurt, though."

"I guess it's a good thing this happened," Robert says bravely. "Now we get to have Grover another day." Robert spills his books on the floor and bends to pick them up. When he looks up, he says, "Daddy doesn't care about him. He just wants to get rid of him. He wants to kill him."

"Oh, Robert, that's not true," says Nancy. "He just doesn't want Grover to suffer."

"But Grover still has half a bottle of Pet-Tabs," Robert says. "What will we do with them?"

"I don't know," Nancy says. She hands Robert his numbers workbook. Like a tape loop, the face of her child as a stranger replays in her mind. Robert has her plain brown hair, her coloring, but his eyes are Jack's—demanding and eerily penetrating, eyes that could pin her to the wall.

After Robert leaves, Nancy lowers the venetian blinds. Her office is brilliantly lighted by the sun, through south-facing windows. The design was accidental, nothing to do with solar energy. It is an old building. Bars of light slant across her desk, like a formidable scene in a forties movie. Nancy's secretary goes home, but Nancy works on, contacting all the parents she couldn't get during working hours. One parent anxiously reports that her child has a swollen lymph node on his neck.

"No," Nancy says firmly. "That is *not* a symptom of hepatitis. But you should ask the doctor about that when you go in for the gamma globulin."

Gamma globulin. The phrase rolls off her tongue. She tries to remember an odd title of a movie about gamma rays. It comes to her as she is dialing the telephone: *The Effect of Gamma Rays on Man-in-the-Moon Marigolds*. She has never known what that title meant.

The office grows dim, and Nancy turns on the lights. The school is quiet, as though the threat of an infectious disease has emptied the corridors, leaving her in charge. She recalls another movie, *The Andromeda Strain*. Her work is like the thrill of watching drama, a threat held safely at a distance. Historians have to be detached, Nancy once said, defensively, to Jack, when he accused her of being unfriendly to shopkeepers and waiters. Where was all that Southern hospitality he had heard so much about? he wanted to know. It hits her now that historians are detached about the past, not the present. Jack has learned some of this detachment: he wants to let Grover go. Nancy thinks of the stark images in his recent photographs—snow, icicles, fences, the long shot of Grover on the hill like a stray wolf. Nancy had always liked Jack's pictures simply for what they were, but Jack didn't see the people or the objects in them. He saw illusions. The vulnerability of the image, he once said, was what he was after. The image was meant to evoke its own death, he told her.

By the time Nancy finishes the scheduling, the night maintenance crew has arrived, and the coffeepot they keep in a closet is perking. Nancy removes her contact lenses and changes into her fleece-lined boots. In the parking lot, she maneuvers cautiously along a path past a mountain of black-stained snow. It is so cold that she makes sparks on the vinyl car seat. The engine is cold, slow to turn over.

At home, Nancy is surprised to see balloons in the living room. The stove is blazing and Robert's face is red from the heat.

"We're having a party," he says. "For Grover."

"There's a surprise for you in the oven," says Jack, handing Nancy a glass of sherry. "Because you worked so hard."

"Grover had ice cream," Robert says. "We got Häagen-Dazs."

"He looks cheerful," Nancy says, sinking onto the couch next to Jack. Her glasses are fogged up. She removes them and wipes them with a Kleenex. When she puts them back on, she sees Grover looking at her, his head on his paws. His tail thumps. For the first time, Nancy feels ready to let the dog die.

When Nancy tells about the gamma globulin, the phrase has stopped rolling off her tongue so trippingly. She laughs. She is so tired she throbs with relief. She drinks the sherry too fast. Suddenly, she sits up straight and announces, "I've got a clue. I'm thinking of a parking lot."

"East or West?" Jack says. This is a game they used to play.

"West."

"Aha, I've got you," says Jack. "You're thinking of the parking lot at that hospital in Tucson."

"Hey, that's not fair going too fast," cries Robert. "I didn't get a chance to play."

"This was before you were born," Nancy says, running her fingers through Robert's hair. He is on the floor, leaning against her knees. "We were lying in the van for a week, thinking we were going to die. Oh, God!" Nancy laughs and covers her mouth with her hands.

"Why were you going to die?" Robert asks.

"We weren't really going to die." Both Nancy and Jack are laughing now at the memory, and Jack is pulling off his sweater. The hospital in Tucson wouldn't accept them because they weren't sick enough to hospitalize, but they were too sick to travel. They had nowhere to go. They had been on a month's trip through the West, then had stopped in Tucson and gotten jobs at a restaurant to make enough money to get home.

"Do you remember that doctor?" Jack says.

"I remember the look he gave us, like he didn't want us to pollute his hospital." Nancy laughs harder. She feels silly and relieved. Her hand, on Jack's knee, feels the fold of the long johns beneath his jeans. She cries, "I'll never forget how we stayed around that parking lot, thinking we were going to die."

"I couldn't have driven a block, I was so weak," Jack gasps.

"You were yellow. *I* didn't get yellow."

"All we could do was pee and drink orange juice."

"And throw the pee out the window."

"Grover was so bored with us!"

Nancy says, "It's a good thing we couldn't eat. We would have spent all our money."

"Then we would have had to work at that filthy restaurant again. And get hepatitis again."

"And on and on, forever. We would still be there, like Charley on the MTA. Oh, Jack, do you *remember* that crazy restaurant? You had to wear a ten-gallon hat—"

Abruptly, Robert jerks away from Nancy and crawls on his knees across the room to examine Grover, who is stretched out on his side, his legs sticking out stiffly. Robert, his straight hair falling, bends his head to the dog's heart.

"He's not dead," Robert says, looking up at Nancy. "He's lying doggo."

"Passed out at his own party," Jack says, raising his glass. "Way to go, Grover!"

# A New-Wave
# Format

Edwin Creech drives a yellow bus, transporting a group of
mentally retarded adults to the Cedar Hill Mental Health Center, where they attend training classes. He is away from 7:00
to 9:30 A.M. and from 2:30 to 5:00 P.M. His hours are so particular that Sabrina Jones, the girl he has been living with for
several months, could easily cheat on him. Edwin devises
schemes to test her. He places a long string of dental floss on
her pillow (an idea he got from a mystery novel), but it remains
undisturbed. She is away four nights a week, at rehearsals for
*Oklahoma!* with the Western Kentucky Little Theatre, and
she often goes out to eat afterward with members of the cast.
Sabrina won't let him go to rehearsals, saying she wants the
play to be complete when he sees it. At home, she sings and
dances along with the movie sound track, and she acts out
scenes for him. In the play, she's in the chorus, and she has
two lines in Act I, Scene 3. Her lines are "And to yer house
a dark clubman!" and "Then out of your dreams you'll go."
Edwin loves the dramatic way Sabrina waves her arms on her
first line. She is supposed to be a fortune teller.
One evening when Sabrina comes home, Edwin is still
up, as she puts on the sound track of *Oklahoma!* and sings
along with Gordon MacRae while she does splits on the living
room floor. Her legs are long and slender, and she still has
her summer tan. She is wearing her shorts, even though it is
late fall. Edwin suddenly has an overwhelming feeling of love
for her. She really seems to believe what she is singing—"Oh,

What a Beautiful Mornin'." When the song ends, he tells her
that.

"It's the middle of the night," he says, teasing. "And you
think it's morning."

"I'm just acting."

"No, you really believe it. You believe it's morning, a beautiful morning."

Sabrina gives him a fishy look, and Edwin feels embarrassed. When the record ends, Sabrina goes into the bedroom
and snaps on the radio. Rock music helps her relax before
going to sleep. The new rock music she likes is monotonous
and bland, but Edwin tells himself that he likes it because
Sabrina likes it. As she undresses, he says to her, "I'm sorry.
I wasn't accusing you of nothing."

"That's O.K." She shrugs. The T-shirt she sleeps in has a
hole revealing a spot of her skin that Edwin would like to
kiss, but he doesn't because it seems like a corny thing to do.
So many things about Sabrina are amazing: her fennel toothpaste and herbal deodorant; her slim, snaky hips; the way she
puts Vaseline on her teeth for a flashier smile, something she
learned to do in a beauty contest.

When she sits on the bed, Edwin says, "If I say the wrong
things, I want you to tell me. It's just that I'm so crazy about
you I can't think sometimes. But if I can do anything better,
I will. I promise. Just tell me."

"I don't think of you as the worrying type," she says, lying
down beside him. She still has her shoes on.

"I didn't used to be."

"You're the most laid back guy I know."

"Is that some kind of actor talk from your actor friends?"

"No. You're just real laid back. Usually good-looking guys
are so stuck up. But you're not." The music sends vibrations
through Edwin like a cat's purr. She says, "I brag on you all
the time to Jeff and Sue—Curly and Laurey."

"I know who Jeff and Sue are." Sabrina talks constantly
about Jeff and Sue, the romantic leads in the play.

Sabrina says, "Here's what I wish. If we had a big pile of

money, we could have a house like Sue's. Did I tell you she's got *woven* blinds on her patio that she made herself? Everything she does is so *artistic.*" Sabrina shakes Edwin's shoulder. "Wake up and talk to me."

"I can't. I have to get up at six."

Sabrina whispers to him, "Sue has the hots for Jeff. And Jeff's wife is going to have a duck with a rubber tail if she finds out." Sabrina giggles. "He kept dropping hints about how his wife was going to Louisville next week. And he and Sue were eating off the same slice of pizza."

"Is that supposed to mean something?"

"You figure it out."

"Would you do me that way?"

"Don't be silly." Sabrina turns up the radio, then unties her shoes and tosses them over Edwin's head into a corner.

Edwin is forty-three and Sabrina is only twenty, but he does not want to believe age is a barrier between them. Sometimes he cannot believe his good luck, that he has a beautiful girl who finds him still attractive. Edwin has a deep dimple in his chin, which reminded his first wife, Lois Ann, of Kirk Douglas. She had read in a movie magazine that Kirk Douglas has a special attachment for shaving his dimple. But Sabrina thinks Edwin looks like John Travolta, who also has a dimple. Now and then Edwin realizes how much older he is than Sabrina, but time has passed quickly, and he still feels like the same person, unchanged, that he was twenty years ago. His two ex-wives had seemed to drift away from him, and he never tried to hold them back. But with Sabrina, he knows he must make an effort, for it is beginning to dawn on him that sooner or later women get disillusioned with him. Maybe he's too laid back. But Sabrina likes this quality. Sabrina has large round gray eyes and limp, brownish-blond hair, the color of birch paneling, which she highlights with Miss Clairol. They share a love of Fudgsicles, speedboats, and *WKRP in Cincinnati.* At the beginning, he thought that was enough to build a relationship on, because he knew so many couples who never shared such simple pleasures, but gradually he has begun to see that it is more complicated than that. Sabrina's liveliness makes him afraid that she will be fickle. He can't bear the thought of losing her, and he doesn't like the idea that his new possessiveness may be the same uneasy feeling a man would have for a daughter.

Sabrina's parents sent her to college for a year, but her father, a farmer, lost money on his hogs and couldn't afford to continue. When Edwin met her, she was working as a waitress in a steak house. She wants to go back to college, but Edwin does not have the money to send her either. In college, she learned things that make him feel ignorant around her. She said that in an anthropology course, for instance, she learned for a fact that people evolved from animals. But when he tried to argue with her, she said his doubts were too silly to discuss. Edwin doesn't want to sound like a father, so he usually avoids such topics. Sabrina believes in the ERA, although she likes to keep house. She cooks odd things for him, like eggplant, and a weird lasagna with vegetables. She says she knows how to make a Big Mac from scratch, but she never does. Her specialty is pizza. She puts sliced dill pickles on it, which Edwin doesn't dare question. She likes to do things in what she calls an arty way. Now Sabrina is going out for pizza with people in the Theatre. Sabrina talks of "the Theatre."

Until he began driving the bus, Edwin had never worked closely with people. He worked on an offshore oil rig for a time, but kept his distance from the other men. He drove a bulldozer in a logging camp out West. In Kentucky, during his marriages, he worked in an aluminum products company, an automotive machine shop, and numerous gas stations, going from job to job as casually as he did with women. He used to think of himself as an adventurer, but now he believes he has gone through life rather blindly, without much pain or sense of loss.

When he drives the bus, he feels stirred up, perhaps the way Sabrina feels about *Oklahoma!* The bus is a new luxury model with a tape deck, AM-FM, CB, and built-in first-aid kit. He took a first-aid course, so he feels prepared to handle emergencies. Edwin has to stay alert, for anything could happen. The guys who came back from Vietnam said it was like this every moment. Edwin was in the army, but he was never sent to Vietnam, and now he feels that he has bypassed some critical stage in his life: a knowledge of terror. Edwin has never had this kind of responsibility, and he has never been around mentally retarded people before. His passengers are like bizarre, overgrown children, badly behaved and unpredictable. Some of them stare off into space, others are hyperactive. A woman named Freddie Johnson kicks aimlessly at the seat in front of her, spouting her ten-word vocabulary. She can say, "Hot! Shorts," "*Popeye* on?" "*Dukes* on!" "Cook supper," and "Go bed." She talks continuously. A gangly man with a clubfoot has learned to get Hershey bars from a vending machine, and every day he brings home Hershey bars, clutching them in his hand until he squeezes them out of shape. A pretty blond woman shows Edwin the braces on her teeth every day when she gets on the bus. She gets confused if Edwin brings up another topic. The noises on the bus are chaotic and eerie— spurts, gurgles, yelps, squeals. Gradually, Edwin has learned how to keep his distance and keep order at the same time. He plays tape-recorded music to calm and entertain the passengers. In effect, he has become a disc jockey, taking requests and using the microphone, but he avoids fast talk. The supervisors at the center have told him that the developmentally disabled—they always use this term—need a world that is slowed down; they can't keep up with today's fast pace. So he plays mellow old sixties tunes by the Lovin' Spoonful, Joni Mitchell, Donovan. It seems to work. The passengers have learned to clap or hum along with the music. One man, Merle Cope, has been learning to clap his hands in a body-awareness class. Merle is forty-seven years old, and he walks two miles—in an hour—to the bus stop, down a country road. He climbs onto the bus with agonizing slowness. When he gets on, he makes an exaggerated clapping motion, as if to congratulate himself for having made it, but he never lets his hands quite touch. Merle Cope always has an eager grin on his face, and when he tries to clap his hands he looks ecstatic. He looks happier than Sabrina singing "Oh, What a Beautiful Mornin'."

On Thursday, November 14, Edwin stops at the junction of a state road and a gravel road called Ezra Combs Lane to pick up a new passenger. The country roads have shiny new green signs, with the names of the farmers who originally settled there three or four generations ago. The new passenger is Laura Combs, who he has been told is thirty-seven and has never been to school. She will take classes in Home Management and Living Skills. When she gets on the bus, the people who were with her drive off in a blue Pacer. Laura Combs, a large, angular woman with buckteeth, stomps deliberately down the aisle, then plops down beside a young black man named Ray Watson, who has been riding the bus for about three weeks. Ray has hardly spoken, except to say "Have a nice day" to Edwin when he leaves the bus. Ray, who is mildly retarded from a blow on the head in his childhood, is subject to seizures, but so far he has not had one on the bus. Edwin watches him carefully. He learned about convulsions in his first-aid course.

When Laura Combs sits down by Ray Watson, she shoves him and says, "Scoot over. And cheer up."

Her tone is not cheerful. Edwin watches in the rear-view mirror, ready to act. He glides around a curve and slows down for the next passenger. A tape has ended and Edwin hesitates before inserting another. He hears Ray Watson say, "I never seen anybody as ugly as you."

"Shut up or I'll send you to the back of the bus." Laura Combs speaks with a snappy authority that makes Edwin wonder if she is really retarded. Her hair is streaked gray and yellow, and her face is filled with acne pits.

Ray Watson says, "That's fine with me, long as I don't have to set by you."

"Want me to throw you back in the woodpile where you come from?"

"I bet you could throw me plumb out the door, you so big."

It is several minutes before it is clear to Edwin that they

are teasing. He is pleased that Ray is talking, but he can't understand why it took a person like Laura Combs to motivate him. She is an imposing woman with a menacing stare. She churns gum, her mouth open.

For a few weeks, Edwin watches them joke with each other, and whenever he decides he should separate them, they break out into big grins and pull at each other's arms. The easy intimacy they develop seems strange to Edwin, but then it suddenly occurs to him what a fool he is being about a twenty-year-old girl, and that seems even stranger. He hears Ray ask Laura, "Did you get that hair at the Piggly Wiggly?" Laura's hair is in pigtails, which seem to be freshly plaited on Mondays and untouched the rest of the week. Laura says, "I don't want no birds nesting in *my* hair."

Edwin takes their requests. Laura has to hear "Mister Bojangles" every day, and Ray demands that Edwin play something from Elvis's Christmas album. They argue over tastes. Each says the other's favorite songs are terrible.

Laura tells Ray she never heard of a black person liking Elvis, and Ray says, "There's a lot about black people you don't know."

"What?"

"That's for me to know and you to find out. You belong on the moon. All white peoples belong on the moon."

"You belong in Atlanta," Laura says, doubling over with laughter.

When Edwin reports their antics one day to Sabrina, she says, "That's too depressing for words."

"They're a lot smarter than you'd think."

"I don't see how you can stand it." Sabrina shudders. She says, "Out in the woods, animals that are defective wouldn't survive. Even back in history, deformed babies were abandoned."

"Today's different," says Edwin, feeling alarmed. "Now they have rights."

"Well, I'll say one thing. If I was going to have a retarded baby, I'd get an abortion."

"That's killing."

"It's all in how you look at it," says Sabrina, changing the radio station.

They are having lunch. Sabrina has made a loaf of zucchini bread, because Sue made one for Jeff. Edwin doesn't understand her reasoning, but he takes it as a compliment. She gives him another slice, spreading it with whipped margarine. All of his women were good cooks. Maybe he didn't praise them enough. He suddenly blurts out so much praise for the zucchini bread that Sabrina looks at him oddly. Then he realizes that her attention is on the radio. The Humans are singing a song about paranoia, which begins, "Attention, all you K Mart shoppers, fill your carts, 'cause your time is almost up." It is Sabrina's favorite song.

"Most of my passengers are real poor country people," Edwin says. "Use to, they'd be kept in the attic or out in the barn. Now they're riding a bus, going to school and having a fine time."

"In the attic? I never knew that. *I'm* a poor country girl and I never knew that."

"Everybody knows that," says Edwin, feeling a little pleased. "But don't call yourself a poor country girl."

"It's true. My daddy said he'd give me a calf to raise if I came back home. Big deal. My greatest dread is that I'll end up on a farm, raising a bunch of dirty-faced younguns. Just like some of those characters on your bus."

Edwin does not know what to say. The song ends. The last line is, "They're looking in your picture window."

While Sabrina clears away the dishes, Edwin practices rolling bandages. He has been reviewing his first-aid book. "I want you to help me practice a simple splint," he says to Sabrina.

"If I broke a leg, I couldn't be in *Oklahoma!*"

"You won't break a leg." He holds out the splint. It is a fraternity paddle, a souvenir of her college days. She sits down for him and stretches out her leg.

"I can't stand this," she says.

"I'm just practicing. I have to be prepared. I might have an emergency."

Sabrina, wincing, closes her eyes while Edwin ties the fraternity paddle to her ankle.

"It's perfect," he says, tightening the knot.

Sabrina opens her eyes and wiggles her foot. "Jim says he's sure I can have a part in *Life with Father*," she says. Jim is the director of *Oklahoma!* She adds, "Jeff is probably going to be the lead."

"I guess you're trying to make me jealous."

"No, I'm not. It's not even a love story."

"I'm glad then. Is that what you want to do?"

"I don't know. Don't you think I ought to go back to school and take a drama class? It'd be a real great experience, and I'm not going to get a job anytime soon, looks like. Nobody's hiring." She shakes her leg impatiently, and Edwin begins untying the bandage. "What do you think I ought to do?"

"I don't know. I never know how to give you advice, Sabrina. What do I know? I haven't been to college like you."

"I wish I were rich, so I could go back to school," Sabrina says sadly. The fraternity paddle falls to the floor, and she says, with her hands rushing to her face, "Oh, God, I can't stand the thought of breaking a leg."

The play opens in two weeks, during the Christmas season, and Sabrina has been making her costumes—two gingham outfits, virtually identical. She models them for Edwin and practices her dances for him. Edwin applauds, and she gives him a stage bow, as the director has taught her to do. Everything Sabrina does now seems like a performance. When she slices the zucchini bread, sawing at it because it has hardened, it is a performance. When she sat in the kitchen chair with the splint, it was as though she imagined her audience. Edwin has been involved in his own performances, on the bus. He emulates Dr. Johnny Fever, on *WKRP*, because he likes to be low-key, cool. But he hesitates to tell Sabrina about his disc jockey role because she doesn't watch *WKRP in Cincinnati* with him anymore. She goes to rehearsals early.

Maybe it is out of resistance to the sappy *Oklahoma!* sound track, or maybe it is an inevitable progression, but Edwin finds himself playing a few Dylan tunes, some Janis Joplin, nothing too hectic. The passengers shake their heads in pleasure or beat things with their fists. It makes Edwin sad to think how history passes them by, but sometimes he feels the same way about his own life. As he drives along, playing these old songs, he thinks about what his life was like back then. During his first marriage, he worked in a gas station, saving for a down payment on a house. Lois Ann fed him on a TV tray while he watched the war. It was like a drama series. After Lois Ann, and then his travels out West, there was Carolyn and another down payment on another house and more of the war. Carolyn had a regular schedule—pork chops on Mondays, chicken on Tuesdays. Thursday's menu has completely escaped his memory. He feels terrible, remembering his wives by their food, and remembering the war as a TV series. His life has been a delayed reaction. He feels as if he's about Sabrina's age. He plays music he did not understand fifteen years ago, music that now seems full of possibility: the Grateful Dead, the Jefferson Airplane, groups with vision. Edwin feels that he is growing and changing for the first time in years. The passengers on his bus fill him with a compassion he has never felt before. When Freddie Johnson learns a new word—"bus"— Edwin is elated. He feels confident. He could drive his passengers all the way to California if he had to.

One day a stringbean girl with a speech impediment gives Edwin a tape cassette she wants him to play. Her name is Lou Murphy. Edwin has tried to encourage her to talk, but today he hands the tape back to her abruptly.

"I don't like the Plasmatics," he explains, enjoying his authority. "I don't play new-wave. I have a golden-oldie format. I just play sixties stuff."

The girl takes the tape cassette and sits down by Laura Combs. Ray Watson is absent today. She starts pulling at her hair, and the cassette jostles in her lap. Laura is wound up too, jiggling her knees. The pair of them make Edwin think of those vibrating machines that mix paint by shaking the cans.

Edwin takes the microphone and says, "If you want a new-wave format, you'll have to ride another bus. Now let's crawl back in the stacks of wax for this oldie but goodie—Janis Joplin and 'A Little Bit Harder.' "

Lou Murphy nods along with the song. Laura's chewing gum pops like BBs. A while later, after picking up another passenger, Edwin glances in the rear-view mirror and sees Laura playing with the Plasmatics tape, pulling it out in a curly heap. Lou seems to be trying to shriek, but nothing comes out. Before Edwin can stop the bus, Laura has thrown the tape out the window.

"You didn't like it, Mr. Creech," Laura says when Edwin, after halting the bus on a shoulder, stalks down the aisle. "You said you didn't like it."

Edwin has never heard anyone sound so matter-of-fact, or look so reasonable. He has heard that since Laura began her classes, she has learned to set a table, make change, and dial a telephone. She even has a job at the training center, sorting seeds and rags. She is as hearty and domineering, yet as delicate and vulnerable, as Janis Joplin must have been. Edwin manages to move Lou to a front seat. She is sobbing silently, her lower jaw jerking, and Edwin realizes he is trembling too. He feels ashamed. After all, he is not driving the bus in order to make a name for himself. Yet it had felt right to insist on the format for his show. There is no appropriate way to apologize, or explain.

Edwin doesn't want to tell Sabrina about the incident. She is preoccupied with the play and often listens to him distractedly. Edwin has decided that he was foolish to suspect that she had a lover. The play is her love. Her nerves are on edge. One chilly afternoon, on the weekend before *Oklahoma!* opens, he suggests driving over to Kentucky Lake.

"You need a break," he tells her. "A little relaxation. I'm worried about you."

"This is nothing," she says. "Two measly lines. I'm not exactly a star."

"What if you were? Would you get an abortion?"

"What are you talking about? I'm not pregnant."

"You said once you would. Remember?"

"Oh. I would if the baby was going to be creepy like those people on your bus."

"But how would you know if it was?"

"They can tell." Sabrina stares at him and then laughs. "Through science."

In the early winter, the lake is deserted. The beaches are washed clean, and the water is clear and gray. Now and then, as they walk by the water, they hear a gunshot from the Land Between the Lakes wilderness area. "The Surrey with the Fringe on Top" is going through Edwin's head, and he wishes he could throw the *Oklahoma!* sound track in the lake, as easily as Laura Combs threw the Plasmatics out the window of the bus. He has an idea that after the play, Sabrina is going to feel a letdown too great for him to deal with.

When Sabrina makes a comment about the "artistic intention" of Rodgers and Hammerstein, Edwin says, "Do you know what Janis Joplin said?"

"No—what?" Sabrina stubs the toe of her jogging shoe in the sand.

"Janis Joplin said, 'I don't write songs. I just make 'em up.' I thought that was clever."

"That's funny, I guess."

"She said she was going to her high school reunion in Port Arthur, Texas. She said, 'I'm going to laugh a lot. They laughed me out of class, out of town, and out of the state.' "

"You sound like you've got that memorized," Sabrina says, looking at the sky.

"I saw it on TV one night when you were gone, an old tape of a Dick Cavett show. It seemed worth remembering." Edwin rests his arm around Sabrina's waist, as thin as a post. He says, "I see a lot of things on TV, when you're not there."

Wild ducks are landing on the water, scooting in like water skiers. Sabrina seems impressed by them. They stand there until the last one lands.

Edwin says, "I bet you can't even remember Janis Joplin.

You're just a young girl, Sabrina. *Oklahoma!* will seem silly to you one of these days."

Sabrina hugs his arm. "That don't matter." She breaks into laughter. "You're cute when you're being serious."

Edwin grabs her hand and jerks her toward him. "Look, Sabrina. I was never serious before in my life. I'm just now, at this point in my life—this week—getting to be serious." His words scare him, and he adds with a grin that stretches his dimple, "I'm serious about *you.*"

"I know that," she says. She is leading the way along the water, through the trees, pulling him by the hand. "But you never believe how much I care about you," she says, drawing him to her. "I think we get along real good. That's why I wish you'd marry me instead of just stringing me along."

Edwin gasps like a swimmer surfacing. It is very cold on the beach. Another duck skis onto the water.

*Oklahoma!* has a four-night run, with one matinee. Edwin goes to the play three times, surprised that he enjoys it. Sabrina's lines come off differently each time, and each evening she discusses the impression she made. Edwin tells her that she is the prettiest woman in the cast, and that her lines are cute. He wants to marry Sabrina, although he hasn't yet said he would. He wishes he could buy her a speedboat for a wedding present. She wants him to get a better-paying job, and she has ideas about a honeymoon cottage at the lake. It feels odd that Sabrina has proposed to him. He thinks of her as a liberated woman. The play is old-fashioned and phony. The love scenes between Jeff and Sue are comically stilted, resembling none of the passion and intrigue that Sabrina has reported. She compared them to Bogart and Bacall, but Edwin can't remember if she meant Jeff and Sue's roles or their actual affair. How did Sabrina know about Bogart and Bacall?

At the cast party, at Jeff's house, Jeff and Sue are publicly affectionate, getting away with it by playing their Laurey and Curly roles, but eventually Jeff's wife, who has made ham, potato salad, chiffon cakes, eggnog, and cranberry punch for sixty people, suddenly disappears from the party. Jeff whizzes off in his Camaro to find her. Sabrina whispers to Edwin, "Look how Sue's pretending nothing's happened. She's flirting with the guy who played Jud Fry." Sabrina, so excited that she bounces around on her tiptoes, is impressed by Jeff's house, which has wicker furniture and rose plush carpets.

Edwin drinks too much cranberry punch at the party, and most of the time he sits on a wicker love seat watching Sabrina flit around the room, beaming with the joy of her success. She is out of costume, wearing a sweatshirt with a rainbow on the front and pots of gold on her breasts. He realizes how proud he is of her. Her complexion is as smooth as a white mushroom, and she has crinkled her hair by braiding and unbraiding it. He watches her join some of the cast members around the piano to sing songs from the play, as though they cannot bear it that the play has ended. Sabrina seems to belong with them, these theatre people. Edwin knows they are not really theatre people. They are only local merchants putting on a play in their spare time. But Edwin is just a bus driver. He should get a better job so that he can send Sabrina to college, but he knows that he has to take care of his passengers. Their faces have become as familiar to him as the sound track of *Oklahoma!* He can practically hear Freddie Johnson shouting out her TV shows: "*Popeye* on! *Dukes* on!" He sees Sabrina looking at him lovingly. The singers shout, "Oklahoma, O.K.!"

Sabrina brings him a plastic glass of cranberry punch and sits with him on the love seat, holding his hand. She says, "Jim definitely said I should take a drama course at Murray State next semester. He was real encouraging. He said, 'Why not be in the play *and* take a course or two?' I could drive back and forth, don't you think?"

"Why not? You can have anything you want." Edwin plays with her hand.

"Jeff took two courses at Murray and look how good he was. Didn't you think he was good? I loved that cute way he went into that dance."

Edwin is a little drunk. He finds himself telling Sabrina about how he plays disc jockey on the bus, and he confesses to her his shame about the way he sounded off about his golden-oldie format. His mind is reeling and the topic sounds trivial, compared to Sabrina's future.

"Why *don't* you play a new-wave format?" she asks him. "It's what *every*body listens to." She nods at the stereo, which is playing "You're Living in Your Own Private Idaho," by the B-52s, a song Edwin has often heard on the radio late at night when Sabrina is unwinding, moving into his arms. The music is violent and mindless, with a fast beat like a crazed parent abusing a child, thrashing it senseless.

"I don't know," Edwin says. "I shouldn't have said that to Lou Murphy. It bothers me."

"She don't know the difference," Sabrina says, patting his head. "It's ridiculous to make a big thing out of it. Words are so arbitrary, and people don't say what they mean half the time anyway."

"You should talk, Miss Oklahoma!" Edwin laughs, spurting a little punch on the love seat. "You and your two lines!"

"They're just lines," she says, smiling up at him and poking her finger into his dimple.

Some of Edwin's passengers bring him Christmas presents, badly wrapped, with tags that say his name in wobbly writing. Edwin puts the presents in a drawer, where Sabrina finds them.

"Aren't you going to open them?" she asks. "I'd be dying to know what was inside."

"I will eventually. Leave them there." Edwin knows what is in them without opening them. There is a bottle of shaving cologne, a tie (he never wears a tie), and three boxes of choco-late-covered cherries (he peeked in one, and the others are exactly the same shape). The presents are so pathetic Edwin could cry. He cannot bring himself to tell Sabrina what happened on the bus.

On the bus, the day before Christmas break, Ray Watson

had a seizure. During that week, Edwin had been playing more Dylan and even some Stones. No Christmas music, except the Elvis album as usual for Ray. And then, almost unthinkingly, following Sabrina's advice, Edwin shifted formats. It seemed a logical course, as natural as Sabrina's herbal cosmetics, her mushroom complexion. It started with a revival of The Doors— Jim Morrison singing "Light My Fire," a song that was so long it carried them from the feed mill on one side of town to the rendering plant on the other. The passengers loved the way it stretched out, and some shook their heads and stomped their feet. As Edwin realized later, the whole bus was in a frenzy, and he should have known he was leading the passengers toward disaster, but the music seemed so appropriate. The Doors were a bridge from the past to the present, spanning those empty years—his marriages, the turbulence of the times—and connecting his youth solidly with the present. That day Edwin taped more songs from the radio—Adam and the Ants, Squeeze, the B-52s, the Psychedelic Furs, the Flying Lizards, Frankie and the Knockouts—and he made a point of replacing the Plasmatics tape for Lou Murphy. The new-wave format was a hit. Edwin believed the passengers understood what was happening. The frantic beat was a perfect expression of their aimlessness and frustration. Edwin had the impression that his passengers were growing, expanding, like the corn in *Oklahoma!*, like his own awareness. The new format went on for two days before Ray had his seizure. Edwin did not know exactly what happened, and it was possible Laura Combs had shoved Ray into the aisle. Edwin was in an awkward place on the highway, and he had to shoot across a bridge and over a hill before he could find a good place to stop. Everyone on the bus was making an odd noise, gasping or clapping, some imitating Ray's convulsions. Freddie Johnson was saying, "*Popeye* on! *Dukes* on!" Ray was on the floor, gagging, with his head thrown back, and twitching like someone being electrocuted. Laura Combs stood hunched in her seat, her mouth open in speechless terror, pointing her finger at Edwin. During the commotion, the Flying Lizards were chanting tonelessly,

"I'm going to take my problems to the United Nations; there ain't no cure for the summertime blues."

Edwin followed all the emergency steps he had learned. He loosened Ray's clothing, slapped his cheeks, turned him on his side. Ray's skin was the color of the Hershey bars the man with the clubfoot collected. Edwin recalled grimly the first-aid book's ironic assurance that facial coloring was not important in cases of seizure. On the way to the hospital, Edwin clicked in a Donovan cassette. To steady himself, he sang along under his breath. "I'm just wild about saffron," he sang. It was a tune as carefree and lyrical as a field of daffodils. The passengers were screaming. All the way to the hospital, Edwin heard their screams, long and drawn out, orchestrated together into an accusing wail—eerie and supernatural.

Edwin's supervisors commended him for his quick thinking in handling Ray and getting him to the hospital, and everyone he has seen at the center has congratulated him. Ray's mother sent him an uncooked fruitcake made with graham cracker crumbs and marshmallows. She wrote a poignant note, thanking him for saving her son from swallowing his tongue. Edwin keeps thinking: what he did was no big deal; you can't swallow your tongue anyway; and it was Edwin's own fault that Ray had a seizure. He does not feel like a hero. He feels almost embarrassed.

Sabrina seems incapable of embarrassment. She is full of hope, like the Christmas season. *Oklahoma!* was only the beginning for her. She has a new job at McDonald's and a good part in *Life with Father.* She plans to commute to Murray State next semester to take a drama class and a course in Western Civilization that she needs to fulfill a requirement. She seems to assume that Edwin will marry her. He finds it funny that it is up to him to say yes. When she says she will keep her own name, Edwin wonders what the point is.

"My parents would just love it if we got married," Sabrina explains. "For them, it's worse for me to live in sin than to be involved with an older man."

"I didn't think I was really older," says Edwin. "But now

I know it. I feel like I've had a developmental disability and it suddenly went away. Something like if Freddie Johnson learned to read. That's how I feel."

"I never thought of you as backward. Laid back is what I said." Sabrina laughs at her joke. "I'm sure you're going to impress Mom and Dad."

Tomorrow, she is going to her parents' farm, thirty miles away, for the Christmas holidays, and she has invited Edwin to go with her. He does not want to disappoint her. He does not want to go through Christmas without her. She has arranged her Christmas cards on a red string between the living room and the kitchen. She is making cookies, and Edwin has a feeling she is adding something strange to them. Her pale, fine hair is falling down in her face. Flour streaks her jeans.

"Let me show you something," Edwin says, bringing out a drugstore envelope of pictures. "One of my passengers, Merle Cope, gave me these."

"Which one is he? The one with the fits?"

"No. The one that claps all the time. He lives with a lot of sisters and brothers down in Langley's Bottom. It's a case of incest. The whole family's backward—your word. He's forty-seven and goes around with this big smile on his face, clapping." Edwin demonstrates.

He pins the pictures on Sabrina's Christmas card line with tiny red and green clothespins. "Look at these and tell me what you think."

Sabrina squints, going down the row of pictures. Her hands are covered with flour and she holds them in front of her, the way she learned from her actor friends to hold an invisible baby.

The pictures are black-and-white snapshots: fried eggs on cracked plates, an oilclothed kitchen table, a bottle of tomato ketchup, a fence post, a rusted tractor seat sitting on a stump, a corn crib, a sagging door, a toilet bowl, a cow, and finally, a horse's rear end.

"I can't look," says Sabrina. "These are disgusting."

"I think they're arty."

Sabrina laughs. She points to the pictures one by one, getting flour on some of them. Then she gets the giggles and can't stop. "Can you imagine what the developers thought when they saw that horse's ass?" she gasps. Her laughter goes on and on, then subsides with a little whimper. She goes back to the cookies. While she cuts out the cookies, Edwin takes the pictures down and puts them in the envelope. He hides the envelope in the drawer with the Christmas presents. Sabrina sets the cookie sheet in the oven and washes her hands.

Edwin asks, "How long do those cookies take?"

"Twelve minutes. Why?"

"Let me show you something else—in case you ever need to know it. The CPR technique—that's cardio-pulmonary resuscitation, in case you've forgotten."

Sabrina looks annoyed. "I'd rather do the Heimlich maneuver," she says. "Besides, you've practiced CPR on me a hundred times."

"I'm not practicing. I don't have to anymore. I'm beyond that." Edwin notices Sabrina's puzzled face. The thought of her fennel toothpaste, which makes her breath smell like licorice, fills him with something like nostalgia, as though she is already only a memory. He says, "I just want you to feel what it would be like. Come on." He leads her to the couch and sets her down. Her hands are still moist. He says, "Now just pretend. Bend over like this. Just pretend you have the biggest pain, right here, right in your chest, right there."

"Like this?" Sabrina is doubled over, her hair falling to her knees and her fists knotted between her breasts.

"Yes. Right in your heart."

# Third Monday

Ruby watches Linda exclaiming over a bib, then a terry cloth sleeper. It is an amazing baby shower because Linda is thirty-seven and unmarried. Ruby admires that. Linda even refused to marry the baby's father, a man from out of town who had promised to get Linda a laundromat franchise. It turned out that he didn't own any laundromats; he was only trying to impress her. Linda doesn't know where he is now. Maybe Nashville.

Linda smiles at a large bakery cake with pink decorations and the message, WELCOME, HOLLY. "I'm glad I know it's going to be a girl," she says. "But in a way it's like knowing ahead of time what you're going to get for Christmas."

"The twentieth century's taking all the mysteries out of life," says Ruby breezily.

Ruby is as much a guest of honor here as Linda is. Betty Lewis brings Ruby's cake and ice cream to her and makes sure she has a comfortable chair. Ever since Ruby had a radical mastectomy, Betty and Linda and the other women on her bowling team have been awed by her. They praise her bravery and her sense of humor. Just before she had the operation, they suddenly brimmed over with inspiring tales about women who had had successful mastectomies. They reminded her about Betty Ford and Happy Rockefeller. Happy . . . Every one is happy now. Linda looks happy because Nancy Featherstone has taken all the ribbons from the presents and threaded them through holes in a paper plate to fashion a funny bridal bouquet. Nancy, who is artistic, explains that this is a tradition at showers. Linda is pleased. She twirls the bouquet, and the ends of the ribbons dangle like tentacles on a jellyfish.

After Ruby found the lump in her breast, the doctor recommended a mammogram. In an X-ray room, she hugged a Styrofoam basketball hanging from a metal cone and stared at the two lights overhead. The technician, a frail man in plaid pants and a smock, flipped a switch and left the room. The machine hummed. He took several X-rays, like a photographer shooting various poses of a model, and used his hands to measure distances, as one would to determine the height of a horse. "My guidelight is out," he explained. Ruby lay on her back with her breasts flattened out, and the technician slid an X-ray plate into the drawer beneath the table. He tilted her hip and propped it against a cushion. "I have to repeat that last one," he said. "The angle was wrong." He told her not to breathe. The machine buzzed and shook. After she was dressed, he showed her the X-rays, which were printed on Xerox paper. Ruby looked for the lump in the squiggly lines, which resembled a rainfall map in a geography book. The outline of her breast was lovely—a lilting, soft curve. The technician would not comment on what he saw in the pictures. "Let the radiologist interpret them," he said with a peculiar smile. "He's our chief tea-leaf reader." Ruby told the women in her bowling club that she had had her breasts Xeroxed.

The man she cares about does not know. She has been out of the hospital for a week, and in ten days he will be in town again. She wonders whether he will be disgusted and treat her as though she has been raped, his property violated. According to an article she read, this is what to expect. But Buddy is not that kind of man, and she is not his property. She sees him only once a month. He could have a wife somewhere, or other girlfriends, but she doesn't believe that. He promised to take her home with him the next time he comes to western Kentucky. He lives far away, in East Tennessee, and he travels the flea-market circuit, trading hunting dogs and pocket knives. She met him at the fairgrounds at Third

Monday—the flea market held the third Monday of each
month. Ruby had first gone there on a day off from work with
Janice Leggett to look for some Depression glass to match Janice's sugar bowl. Ruby lingered in the fringe of trees near the
highway, the oak grove where hundreds of dogs were whining
and barking, while Janice wandered ahead to the tables of
figurines and old dishes. Ruby intended to catch up with Janice
shortly, but she became absorbed in the dogs. Their mournful
eyes and pitiful yelps made her sad. When she was a child,
her dog had been accidentally locked in the corncrib and died
of heat exhaustion. She was aware of a man watching her watching the dogs. He wore a billed cap that shaded his sharp eyes
like an awning. His blue jacket said HEART VALLEY COON CLUB
on the back in gold-embroidered stitching. His red shirt had
pearl snaps, and his jeans were creased, as though a woman
had ironed them. He grabbed Ruby's arm suddenly and said,
"What are you staring at, little lady! Have you got something
treed?"

He was Buddy Landon, and he tried to sell her a hunting
dog. He seemed perfectly serious. Did she want a coonhound
or a bird dog? The thing wrong with bird dogs was that they
liked to run so much they often strayed, he said. He recommended the Georgia redbone hound for intelligence and pa-
tience. "The redbone can jump and tree, but he doesn't bark
too much," he said. "He don't cry wolf on you, and he's a
good fighter."

"What do I need a coon dog for?" said Ruby, wishing he
had a good answer.

"You must be after a bird dog then," he said. "Do you
prefer hunting ducks or wild geese? I had some hounds that
led me on a wild-goose chase one time after an old wildcat.
That thing led us over half of Kentucky. That sucker never
*would* climb a tree! He wore my dogs out." He whooped and
clapped his hands.

There were eight empty dog crates in the back of his
pickup, and he had chained the dogs to a line between two
trees. Ruby approached them cautiously, and they all leaped

into the air before their chains jerked them back.

"That little beagle there's the best in the field," Buddy said to a man in a blue cap who had sidled up beside them.

"What kind of voice has he got?" the man said.

"It's music to your ears!"

"I don't need a rabbit dog," the man said. "I don't even have any rabbits left in my fields. I need me a good coon dog."

"This black-and-tan's ambitious," said Buddy, patting a black spot on a dog's head. The spot was like a little beanie. "His mama and daddy were both ambitious, and *he*'s ambitious. This dog won't run trash."

"What's trash?" Ruby asked.

"Skunk. Possum," Buddy explained.

"I've only knowed two women in my life that I could get out coon hunting," the man in the blue cap said.

"This lady claims she wants a bird dog, but I think I can make a coon hunter out of her," said Buddy, grinning at Ruby.

The man walked away, hunched over a cigarette he was lighting, and Buddy Landon started to sing "You Ain't Nothin' But A Hound Dog." He said to Ruby, "I could have been Elvis Presley. But thank God I wasn't. Look what happened to him. Got fat and died." He sang, " 'Crying all the time. You ain't never caught a rabbit . . .' I love dogs. But I tell you one thing. I'd never let a dog in the house. You know why? It would get too tame and forget its job. Don't forget, a dog is a dog."

Buddy took Ruby by the elbow and steered her through the fairgrounds, guiding her past tables of old plastic toys and kitchen utensils. "Junk," he said. He bought Ruby a Coke in a can, and then he bought some sweet corn from a farmer. "I'm going to have me some roastin' ears tonight," he said.

"I hear your dogs calling for you," said Ruby, listening to the distant bugle voices of the beagles.

"They love me. Stick around and you'll love me too."

"What makes you think you're so cute?" said Ruby. "What makes you think I need a dog?"

He answered her questions with a flirtatious grin. His belt

had a large silver buckle, with a floppy-eared dog's head en-
graved on it. His hands were thick and strong, with margins
of dirt under his large, flat nails. Ruby liked his mustache and
the way his chin and the bill of his cap seemed to yearn toward
each other.

"How much do you want for that speckled hound dog?"
she asked him.

He brought the sweet corn and some steaks to her house
that evening. By then, the shucks on the corn were wilting.
Ruby grilled the steaks and boiled the ears of corn while Buddy
unloaded the dogs from his pickup. He tied them to her clothes-
line and fed and watered them. The pickup truck in Ruby's
driveway seemed as startling as the sight of the "Action News"
TV van would have been. She hoped her neighbors would
notice. She could have a man there if she wanted to.

After supper, Buddy gave the dogs the leftover bones and
steak fat. Leaping and snapping, they snatched at the scraps,
but Buddy snarled back at them and made them cringe. "You
have to let them know who's boss," he called to Ruby, who
was looking on admiringly from the back porch. It was like
watching a group of people playing "May I?"

Later, Buddy brought his sleeping roll in from the truck
and settled in the living room, and Ruby did not resist when
he came into her bedroom and said he couldn't sleep. She
thought her timing was appropriate; she had recently bought
a double bed. They talked until late in the night, and he told
her hunting stories, still pretending that she was interested
in acquiring a hunting dog. She pretended she was, too, and
asked him dozens of questions. He said he traded things—anything he could make a nickel from: retreaded tires, cars, old
milk cans and cream separators. He was fond of the dogs he
raised and trained, but it did not hurt him to sell them. There
were always more dogs.

"Loving a dog is like trying to love the Mississippi River,"
he said. "It's constantly shifting and changing color and sound
and course, but it's just the same old river."

Suddenly he asked Ruby, "Didn't you ever get married?"

"No."

"Don't it bother you?"

"No. What of it?" She wondered if he thought she was a lesbian.

He said, "You're too pretty and nice. I can't believe you never married."

"All the men around here are ignorant," she said. "I never wanted to marry any of them. Were you ever married?"

"Yeah. Once or twice is all. I didn't take to it."

Later, in the hospital, on Sodium Pentothol, Ruby realized that she had about a hundred pictures of Clint Eastwood, her favorite actor, and none of Buddy. His indistinct face wavered in her memory as she rolled down a corridor on a narrow bed. He didn't have a picture of her, either. In a drawer somewhere she had a handful of prints of her high school graduation picture, taken years ago. Ruby Jane MacPherson in a beehive and a Peter Pan collar. She should remember to give him one for his billfold someday. She felt cautious around Buddy, she realized, the way she did in high school, when it had seemed so important to keep so many things hidden from boys. "Don't let your brother find your sanitary things," she could hear her mother saying.

In the recovery room, she slowly awoke at the end of a long dream, to blurred sounds and bright lights—gold and silver flashes moving past like fish—and a pain in her chest that she at first thought was a large bird with a hooked beak suckling her breast. The problem, she kept thinking, was that she was lying down, when in order to nurse the creature properly, she ought to sit up. The mound of bandages mystified her.

"We didn't have to take very much," a nurse said. "The doctor didn't have to go way up under your arm."

Someone was squeezing her hand. She heard her mother telling someone, "They think they got it all."

A strange fat woman with orange hair was holding her hand. "You're just fine, sugar," she said.

When Ruby began meeting Buddy at the fairgrounds on Third Mondays, he always seemed to have a new set of dogs. One morning he traded two pocket knives for a black-and-tan coonhound with limp ears and star-struck eyes. By afternoon, he had made a profit of ten dollars, and the dog had shifted owners again without even getting a meal from Buddy. After a few months, Ruby lost track of all the different dogs. In a way, she realized, their identities did flow together like a river. She thought often of Buddy's remark about the Mississippi River. He was like the river. She didn't even have an address for him, but he always showed up on Third Mondays and spent the night at her house. If he'd had a profitable day, he would take her to the Burger Chef or McDonald's. He never did the usual things, such as carry out her trash or open the truck door for her. If she were a smoker, he probably wouldn't light her cigarette.

Ruby liked his distance. He didn't act possessive. He called her up from Tennessee once to tell her he had bought a dog and named it Ruby. Then he sold the dog before he got back to town. When it was Ruby's birthday, he made nothing of that, but on another day at the fairgrounds he bought her a bracelet of Mexican silver from a wrinkled old black woman in a baseball cap who called everybody "darling." Her name was Gladys. Ruby loved the way Buddy got along with Gladys, teasing her about being his girlfriend.

"Me and Gladys go 'way back," he said, embracing the old woman flamboyantly.

"Don't believe anything this old boy tells you," said Gladys with a grin.

"Don't say I never gave you nothing," Buddy said to Ruby as he paid for the bracelet. He didn't fasten the bracelet on her wrist for her, just as he never opened the truck door for her.

The bracelet cost only three dollars, and Ruby wondered if it was authentic. "What's *Mexican* silver anyway?" she asked.

"It's good," he said. "Gladys wouldn't cheat me."

Later, Ruby kept thinking of the old woman. Her merchandise was set out on the tailgate of her station wagon—odds and ends of carnival glass, some costume jewelry, and six Barbie dolls. On the ground she had several crates of banties and guineas and pigeons. Their intermingled coos and chirps made Ruby wonder if Gladys slept in her station wagon listening to the music of her birds, the way Buddy slept in his truck with his dogs.

The last time he'd come to town—the week before her operation—Ruby traveled with him to a place over in the Ozarks to buy some pit bull terriers. They drove several hours on interstates, and Buddy rambled on excitedly about the new dogs, as though there were something he could discover about the nature of dogs by owning a pit bull terrier. Ruby, who had traveled little, was intensely interested in the scenery, but she said, "If these are mountains, then I'm disappointed."

"You ought to see the Rockies," said Buddy knowingly. "Talk about mountains."

At a little grocery store, they asked for directions, and Buddy swigged on a Dr Pepper. Ruby had a Coke and a bag of pork rinds. Buddy paced around nervously outside, then unexpectedly slammed his drink bottle in the tilted crate of empties with such force that several bottles fell out and broke. At that moment, Ruby knew she probably was irrevocably in love with him, but she was afraid it was only because she needed someone. She wanted to love him for better reasons. She knew about the knot in her breast and had already scheduled the mammogram, but she didn't want to tell him. Her body made her angry, interfering that way, like a nosy neighbor.

They drove up a winding mountain road that changed to gravel, then to dirt. A bearded man without a shirt emerged from a house trailer and showed them a dozen dogs pacing in makeshift kennel runs. Ruby talked to the dogs while Buddy and the man hunkered down together under a persimmon tree. The dogs were squat and broad-shouldered, with squinty eyes. They were the same kind of dog the Little Rascals had had in the movies. They hurled themselves against the shaky wire, and Ruby told them to hush. They looked at her with cocked heads. When Buddy finally crated up four dogs, the owner looked as though he would cry.

At a motel that night—the first time Ruby had ever stayed in a motel with a man—she felt that the knot in her breast had a presence of its own. Her awareness of it made it seem like a little energy source, like the radium dial of a watch glowing in the dark. Lying close to Buddy, she had the crazy feeling that it would burn a hole through him.

During *The Tonight Show,* she massaged his back with baby oil, rubbing it in thoroughly, as if she were polishing a piece of fine furniture.

"Beat on me," he said. "Just like you were tenderizing steak."

"Like this?" She pounded his hard muscles with the edge of her hand.

"That feels wonderful."

"Why are you so tensed up?"

"Just so I can get you to do this. Don't stop."

Ruby pummeled his shoulder with her fist. Outside, a dog barked. "That man you bought the dogs from looked so funny," she said. "I thought he was going to cry. He must have loved those dogs."

"He was just scared."

"How come?"

"He didn't want to get in trouble." Buddy raised up on an elbow and looked at her. "He was afraid I was going to use those dogs in a dogfight, and he didn't want to be traced."

"I thought they were hunting dogs."

"No. He trained them to fight." He grasped her hand and guided it to a spot on his back. "Right there. Work that place out for me." As Ruby rubbed in a hard circle with her knuckles, he said, "They're good friendly dogs if they're treated right."

Buddy punched off the TV button and smoked a cigarette in the dark, lying with one arm under her shoulders. "You know what I'd like?" he said suddenly. "I'd like to build me a log cabin somewhere—off in the mountains maybe. Just a place for me and some dogs."

"Just you? I'd come with you if you went to the Rocky Mountains."

"How good are you at survival techniques?" he said. "Can you fish? Can you chop wood? Could you live without a purse?"

"I might could." Ruby smiled to herself at the thought.

"Women always have to have a lot of baggage along— placemats and teapots and stuff."

"I wouldn't."

"You're funny."

"Not as funny as you." Ruby shifted her position. His hand under her was hurting her ribs.

"I'll tell you a story. Listen." He sounded suddenly confessional. He sat up and flicked sparks at the ashtray. He said, "My daddy died last year, and this old lady he married was just out to get what he had. He heired her two thousand dollars, and my sister and me were to get the homeplace—the house, the barn, and thirty acres of bottomland. But before he was cold in the ground, she had stripped the place and sold every stick of furniture. Everything that was loose, she took."

"That's terrible."

"My sister sells Tupperware, and she was in somebody's house, and she recognized the bedroom suit. She said, 'Don't I know that?' and this person said, 'Why, yes, I believe that was your daddy's. I bought it at such-and-such auction.' "

"What an awful thing to do to your daddy!" Ruby said.

"He taught me everything I know about training dogs. I learned it from him and he picked it up from his daddy." Buddy jabbed his cigarette in the ashtray. "He knew everything there was to know about field dogs."

"I bet you don't have much to do with your stepmother now."

"She really showed her butt," he said with a bitter laugh. "But really it's my sister who's hurt. She wanted all those keepsakes. There was a lot of Mama's stuff. Listen, I see that kind

of sorrow every day in my line of work—all those stupid, homeless dishes people trade. People buy all that stuff and decorate
with it and think it means something."

"I don't do that," Ruby said.

"I don't keep anything. I don't want anything to remind
me of *any*thing."

Ruby sat up and tried to see him in the dark, but he was
a shadowy form, like the strange little mountains she had seen
outside at twilight. The new dogs were noisy—bawling and
groaning fitfully. Ruby said, "Hey, you're not going to get them
dogs to fight, are you?"

"Nope. But I'm not responsible for what anybody else
wants to do. I'm just the middleman."

Buddy turned on the light to find his cigarettes. With relief,
Ruby saw how familiar he was—his tanned, chunky arms, and
the mustache under his nose like the brush on her vacuum
cleaner. He was tame and gentle, like his best dogs. "They
make good watchdogs," he said. "Listen at 'em!" He laughed
like a man watching a funny movie.

"They must see the moon," Ruby said. She turned out
the light and tiptoed across the scratchy carpet. Through a
crack in the curtains she could see the dark humps of the
hills against the pale sky, but it was cloudy and she could not
see the moon.

Everything is round and full now, like the moon. Linda's
belly. Bowling balls. On TV, Steve Martin does a comedy routine, a parody of the song, "I Believe." He stands before a
gigantic American flag and recites his beliefs. He says he doesn't
believe a woman's breasts should be referred to derogatorily
as jugs, or boobs, or Winnebagos. "I believe they should be
referred to as hooters," he says solemnly. Winnebagos? Ruby
wonders.

After the operation, she does everything left-handed. She
has learned to extend her right arm and raise it slightly. Next,
the doctors have told her, she will gradually reach higher and
higher—an idea that thrills her, as though there were something tangible above her to reach for. It surprises her, too, to

learn what her left hand has been missing. She feels like a newly blind person discovering the subtleties of sound.

Trying to sympathize with her, the women on her bowling team offer their confessions. Nancy has such severe monthly cramps that even the new miracle pills on the market don't work. Linda had a miscarriage when she was in high school. Betty admits her secret, something Ruby suspected anyway: Betty shaves her face every morning with a Lady Sunbeam. Her birth-control pills had stimulated facial hair. She stopped taking the pills years ago but still has the beard.

Ruby's mother calls these problems "female trouble." It is Mom's theory that Ruby injured her breasts by lifting too many heavy boxes in her job with a wholesale grocer. Several of her friends have tipped or fallen wombs caused by lifting heavy objects, Mom says.

"I don't see the connection," says Ruby. It hurts her chest when she laughs, and her mother looks offended. Mom, who has been keeping Ruby company in the afternoons since she came home from the hospital, today is making Ruby some curtains to match the new bedspread on her double bed.

"When you have a weakness, disease can take hold," Mom explains. "When you abuse the body, it shows up in all kinds of ways. And women just weren't built to do man's work. You were always so independent you ended up doing man's work and woman's work both."

"Let's not get into why I never married," says Ruby.

Mom's sewing is meticulous and definite, work that would burn about two calories an hour. She creases a hem with her thumb and folds the curtain neatly. Then she stands up and embraces Ruby carefully, favoring her daughter's right side. She says, "Honey, if there was such of a thing as a transplant, I'd give you one of mine."

"That's O.K., Mom. Your big hooters wouldn't fit me."

At the bowling alley, Ruby watches while her team, Garrison Life Insurance, bowls against Thomas & Sons Plumbing. Her team is getting smacked.

"We're pitiful without you and Linda," Betty tells her.

"Linda's got too big to bowl. I told her to come anyway and watch, but she wouldn't listen. I think maybe she *is* embarrassed to be seen in public, despite what she said."

"She doesn't give a damn what people think," says Ruby, as eight pins crash for Thomas & Sons. "Me neither," she adds, tilting her can of Coke.

"Did you hear she's getting a heavy-duty washer? She says a heavy-duty holds forty-five diapers."

Ruby lets a giggle escape. "She's not going to any more laundromats and get knocked up again."

"Are you still going with that guy you met at Third Monday?"

"I'll see him Monday. He's supposed to take me home with him to Tennessee, but the doctor said I can't go yet."

"I heard he didn't know about your operation," says Betty, giving her bowling ball a little hug.

Ruby takes a drink of Coke and belches. "He'll find out soon enough."

"Well, you stand your ground, Ruby Jane. If he can't love you for yourself, then to heck with him."

"But people always love each other for the wrong reasons!" Ruby says. "Don't you know that?"

Betty stands up, ignoring Ruby. It's her turn to bowl. She says, "Just be thankful, Ruby. I like the way you get out and go. Later on, bowling will be just the right thing to build back your strength."

"I can already reach to here," says Ruby, lifting her right hand to touch Betty's arm. Ruby smiles. Betty has five-o'clock shadow.

The familiar crying of the dogs at Third Monday makes Ruby anxious and jumpy. They howl and yelp and jerk their chains—sound effects in a horror movie. As Ruby walks through the oak grove, the dogs lunge toward her, begging recognition. A black Lab in a tiny cage glares at her savagely. She notices dozens of blueticks and beagles, but she doesn't see Buddy's truck. As she hurries past some crates of ducks and rabbits and pullets, a man in overalls stops her. He is holding a pocket knife and, in one hand, an apple cut so precisely that the core is a perfect rectangle.

"I can't 'call your name," he says to her. "But I know I know you."

"I don't know *you*," says Ruby. Embarrassed, the man backs away.

The day is already growing hot. Ruby buys a Coke from a man with a washtub of ice and holds it with her right hand, testing the tension on her right side. The Coke seems extremely heavy. She lifts it to her lips with her left hand. Buddy's truck is not there.

Out in the sun, she browses through a box of *National Enquirers* and paperback romances, then wanders past tables of picture frames, clocks, quilts, dishes. The dishes are dirty and mismatched—odd plates and cups and gravy boats. There is nothing she would want. She skirts a truckload of shock absorbers. The heat is making her dizzy. She is still weak from her operation. "I wouldn't pay fifteen dollars for a corn sheller," someone says. The remark seems funny to Ruby, like something she might have heard on Sodium Pentothol. Then a man bumps into her with a wire basket containing two young gray cats. A short, dumpy woman shouts to her, "Don't listen to him. He's trying to sell you them cats. Who ever heard of buying cats?"

Gladys has rigged up a canvas canopy extending out from the back of her station wagon. She is sitting in an aluminum folding chair, with her hands crossed in her lap, looking cool. Ruby longs to confide in her. She seems to be a trusty fixture, something stable in the current, like a cypress stump.

"Buy some mushmelons, darling," says Gladys. Gladys is selling banties, Fiestaware, and mushmelons today.

"Mushmelons give me gas."

Gladys picks up a newspaper and fans her face. "Them seeds been in my family over a hundred years. We always saved the seed."

"Is that all the way back to slave times?"

Gladys laughs as though Ruby has told a hilarious joke. "These here's my roots!" she says. "Honey, we's *in* slave times, if you ask me. Slave times ain't never gone out of style, if you know what I mean."

Ruby leans forward to catch the breeze from the woman's newspaper. She says, "Have you seen Buddy, the guy I run around with? He's usually here in a truck with a bunch of dogs?"

"That pretty boy that bought you that bracelet?"

"I was looking for him."

"Well, you better look hard, darling, if you want to find him. He got picked up over in Missouri for peddling a hot TV. They caught him on the spot. They'd been watching him. You don't believe me, but it's true. Oh, honey, I'm sorry, but he'll be back! He'll be back!"

In the waiting room at the clinic, the buzz of a tall floor fan sounds like a June bug on a screen door. The fan waves its head wildly from side to side. Ruby has an appointment for her checkup at three o'clock. She is afraid they will give her radiation treatments, or maybe even chemotherapy. No one is saying exactly what will happen next. But she expects to be baptized in a vat of chemicals, burning her skin and sizzling her hair. Ruby recalls an old comedy sketch, in which one of the Smothers Brothers fell into a vat of chocolate. Buddy Landon used to dunk his dogs in a tub of flea dip. She never saw him do it, but she pictures it in her mind—the stifling smell of Happy Jack mange medicine, the surprised dogs shaking themselves afterward, the rippling black water. It's not hard to imagine Buddy in a jail cell either—thrashing around sleeplessly in a hard bunk, reaching over to squash a cigarette butt on the concrete floor—but the image is so inappropriate it is like something from a bad dream. Ruby keeps imagining different scenes in which he comes back to town and they take off for the Rocky Mountains together. Everyone has always said she had imagination—imagination and a sense of humor.

A pudgy man with fat fists and thick lips sits next to her

on the bench at the clinic, humming. With him is a woman in a peach-colored pants suit and with tight white curls. The man grins and points to a child across the room. "That's my baby," he says to Ruby. The little girl, squealing with joy, is riding up and down on her mother's knee. The pudgy man says something unintelligible.

"He loves children," says the white-haired woman.

"My baby," he says, making a cradle with his arms and rocking them.

"He has to have those brain tests once a year," says the woman to Ruby in a confidential whisper.

The man picks up a magazine and says, "This is my baby." He hugs the magazine and rocks it in his arms. His broad smile curves like the crescent phase of the moon.

## ACKNOWLEDGMENTS

"Shiloh," "Offerings," "Nancy Culpepper," and "Third Monday" appeared originally in *The New Yorker*. "Detroit Skyline, 1949," "A New-Wave Format," "Drawing Names," and "The Retreat" appeared originally in *Atlantic Monthly*. "Still Life with Watermelon" first appeared in *Redbook*. "Old Things" first appeared in somewhat different form in *The North American Review*. "The Climber" first appeared in the *Washington Post Magazine*. "Residents and Transients" first appeared in *New Boston Review*. "The Ocean" first appeared in somewhat different form in *Bloodroot* under the title "Recreation." "Graveyard Day" first appeared in somewhat different form in *Ascent*.

Grateful acknowledgment is made to the following for permission to reprint: The lyrics "Everybody wants to do The Horizontal Bop" in *Rookers* from the song "The Horizontal Bop," words and music by Bob Seger; copyright © 1979, 1980 Gear Publishing Co.; from the album entitled *Against the Wind* on Capitol Records. The lyrics "I'm just wild about saffron" in *A New-Wave Format* from the song "Mellow Yellow," written and sung by Donovan Leitch; copyright © 1966 by Donovan Music Ltd.; sole selling agent Peer International Corporation; used by permission, all rights reserved. The lyrics "You ain't nothing but a hound dog" and "Crying all the time. You ain't never caught a rabbit..." in *Third Monday* from the song "Hound Dog," by Jerry Leiber and Mike Stoller; copyright © 1956 by Elvis Presley Music & Lion Publishing Co., Inc., copyright assigned to Gladys Music & MCA Music, A Division of MCA Inc.; all rights controlled by Chappell & Co., Inc. (Intersong Music, Publisher), international copyright secured; all rights reserved, used by permission. The lyrics "Don't go walking down lovers' lane/With anyone else but me/Till I come marching home" in *The Ocean* from the song "Don't Sit Under the Apple Tree," by Brown, Stept, and Tobias; copyright © 1942, 1954 Robbins Music Corporation, renewed 1970 Robbins Music Corporation and Ched Music Corporation; all rights reserved, used by permission. The lyrics "Attention, all you K Mart Shoppers, fill your carts, cause your time is almost up" and "They're looking in your picture window" in *A New-Wave Format* from the song "Get You Tonight," by Sterling Storm; copyright © 1981 by Sterling Storm, from The Humans' LP: "*Happy Hour*"/IRS Records; published by Walk Away From Music. The lyrics "I'm going to take my problems to the United Nations; there ain't no cure for the summertime blues" in *A New-Wave Format* from "Summertime Blues," by Jerry Capehart and Eddie Cochran; copyright © 1958 Warner-Tamerlane Publishing Corp., Rightsong Music, Elvis Presley Music & Gladys Music; all rights reserved, used by permission.